THE
CODIST

THE AARON CHRONICLES

THE CODIST

ERIC E. WALKER

TATE PUBLISHING
AND ENTERPRISES, LLC

Published by Tate Publishing & Enterprises, LLC
127 E. Trade Center Terrace | Mustang, Oklahoma 73064 USA
1.888.361.9473 | www.tatepublishing.com

Tate Publishing is committed to excellence in the publishing industry. The company reflects the philosophy established by the founders, based on Psalm 68:11,
"The Lord gave the word and great was the company of those who published it."

Book design copyright © 2015 by Tate Publishing, LLC. All rights reserved.
Cover and Layout Design by Christina Hicks

Published in the United States of America

ISBN: 978-1-68207-060-4
Fiction / Christian / Suspense
15.05.27

To my best friend for life.

CHAPTER 1

Jake Aaronson's eyes darted back and forth scanning a wall of LCD monitors as if he was lost in a state of permanent REM sleep, but he was not asleep by any stretch of the imagination. He was not like the other analysts with their MIT PhD's and algorithms; his brain was innately programmed to see the patterns. Not only could Jake's brain see the patterns, he could create the patterns.

Jake worked in an ultra top-secret panopticon that did not exist in the public's mind and was hidden from 99.9% of the government's officials. Only the President, the Director of the NSA, and the twenty-four hand-picked Analysts assigned to write queries and monitor the facility were allowed inside the room. All other cleared personnel were fed data for further analysis without knowing the exact location or source of the intelligence. Few could imagine the magnitude of a six-story-high wall, spanning a 100-foot-diameter room, filled with clusters of 120" LCD displays. The design was comparable in size to the United States Capitol Building Rotunda. The walls danced with flashing data, code, images, security camera feeds, email, electronic forms, and live streaming internet data from almost every country in the world. All the team members except Jake were responsible for writing search strings to harvest data from tens of millions of sources connected to many thousands of servers across the globe. No company, individual or government was immune from the prying eyes of the various systems, developed under names like XKeyscore, Narus' Semantic Traffic Analyzer (STA), which were designed to mine data from every source imaginable. These data mining systems worked around the clock to sniff out terrorists and enemies of the State.

Jake was unique in his role. He was not assigned to sit behind a computer terminal and write queries. While the other Analysts were responsible for specific clusters of panels and the data feeds to their queries, Jake was responsible for walking the circumference of the panopticon to look for patterns. Any patterns. To reach the middle and higher tiers of the LCD panels, Jake would enter a capsule and sit behind a command center console mounted on a hydraulic arm. From there he could guide the arm up, down, and in a 360-degree circle, giving him close up access to any panels or clusters of panels that caught his eye.

All over the world there were countless programmers and hackers using every bit of the latest technology to break into and out of the next best operating system or security software. Algorithms and search strings abounded throughout the world of cyber security. There was, however, one thing they could not replace. The human mind and its creative powers still trumped technology.

Jake Aaronson saw what even the sophisticated software could not see; the patterns that escaped the computer's eye. He knew how to write code, and he knew how to break code, but he was the best at seeing the patterns others could not. It was a gift from God that he alone possessed.

He had distinguished himself, both academically and in the Israeli intelligence community, before returning to the United States to join the National Security Agency (NSA) on assignment as a civilian contractor. His return was facilitated after being recruited by one of Washington, DC's most powerful intelligence operations and power brokers.

There was nothing personal about his job. In fact, the impersonal nature of the job was its most attractive feature. It was not that Jake wasn't strikingly handsome and could have had a vibrant social life. At thirty-four years old, Jake was doing what he passionately loved. He loved the patterns, the puzzles, the code, and the challenge more than anything else in his life.

It wasn't long before he became acclimated to his new work environment. He had already proven his ability to solve some cases and build some allies. He was making a difference and he felt good about the work he was doing. This new position brought him back home after many years of living in Israel and afforded him the chance to build a new life. He could choose his own cases and had access to the vast resources of the NSA.

It wasn't long before a new case surfaced that seemed to pick Jake instead of the other way around. This case was personal and would take him out of his comfort zone. He would be forced to draw upon every skill he had ever mastered and ones he didn't even know he possessed. His family heritage, his identity, and his gifts would all come into play. He thought he was prepared for any case that came his way, but it would take more than preparation and training to defeat the greatest threat to the Jewish people since the Holocaust.

CHAPTER 2

It was six months after Jake's second birthday that Uncle Saul came to visit for the first time. Uncle Saul was the family playboy who loved being an investment banker, and the world travel that came along with it, more than the idea of settling down and having a family. Jake was his only nephew and he brought him a gift. Not knowing what a two-and-a-half-year-old would like, Uncle Saul brought Jake a Rubik's Cube. Jake's mother, Lydia, chided her older brother for the age inappropriateness of the gift and went into her auto-tirade about settling down and building a family of his own. The conversation was quickly interrupted by an unmistakable clicking sound that stunned Lydia and her brother

Sitting on the floor was Jake twisting and turning the Rubik's Cube as if he knew what he was supposed to do. Red to red. Green to green. White to white. Blue to blue. Orange to orange. Yellow to yellow. They stared at him as he worked with a focus and a determination that was as age incongruous as the toy itself. After thirty minutes it was done. The Rubik's Cube puzzle had been solved by a child under the age of three. It had to be a fluke. As they took the cube from Jake and untwisted it and handed it back to him his face lit up with a grin of heavenly joy. Ten minutes later the puzzle was solved again. It was no fluke.

Certainly it fell short of the record of the youngest person, who was 3 years 118 days old when she solved the cube in 1:39.33, but nonetheless it was impressive to say the least.

As Jake grew older his fascination with puzzles grew exponentially. His off-the-chart mastery challenged his parents to find more ways to keep him stimulated. While his peers where playing with Nintendo, Jake was consumed with anagrams, word searches and puzzles of every kind. At age six he had mastered every level of cryptic code dating back from World War 2 to the present day. He became so bored with the limitations of the current coding systems that he created his own coding systems. By age ten he had created over 1000 different coding methods, and one of his simple pleasures was to memorize the spelling of his own name in every system that he learned or developed.

In spite of Jake's unique abilities and interests, his parents had always agreed to involve him in traditional activities as best they could. Like the rest of his Jewish friends in the Washington suburb of Bethesda, Maryland, he would soon begin Bar Mitzvah training to complete this rite of passage at age thirteen.

Up until now Jake had only been taught English in school and self taught the language of cyphers and codes. He accompanied his parents to the synagogue in his neighborhood on those occasions when his mother could motivate his father to go. That worked out to only be two or three times a year. It was there he heard

Hebrew, but didn't really pay much attention to it. One thing he did notice was how uncomfortable his father seemed to be when everyone would pay special attention to him just because he was somehow related to the Aaron of the Bible. His father's role in the diplomatic circles of Washington drew enough attention and this recognition at the synagogue just seemed to make things worse. Both their significance would later matter, but at this stage of his life it just didn't seem to have much relevance.

The process he began was like so many Jewish boys before him by going to Hebrew School and learning the fundamentals of Biblical Hebrew. Although Jake was born in Israel, his family returned to the United States before his first birthday. He would be required to actually learn the who, what, where and why of the first five books of the Bible, the Torah. Jake was doing this because it was expected of him. It was tradition. His father, and his father's father, and every generation of Aaronson were trained in a similar fashion. Jake would follow in the footsteps of his ancestors and be called to stand before the congregation and read from the Torah.

It was Jake's nature to dig below the surface of everything he studied and search for the patterns. This would be no different; he would embrace what was taught and make his family proud. This required study of the first five books of the Bible would lay a foundation of understanding beyond his wildest imagination.

CHAPTER 3

Across the globe Hakeem Baba rolled his eyes as he listened to the old men discuss their plans. They talked endlessly about annihilation, jihad terrorist attacks, and more of the same methods that had only planted fear in the hearts of the West, but had made no real progress in the battle for the elimination of Israel and the United States. Friends his own age shared his frustration. They had endured years of training, yet sat idly by listening to the yammering of old men who had yet to strike the deathblow to the underbelly of the enemy against whom they were so unified.

Hakeem and his friends Numair, Mahfuz, Jafar, and Farooq were sons of diplomats and received some of their education in the finest schools in America. Their English was flawless and their lineage given away by their names alone. Their mothers were all of European origin, carefully selected to pass along their fair coloring to the ones chosen to carry out the ultimate plans of global domination. They also shared a rather macabre coincidence. All of their mothers died during childbirth. These five were being groomed to take over the leadership of the Iranian Guardian Council. They felt trapped. It seemed that all they could do was bide their time until the Elders died in order for them to take their rightful places

Hakeem grew more and more impatient. "Their plans are old," Hakeem whispered to Farooq. "When will they do something more than train children to strap on vests and blow themselves up and promise they will be remembered as heroes? I cannot even remember the names of the ones who died last year, let alone the many who gave their lives all the years we have been listening to their plans. How can we continue to bask in the glory of September 11, 2001, when we have done so little since? Each one of you has been strategically placed across Europe, yet, all we can do is sit and wait for instructions and nothing has changed. There is a reason we are all together again this night. I have waited until we could all be in the same city at the same time without drawing any attention. The funeral of our beloved friend Numair's father has provided us the perfect cover to meet in one place after our many years away."

"I have a plan," Hakeem continued. "It will destroy the heart of the Little Satan forever. You and the others say you are willing to do anything for Allah. The time has come to join the elders or me. If you are in, the others will join us. Farooq, can I count on you?

Farooq's eyes grew wide with a newfound excitement as he nodded his head in agreement. Hakeem continued, "I leave it to you to speak to the other three and meet me tonight after the evening prayers behind the café where we played as young boys. Whoever is there will share in this glorious plan to rip the very heart out of our enemy. Whoever is not, is dead to us."

CHAPTER 4

Hakeem and his friends grew up in traditional Muslim homes in Tehran submitting to the training of Islam and the teachings of the Koran. Private tutors schooled them until they excelled in math, science and English and could compete for admission to America's top universities. By the time the boys turned ten each of their fathers were given a new assignment in another Muslim country. Hakeem and his father moved to Ankara, Turkey. By age thirteen he and his four friends were not only academically skilled, but physically trained and entrenched in the ideology of Islam. They were prepared to answer the call to serve and give their lives on a moment's notice. The plans for their future had been in place since their birth, and each of the five were personally selected for a specific criterion known only to the Ayatollah.

Hakeem never thought of himself as different than the other four, and when he was told they were moving to the Washington, DC, suburb of Bethesda, Maryland, because of his father's new job, he did not give it a second thought. He knew this was a part of the overall plan, but was not concerned that he was being given it one piece at a time. He was raised not to question, but to obey and be ready for his next set of instructions.

His father's diplomatic training, and new role as Under Secretary to the Ambassador of Turkey, provided the means for him and his father to relocate without drawing any attention from anyone. They had been fully vetted and their moderate public image made for the perfect entre' into the American foreign relations spheres of influence. Hakeem was just another teenager who was leaving his friends behind and relocating because of his father's job. He would adopt the appropriate amount of respect required of a diplomat's son, seasoned with enough appearance of rebellion to easily insert himself into the American society that he had been trained to infiltrate.

"My son," Hakeem's Father began. "We have waited for this moment since you were born. Our faithfulness to Allah has provided us with the opportunity to go to America and take our place in history. Upon our arrival in Washington you will be enrolled in the Winchester Academy. You will board there so that both of us can do what we have been charged with doing. It will not be easy, my son, as you will live with your sworn enemy. You must not allow them to provoke you. You must keep a watchful eye on everyone, as you too may be watched. Let it appear that you can be trusted and that you are a true friend, but do not let your guard down for even a minute. This is all part of the plan and you are a soldier trained for this very assignment. Learn all you can. Become one of them, so that you may be accepted into the inner circle. Do not forget what you have been taught. Nothing is impossible for the willing. Remember who you belong to and why you were chosen as one of The Five."

Hakeem looked his father in the eye and stood with his shoulders back and his head held high as he said, "Father, I will not let you down. I will do as instructed and be faithful to the family name and most of all to the teachings of Muhammad. Allah be praised!"

CHAPTER 5

As Jake Aaronson was finishing his last year of middle school with a perfect record of academic excellence, his parents had come to a crossroads in deciding where Jake would attend high school. As the Deputy Secretary of State, Jake's father, Norman, was the highest-ranking Jewish government official in America and served as the alter ego to the Secretary of State himself. His combination of experiences in Foreign and Domestic relations uniquely qualified him for the position as he had previously served as an Attaché to the US Ambassador to Israel where Jake was born.

The decision to send Jake to the prestigious Winchester Academy in Bethesda would offer the best education coupled with the exposure Jake would have to other international dignitaries' children. The Winchester alumni read like a Who's Who of Accomplishment and boasted an unequalled 98.9% Ivy League College Acceptance. Noted physicists, doctors, diplomats, and authors counted Winchester as their own launch pad. Among its other more notable but less publicized accomplishments was its contribution to the ranks of the NSA, CIA and other Intelligence Agencies.

Norman Aaronson's unique position made him aware of the early recruiting of Winchester students for the intelligence community, and he had always thought of his son as being a perfect candidate. As important as this was to Norman, he could never mention this to his wife, Lydia. She had dreams of Jake becoming a world-renowned scientist who would discover the cure for cancer because of his uncanny ability to see the patterns in everything. She thought he would be able to look at DNA and discover some pattern never seen before. She also had no desire to see her son live in the world of government and politics where he would be treated like an asset in the worst possible way. Her biggest fear was having her son's gift used for military weaponry and turning this pure-hearted talent into a commodity to be leveraged into a tool of manipulation and destruction.

Lydia was leaning towards The Academy of Arts & Sciences, renowned for its academia and the added advantage of not offering boarding. As their only child, this would keep Jake at home for at least another four years. Lydia only knew part of her husband's motivation for leaning toward Winchester and was operating under the assumption that her art of persuasion would give her an advantage over her more diplomatically oriented husband.

Lydia's battle strategy was bulletproof. You would think after having played the same hand every time she wanted Norman to give in to her plans that he would see through it, but he never seemed to see it coming. Maybe he just enjoyed it, but regardless, he never let on that he knew her strategy.

Unlike most Washington, DC, commuters, Norman had the benefit of a driver and a government car. You would think the ride would give him the luxury to unwind from the stresses of his high office, but there was never silence as his car phone chimed with one message after another from people he could not afford to ignore.

As soon as he walked in the door he recognized the familiar set-up and immediately took mental inventory of important family dates that either he or his assistant had forgotten. None came to mind. He thought, "What am I missing? What decision do we have to make important enough for Lydia to prepare his favorite meal?" The table was set just for two. Where was Jake?

His mental gymnastics were interrupted when he heard Lydia descending the circular staircase. As he beheld his wife, his eyes drank in the makeup, the hair, the outfit he lovingly refereed to as "access wear," and he knew she was dressed in full battle gear.

The thought jumped into his head, "This time I will hold my ground, no matter what the issue." In the past he had been resolute, but wavered at her charm. He could see she was up to something. He knew he loved her and would fall for her persuasiveness almost every time. All he could do was smile and think, "Let the games begin!"

The longer-than-usual welcome home kiss was just the opening volley as she helped Norman take off his suit coat, rubbed his neck, and then leaned in close and whispered in a low voice, "I'm glad you're home. Come, let's sit by the fire for a few minutes before dinner and relax." As obvious as it was, Norman found himself taking her outstretched hand and being led into the family room where a fire was blazing and the lights were turned low.

Lydia began with the warm-up questions that Norman had come to expect when he was being set up for a serious discussion. She started with, "How was your day?" Norman took the cue and gave a fainthearted recount of the meeting and policies that were being discussed, making every attempt to avoid detail and skim the surface.

Lydia followed with, "You know we have to make a decision about Jake's high school, and I was thinking of all the advantages to The Academy of Arts and Sciences. It's clear to me how well their environment would suit Jake's particular interest."

In an attempt to make the conversation a little lighter Norman replied, "I had hoped to make it to dessert before we had this discussion. Since you have opened the door, let's get through this and see if dinner is even an option after we are done talking."

That was all it took to give Lydia the opportunity to deliver the speech she had been preparing for weeks, " Norman, you and I both know how about Jake's unique gifts. He is not like the other boys who go to Winchester. He doesn't have the social skills and all he is interested in is computers and those codes and queries he is always working on. Winchester is all about training up and educating men of distinction to feed into the Ivy League colleges that pump out doctors, physicists, politicians, and Nobel Prize candidates. They lump diplomats' kids in with everyone else and it's hard enough for Jake to talk to a girl in his Hebrew school let alone a world-travelled, well-rounded, bilingual academic scholar from another country."

Lydia stood to her feet, took a deep breath and fired the final shot as she said, "And as his mother, I know what's best for our son, and I say he is staying at home for the next four years and going to The Academy of Arts and Sciences."

Just as Lydia delivered her closing statement, Norman's phone rang and it was an urgent call from the State Department. Lydia knew this discussion was over for now, but she would not let it end here.

Unbeknownst to Lydia this was to be a battle that she could never win. Jake had overheard Norman and Max Hirschberg discussing their plans to send Jake to Winchester and recruit him into the ranks of the intelligence community. He was fascinated by this discussion and spoke to his father in confidence. He shared that he knew of their plans and was fully supportive and excited at the prospect. He understood his mother would not readily agree, but would leave that to his father. The die had been cast, and Jake's future had been decided long ago by a power much greater than either of his parents could have imagined.

CHAPTER 6

A line of chauffeur-driven black limousines inched forward, proudly displaying diplomatic plates from every imaginable country. To the unknowing eye, this would appear to be a gathering of Heads of State, but as prophetic an image as that would paint, it was simply check-in day at the Winchester Academy.

A team of well-dressed, well-mannered, and well-trained uniformed concierges met each vehicle. As the driver opened the door to deliver his occupant, the concierge would extend a welcoming hand and a greeting in the native language of every arrival. Drivers were handed a packet of information directing them to the designated address for them to unload the personal belongings of the passengers. The students were escorted into Meanly Hall, where they would gather for the official Welcome Reception.

Every new student was greeted by an upperclassman who would be their mentor during their first semester at Winchester. This system was put in place in 1896 by Siegfried Winchester, the Founding Father of the Academy. It was his vision to empower each person and the school's motto, "*NIL VOLENTIBUS ARDUUM* – NOTHING IS IMPOSSIBLE FOR THE WILLING," reflected his commitment to developing servant leaders.

Each year those who passed the most stringent admission requirements were selected to fill one of only thirty-four openings. Every student and their families were vetted as if they were being appointed to a high-level government role. In fact, for many, this vetting would be an inherent part of their lives from this point forward. The academic requirements alone were enough to weed out 90% of the applicants who did not score in the top 1% on both the SAT and the ACT. These test scores, plus a perfect 4.0 or higher throughout their elementary and middle school years added to the exclusivity of the school's alumni. The applicants' conduct had to be impeccable and they had to be recognized as model citizens in their respective communities. Activities and team membership were plusses, but being the leader was much more important than just being a member of an organization or a team.

The mentors escorted their new charges down a tree-lined sidewalk to a round building with a brass plate above the doorway, which read, "MEANLY HALL – MEN OF DISTINCTION GATHER HERE." As they entered, they could hear the sounds of voices coming from the auditorium straight ahead of them.

Upperclassmen were seated on the right side and incoming freshman, along with faculty, sat on the left. Headmaster Prescott Reed called the room to order and gave his usual opening welcome to the new Class of 1999 and gave his charge to students and faculty alike.

It was now time for the pairing of incoming students and their roommate assignments and introductions. The tradition of permanent roommate assignments was designed to break down every cultural, social, economic and racial barrier between the students. This was designed to prepare them for their entrance into institutes of higher learning and position them to assume leadership roles regardless of their national origin.

The pairings were as varied as the nations represented. Of the seventeen sets of new roommates called, none garnered as much of a murmuring as the very obvious Jewish name of Jacob Aaronson and the very obvious Arabic name of Hakeem Baba. As they made their way down the aisle escorted by their mentors, there was a palpable tension in the room.

Each was introduced to the other and was to extend a warm handshake and then take their seats side by side. This was to be their roommate and companion for the next four years of their life. As Jake extended his hand in friendship, Hakeem continued his stone cold stare, took Jake's hand, and quickly let it go after one very embittered up and down. Jake sensed a powerful darkness and a feeling of trepidation he had never felt before. Silently he took his seat next to Hakeem, hoping his new roommate would not sense the intensity of his discomfort and fear.

CHAPTER 7

Jake and Hakeem's bags had already been delivered to their dormitory apartment and the sound of the door closing began their first moments alone with each other. They were standing in a professionally decorated living room centrally located with each bedroom on opposite ends of the main room. There was a couch facing a large bookcase filled with leather-bound editions of the classics, two leather chairs, each with its own reading lamp and end table, and a coffee table. Next to the bookcase was a gas log fireplace. Neatly placed in the corner was a kitchenette equipped with a sink, small refrigerator, microwave, cook top with a teapot, and a toaster oven. There were also cabinets and drawers fully stocked with all the basics. A small selection of grocery items was available in the commissary.

Hakeem did not take his eyes off of Jake as he reached for his own suitcases, picked them up and headed toward the bedroom door with his name on it. The last sound Jake heard was the slamming of his new roommate's door. Now alone, Jake took his bags to his room and closed the door quietly.

Every two-bedroom dormitory apartment was identically laid. Everything a student would need was provided for them: double bed, dresser, chest of drawers, walk-in closet, desk, credenza, bookshelves already filled with textbooks and reference materials, a new Power Macintosh, a 28.8KB modem and a new Color StyleWriter Inkjet Printer.

The décor was Ralph Lauren, and sitting on top of the down comforter on each bed was a sealed dossier clearly marked FOR YOUR EYES ONLY. Jake stood for a moment taking it all in and wondering what he should do first. Curiosity won over logic, and instead of unpacking his bags and putting his clothing and personal belongings away, he sat down on the bed carefully examining the envelope.

Jake assumed the packet would contain such mundane items as class schedules, dormitory rules and regulations, a map of the campus, etc. He tore the tape off the flap and poured the contents of the packet onto the bed. There lying before him was everything he expected with the exception of one smaller sealed envelope with the name Hakeem Baba on it. He thought to himself, "Was this a mistake? Was this a test to see if I would take an envelope that had my roommate's name on it and peak inside? Was this meant for me or for Hakeem?" There were no other markings on the envelope and Jake scanned through all the other documents in the packet to see if there were any instructions pertaining to the envelope. None were found.

Finding no instructions, Jake kicked his analytical puzzle-solving skills into high gear and in seconds knew the same challenge was being reviewed by each of the thirty-four incoming freshman. A smile spread over his face as he took a little pity on the less skilled problem solvers and heard the chatter in the hallway as some of his new classmates began asking each other if they got an envelope with the wrong name on it. A voice over a loud speaker announced each student was to complete their unpacking and read the contents of their orientation packages in their entirety until the dinner bell rang. Jake heard the scurrying of feet and the closing of doors all the way down the hall as he chuckled to himself and opened the envelope with Hakeem's name on it.

The envelope contained two sheets of high-quality linen paper bearing the seal and watermark of the Winchester Academy. There was also a three-by-five index card with the disclaimer on it that read:

"The information contained herein is

<u>FOR YOUR EYES ONLY</u>

<u>HIGHLY CONFIDENTIAL.</u>

Any discussion of the contents will be cause for immediate dismissal.

You are to destroy this note and the accompanying documents before leaving your room – TODAY"

Jake's mind moved back into analysis mode as he scrolled through a mental checklist of questions. "Why the confidentiality? Why the penalty? Was this some type of test?"

Jake set the index card down and began reading the two sheets of information containing a complete briefing on his roommate Hakeem Baba.

Name: Hakeem Nisralla Baba

Date of Birth: September 11, 1980

Height: 5' 10"

Weight: 160#

Hair Color: Brown

Eyes: Black

Skin: Fair

Place of Birth: Tehran, Iran

Current Residence: Ankara, Turkey

Father's Name: Akram Abdullah Baba

Father's Position: Under Secretary to Turkish Ambassador

Mother: Deceased

Siblings: None

Religion: Muslim, Observant

Politics: Moderate

Academic Ranking: Privately tutored from age 2-14

Languages Spoken: Turkish, Arabic, Farsi, Hebrew, English, Spanish, French, German, and Russian

IQ: 179 (Exceptionally Gifted)

SAT Scores – 1600

ACT Score – 36

Special Skills: Languages, Physics, and Martial Arts

Just as Jake was feeling a bit overwhelmed by the language and martial arts skills of his roommate, his mind flashed back to his last private conversation with his father before he left for Winchester. He could hear his father's voice saying to him, "Son, you are about to take a step into your future. From the time you were born I knew you were destined for something special. You have a mind that sees and analyzes like no one else I have ever known. No matter how small an assignment may seem, use your gifts to look beneath the surface of everything for its true meaning."

Jake paused and thought about his father's words. For just a brief moment he looked outside the dormitory window to process what he recalled and then returned to his father's words of instruction.

"Everything in life is a test. You must prove trustworthy in all things even if you don't understand their meaning at the time. Over the course of these next four years you will face personal, physical, emotional, intellectual and spiritual challenges that you may not feel you have the ability to overcome. I believe you have everything it takes to rise to these challenges. Trust no one. Keep your eyes and ears open as not everything may be as it appears. Remember this always, nothing is impossible for the willing."

Jake picked up the pages containing Hakeem's profile and read it again using the new lens of his father's charge. More confident now of his own abilities, Jake analyzed the significance of both the contents of the profile and the instructions on the index card.

Because of Jake's photographic memory, he knew he could draw on the contents of this profile by searching the intricate filing system that existed in his brain. All he had to do was close his eyes and picture himself sitting on this bed, reading this profile, and the contents would immediately appear in his mind's eye. Somehow he knew this was an important gift that would prove most useful over the coming days.

Since Jake had overheard some of the chatter in the hallway earlier he assumed that each student was given a confidential profile about their roommates. He thought carefully and asked himself, "How did they know students were in the hall? Was that just a random announcement or could they have seen or even heard what was going on?"

Before he left his room to carry out the final instruction of destroying the profile, Jake took a few more minutes to examine his room and its contents. Now the puzzle solving began and Jake's senses were on high alert.

CHAPTER 8

Hakeem was agitated about his roommate assignment and paced back and forth ignoring the envelope sitting on top of his bed. His thoughts raged in his head, "Is this someone's idea of a sick joke that starts out, 'a Muslim and a Jew are roommates for four years...'" He found no humor in his circumstances and angrily pounded his fist on the desk so hard that his computer shook and floppy disks tumbled over. As he began to set items back in their place, something in the corner under the shelf above the computer caught his eye. He moved the computer on to the floor to give himself access to the spot, and there he could make out the unmistakable shape of a lens inset into the wall. Next to it was a mesh-covered spot no bigger around than a pencil eraser. He could only assume it was a microphone based upon its shape and size.

His father had researched Winchester and knew of its deep connection to the intelligence community. It was therefore no surprise he was under the watchful eye of those in charge. He could hear his father's voice in his head as he replayed his instructions, "Do what you must to protect your mind from becoming westernized. Lead them to believe you are open to new ideas and new ways. Show them you are willing to be faithful to whatever they ask of you. Let no one in. You are there to learn all you can about the weak westerners and their liberal attitudes. You have been physically, mentally, and emotionally trained to accomplish our goals. Show them how a leader excels at all he does. Remember, nothing is impossible for the willing. You are under Allah's protection, my son."

His father's voice had a calming effect and Hakeem composed himself and put his room back in order. He would play along with their surveillance and do nothing to draw any attention to his discovery.

He calmly sat on the edge of his bed and reached over to examine the envelope with Jake Aaronson's name on it. Without hesitation he tore it open to extract its contents. After reading the instruction card carefully, he focused his attention on his roommate's profile.

Name: Jacob Eleazar Aaronson
Date of Birth: July 18, 1980
Height: 5' 6"
Weight: 130#
Hair Color: Brown
Eyes: Blue
Skin: Fair
Place of Birth: Netanya, Israel
Current Residence: Bethesda, Maryland
Father's Name: Norman David Aaronson
Father's Position: Deputy Secretary of State
Mother: Lydia Abrams Aaronson
Siblings: None
Religion: Jewish, Conservative

Politics: Moderate

Academic Ranking: 1

Languages Spoken: English

IQ: 183 (Profoundly Gifted)

SAT Scores – 1600

ACT Score – 36

Special Skills: Puzzles, cryptography, cryptology

Hakeem arrogantly mumbled to himself, "So, he is small, weak, highly intelligent and Jewish. He poses no threat whatsoever, yet they have chosen him as my roommate. I must watch him carefully as there must be more to him than they are telling me. I will do as I am instructed and show them how a leader maintains his composure. I must study this Jake Aaronson closely and even become his friend. I can learn much more on the inside than from the outside."

Just as Hakeem was finishing his thoughts the dinner bell rang and he had not yet destroyed the document. He would burn the pages in the fireplace on his way out and would never mention their contents to anyone. He gathered his things, and just as he opened his bedroom door, he saw Jake putting something into the fireplace. He quietly closed his door and waited until Jake left the apartment before he, too, tossed his papers into the fire and watched them burst into flames. He waited to be sure there was nothing but ash before he made his way to the dining hall for his first meal at Winchester.

CHAPTER 9

The dining hall at Winchester was set with seventeen round tables of eight. Each table was seated with two roommates, their mentors, and four other upper classmen. Faculty did not mix with students and had their own dining room.

Each student was served a meal specifically designed to meet his nutritional needs. Special plates were prepared for those with any dietary restrictions based upon their religious observances or allergies. In the center of each table was a metal placard holder containing a card with that meal's designated topic of conversation. Since this was the first meal, tonight's discussion would center on personal introductions and general questions and answers to familiarize the new students with Winchester life.

The first to speak was a tall Afrikaner with a distinct accent. "My name is Jacobus Coetzee and I am from South Africa." He began. "My father is the attaché to the embassy in Washington. I am pleased to meet you and am here to learn."

"Pierre Deveraux is my name and I am from Paris. No need to tell you that I am French, that goes without saying. I will be surprised if we last here in America. The food is so disappointing."

The next to introduce himself was Vladimir Polokov from Moscow. In a thick Russian accent and with all the arrogance he could muster he declared, "My father is here, but I cannot discuss what he does. Of course it is very important or we would not be here. I am considered by most to be a virtuoso on the violin. I am sure you have heard of such an instrument."

Hakeem Baba spoke next suspicious of his classmates and simply stated, "Hakeem Baba from Turkey. We are here in the Washington area serving our country's Ambassador."

Finally, Jake Aaronson introduced himself by saying, "I am Jacob Aaronson, my friends call me Jake. I grew up around here and am happy to help you get your bearings."

This was the first social interaction between Hakeem and Jake, and each held his own during the table talk. They were both mindful to keep all discussion as superficial as possible as they carefully observed each other. Each was guarded in his own way and remained as minimally engaged as possible.

Jake took mental snapshots of each table and surveyed the room for any patterns. He would review and examine his mental notes later when alone in his room. Hakeem tried to remain inconspicuous as he noticed the base of the metal centerpiece was decorated with etched florets each containing what appeared to be a small lens. It, like the hidden camera in his room, had a small mesh object adjacent to it concealing the microphone beneath.

At exactly 7:00PM all four upperclassmen at each table stood to their feet and bid the new students a good evening and departed the dining hall. The mentors and their charges remained seated and the discussion took on a more direct tone.

At Jake and Hakeem's table, Hakeem's mentor Lawrence Worthington addressed the smaller group in his very proper British accent. His speech began with a firmly stated, "You are expected to conduct yourselves in a manner worthy of the Winchester name. During your tenure here your primary focus will be both personal and academic excellence. Anything less than your best in every situation will not be tolerated. We have a system of peer-based accountability, and any upperclassman may call you out at any time your conduct is unbecoming of the Winchester Standard." Without pausing for any confirmation Lawrence continued, "Trustworthiness is the highest of all character traits, and you will be entrusted with much during your time here at Winchester, no matter how long or how short a period that may be. What you do with that is up to you. You will be challenged beyond your comfort level academically, physically and emotionally. Your destiny is in your hands. Remember, nothing is impossible for the willing."

He closed with these words; "Breakfast is served at 6:30AM, and the dining hall doors close at exactly 6:30AM. Rest well and we will see if we will see you tomorrow. Goodnight." With that Lawrence and Jake's mentor, Yuri

Belenko, stood, pushed their chairs back into place, and left.

All that remained at each of the seventeen tables were the new students. Slowly each arose from their seats and exited. Some left in pairs, and others, like Jake and Hakeem, made their way solo out of the dining hall deep in their own thoughts.

As Jake took a circuitous route back to the dormitory, he replayed Lawrence Worthington's words in his head, "We will see if we will see you tomorrow," over and over until it registered that some had already violated the code when they openly discussed the confidential packets in the hallway. Jake would compare who was at breakfast the next morning with the mental photograph he had taken to see how many would be missing. In the meantime, there was work to be done unpacking and taking inventory of what else was in his room that was not so obvious.

Hakeem's route was more direct as he was intent on making it back to the apartment before his roommate so he could further search out other recording devices. He knew it would not be long before his search would uncover what he already had confirmed—that every student was being monitored. The only thing he did not yet know was why, but he would not rest until he figured it out.

Hakeem had completed his inspection and was in his room when Jake returned. Remembering his personal commitment to show them how a leader conducts himself, he opened the door to his bedroom and greeted Jake by saying, "Maybe we should sit down, talk, and get to know each other a little better."

As surprised as Jake was at the overture, he accepted and the two sat on the couch facing the fire. Hakeem began benignly, "So what do you think of all this?"

Jake's experience at small talk was limited at best, and he replied in typical Jake fashion with, "Precisely what are you asking?"

Hakeem looked Jake straight in the eye and laughed so loudly that it made Jake join him in the realization that it was really a funny response. Their laughter seemed to bring the two one step closer and ease the tension in the room.

As the laughter died down, Jake responded candidly, "I haven't really had time to process a lot of what I have seen. My first impression is there is much more here than meets the eye. It is certainly more serious than I thought it would be, but I am quite comfortable being serious."

Hakeem laughed at this response and confirmed, "I can see you are quite the serious one. Yes, I agree there is more here than either one of us knows. I can already tell they have a reason for everything they do here. Nothing is left to chance, and you and I rooming together must be a part of that plan. We come from two different worlds, and yet, we are expected to live harmoniously."

Jake paused a moment and then asked, "Where are you from that makes you think we are so different?"

The question initially caught Hakeem off balance, as he was certain Jake knew the answer already, but he knew he must play along and replied, "I was born in Iran and later on my father and I moved to Turkey. You must admit that is a different world than you come from."

Jake took this opportunity to share that he was born in Israel and his family came back to the United States before his first birthday. He had hoped to bridge the gap between them by showing they were both from the Middle East, but this seemed to agitate Hakeem instead.

Hakeem stood to his feet and seemed to lose his previous control when he declared, "This is exactly my point. We are from two different worlds that can never coexist. You and I are nothing alike."

At this, Jake mustered every bit of character in his being and rose to his feet to stand facing Hakeem. The much taller and stronger Hakeem towered over his smaller roommate, yet Jake boldly looked him squarely in the eyes as he took his foot and drug it across the carpet clearly drawing a line between them.

Jake laid down a challenge that was sure to start a fight as he said, "I dare you to step over this line." Hakeem was not one to back down from a challenge, and especially one issued by a puny adversary. Defiantly Hakeem stepped forward, crossing the line, and stood facing Jake, with only an inch or two separating them. The breath from Hakeem's flared nostrils washed over Jake's forehead as Jake proclaimed the words, "Now you are on my side!"

Hakeem's intellect won over his sense of offense and again he burst out into laughter in response to his roommate. Jake had won over his potential nemesis and was comforted by Hakeem's words, "You have heart, my little friend. We shall remain on the same side."

Their day ended on this note as they returned to their own rooms to process even more than they had anticipated.

CHAPTER 10

Jake rolled over at the sound of his clock radio's alarm and jumped to his feet anxious to start his first full day at Winchester, even at 5:30AM. He remembered the guidelines in the student handbook that every bed must be made daily and rooms kept neat. By 5:45 he had made his bed, brushed his teeth, and changed into his uniform. Already neatly hung in his closet were his Brook's Brothers' Blue Oxford cloth button-down shirt, Dockers khaki pants, and the Member's Only windbreaker with the Winchester Crest proudly displayed over his heart. He threw his already prepared Winchester backpack over his shoulder. It was fully laden with books, athletic gear, and all the items necessary to take on the day that lay ahead.

He was sure he would be the first out of the door and thought to himself, "This would be a good time to look around while everyone else is still waking up." He left his bedroom and paused to hear if Hakeem was up yet. Hearing him still in his room, Jake left without saying a word, quietly closing the door behind him.

No one else was in the hall, and Jake made his way downstairs and out into the Quad without running into anyone. It was still just before sunrise, and the glow of the mercury vapor bulbs washed the sidewalk with a crisscross pattern of light.

Jake took notice of the closed circuit TV video cameras mounted on the corners of each building he passed and on every seventh light pole. He saw a network of wires dropping down the sides of every building into a pipe sticking a few inches out of the ground. Jake began to wonder where all these wires were going and pulled out his campus map and began matching each building he saw with its respective location on the map. He counted seventeen named buildings on the map, but his mental count was eighteen. He had only a few more minutes to get to the dining hall in time for breakfast and would have to review his miscount later. His day was full with the start of classes and meeting his new professors. He caught himself being excited about this new adventure and the challenges that lay ahead, but also had a piece of the puzzle out of order. He knew that would haunt him all day until he could reconcile the number of buildings.

The line to the Dining Hall was not as long as Jake had expected and he arrived with plenty of time to spare. The room was still configured the same way it had been at dinner, but there was a noticeable difference in the number of empty chairs at some of the tables. There was still time before the doors closed, but the last one to take their seat was Hakeem. Jake counted five empty spots around the room and noticed right away they all were where incoming freshman had sat the night before.

Jake nudged Hakeem and tried to get him to look in the same direction to notice what he had observed, but something was keeping Hakeem from acknowledging Jake's efforts. He seemed to be staring at the centerpiece that contained this meal's subject card. Jake followed his eyes and noticed they were not on the card, but on the bottom of the stand. He focused where Hakeem was focusing and he became aware of the lens embedded in each etched floret at the bottom of the base. Jake was now as aware as Hakeem that a lens was positioned in front of each of the eight occupants at the table and they were being watched. He, too, noticed the mesh-covered spots adjacent to the lens and knew it covered a microphone as well.

At precisely 7:00AM, Hakeem's mentor, Lawrence Worthington, in perfect harmony with the mentors at every other table, reached out and took the placard off the center stand and began to read aloud. In perfect unison seventeen voices could be heard reciting the same words, "Today begins your first full day at Winchester. Your time here is planned to maximize your personal growth and no two schedules are exactly the same. You are to be where you are expected to be at the time assigned to you. Do not be confused by the staggered nature of the schedule. Your schedule pertains to you and you alone. Lunch is served here at 12:00PM and the doors close precisely at 12:00PM. Attendance at all meals, functions, meetings, and classes is mandatory. Tardiness will not be tolerated. You have everything you need for the entire day and will return to your rooms to prepare for dinner with plenty of time to spare. You are dismissed."

Upon dismissal, all 136 students minus the five absentees stood with such precise timing that it would have appeared to be a synchronized movement. Their exit out the doors was much less orderly as each rushed to make it to their first class on time.

Jake tried to catch up to Hakeem to discuss what he saw at the base of the placard stands and to talk about the missing five. He looked, but Hakeem was already twenty yards ahead of him and on a path in a different direction.

Jake had not forgotten about the unmarked Building 18, and on his way to his first class he thought he saw a building not shown on the map. His route for the reminder of the day would take him to the opposite side of the campus and he would not have another opportunity to check it out until the following day. He did, however, make mental notes of camera locations on every building he passed and would plot them out later that night in his room. There was a pattern here, and he would figure it out in typical Jake Aaronson fashion.

It was already quite obvious the Winchester Academy was much more than what the brochure contained. It was now Jake's personal mission to find out all he could. By the time he arrived at his first class of the day, there was a smile on his face that could not hide his excitement.

CHAPTER 11

Every class at the Winchester Academy was populated by a full cross-section of students regardless of their traditional status as freshman, sophomore, junior or senior. Jake's class schedule was heavily weighted towards math and science. The only class he had in common with Hakeem was Calculus. Some classes had up to twelve students and others as little as four. All the teachers had their PhD's and taught multiple classes within their respective discipline.

There were no intramural teams at such a small-specialized school like Winchester; however, there was still tremendous emphasis placed on physical fitness. Mornings were devoted to academics and afternoons were for physical development. The classes offered were all focused on martial arts and was on everyone's schedule after lunch.

Jake had never taken even so much as a beginner's class in any sport. He was on the verge of intimidation at the thought of spending three hours every day in this one area. He had never been intellectually intimated by anyone, but physically, he was not so confident. If his body were in the same shape as his mind, he would have been ripped with muscles, but it wasn't.

After lunch, Jake returned to his room and changed into the white gi hanging in his closet.

He wrapped the white belt around his waist and headed off to his very first karate class. The smile that was there earlier when he was on his way to his morning classes was replaced with a worried look tinged with a fear.

In stark contrast to Jake's lack of martial art's training, Hakeem was already an expert with many years of training. He had already changed into his dobok, proudly tied with his black belt, and sprinted to his advanced taekwondo class with great enthusiasm.

The Pittman Athletic Center was unlike any other Jake had ever seen. In the center, where you would expect a basketball court, were six fully padded open ceiling rooms. On the second floor was a catwalk extending all the way around and served as an observation deck providing an overhead view into each room. No sound could be heard between the rooms; however, the observation deck was constructed with six parabolic microphones aimed at each room. There were six headphone equipped observation platforms. Hidden next to the microphone inside the parabolic dish was a lipstick camera providing a video feed. Every room was separately audio and video recorded. Through the use of motion activation, every room could be recorded automatically.

There was a running track outside of the classrooms resembling a beltway with exit ramps leading into the six padded rooms. Above the entrance to each room was a number. Jake entered his assigned room number one and Hakeem entered room number five. The only time they would see each other during their three-hour class was the mandatory twenty-five laps around the track after the thirty-minute warm up period was complete.

Hakeem's smile was plastered to his face as he lapped his roommate for the third time and finished his twenty-five-lap run. Jake never saw Hakeem run past him as he struggled to keep his legs moving just hoping he would live through this torture.

Completely spent, Jake made his way around the track and entered room number one. He was the last to arrive and class had already continued without him. Dr. Mimura looked at Jake and waited for him to bow in recognition of his late entry. Jake could barely catch his breath and see through his sweat-filled eyes as Dr. Mimura approached. Jake leaned in as his instructor spoke at a very low whisper, "Never let this happen again. Nothing is impossible for the willing."

Jake thought to himself, "I am willing, even if it kills me. And it just might."

For the next two hours Jake found an inner strength he never knew existed and kept up with his classmates. By the time he made it back to his room he was too exhausted to try and talk to Hakeem about anything. All he had the strength to do was shower, dress, and walk to the dining hall in time for dinner.

Jake's legs burned, his arms hurt, and had cramps in places he had never felt before. He was too tired to even notice that the five chairs that had been empty were now filled at all the tables. He was so fatigued he barely heard the evening topic and did not participate in any of the table discussion. Eating was physically challenging as his arms were like noodles. All he could think of was his bed.

The only obstacle between Jake and his bed was the long walk from the dining hall. To keep his mind off the searing pain that consumed his body, he counted every step between the dining hall and his room. In his final physical act of the night, he threw his clothes on the floor and crawled into bed. It took every bit of his remaining strength to set his alarm for 3:30AM so he could wake and do his homework.

CHAPTER 12

Although Jake and Hakeem were room-mates, there was little interaction between them during the course of the first week. Both schedules were full and their exit and entry into the dorm room never seemed to coincide. They shared one class and Hakeem continued to lap Jake on the track daily, but even at meals there was no chance to talk. Every day was planned except Sunday. This afforded each student the chance to catch up on sleep as Sunday Brunch was not until 10:30AM. Some students opted to attend the chapel for non-denominational services, but few chose this over the added hours of sleep. The afternoons were free and the dining hall had a self-serve sandwich bar open from 1:00-3:00PM.

Hakeem seemed somewhat aloof as Jake greeted him in their kitchenette with a very cheerful "Good Morning." Hakeem nodded, gave a half smile, poured his coffee, and started back to his room. Jake called after him, "Wait, Hakeem, there are things I want to talk to you about. Things I've seen and know that you have too."

Hakeem spun around, almost spilling his coffee, as he cast his eyes on a spot in the ceiling and turned back and proceeded into his room. In less than a minute he emerged with his Calculus textbook and a notepad. He motioned for Jake to meet him at the table and sat down next to him. As Jake sat down, Hakeem spoke up and said, "Please help me understand this problem I am struggling with."

Jake was clearly confused by Hakeem's actions and replied, "Sure, but it's Sunday and we have plenty of time to study later." Just as he finished saying that, Jake looked down and saw Hakeem had scrawled across a sheet of paper inside his open textbook "Meet me by the fountain in 10 minutes. Say nothing more."

Jake took the hint and said, "Hakeem, I will help you later. It is too nice outside to sit in here and waste our free time." He got up from the table, went into his room, changed into his sweats, and left the dorm room. Five minutes later Hakeem did the same.

They arrived at the fountain in the center of the quad at almost the exact same time. Hakeem was facing the fountain as he said to Jake, "What is it that you have to tell me?"

Jake replied, "Why did we have to leave our room to talk about what I wanted to talk about there? Is something wrong?"

Hakeem answered, "What we say and what we do can be heard and seen except in our bathroom and here at the fountain. Would you not think it odd for me to invite you into my bathroom to have a conversation? We come from different places, but surely this is not something you would find normal in your culture, is it?"

Jake laughed and assured Hakeem that he was correct in his assessment. Then Jake asked him, "How do you know they can see and hear everything?

Hakeem stepped closer to Jake, and for the second time in their brief relationship Jake could feel Hakeem's breath on his face. Hakeem sharply retorted, "Do you think I am a fool? You pretend you do not know and want me to tell you what I know. Is this some game you are playing with me? How do I know I can trust you?"

Jake stepped back so that he could compose himself and gave his assurance, "We are on the same side, remember?"

Hakeem's defensive posture softened and he nodded in affirmation. Quickly looking around to make sure no one else was within earshot he said, "Yes, I remember, but humor me by telling what you know first and then I will share what I have seen. You are the one who indicated you had something you wanted to discuss with me."

Jake began excitedly, " Did you notice the five missing students and then five new ones showing up? Did you see the cameras and the microphones in Pittman? Did you see that every building has cameras mounted on the outside? I know you saw the microphones on the dining tables. Did you notice that there are seventeen buildings on the campus map, but there are actually eighteen buildings?"

Hakeem laughed out loud as he told Jake slow down and take a breath. "I have observed much of what you just spoke of, but not all. I am impressed with these observations and will share with you what I have found." He continued, "In our rooms under the shelf above the computer is a microphone. There is also a camera that is aimed at the keyboard and the monitor. A microphone and camera are also mounted in the overhead light in the living room. That is why I hid the note inside my textbook, so it could not be seen on the overhead camera."

Jake was wide eyed as he said, "Why do you think everything is so closely watched? What is this place? Do you think it is some kind of training camp? I know I feel like I am in some type of military school without the uniforms, marching, and saluting. Do you think it is just for protection because of our parents and their positions? Do you think the teachers have guns? Do you think that the extra building is a bomb shelter?"

Again Hakeem laughed at his roommate. "Calm down, my little friend. You are so serious and have so many questions. I am not sure what it is all about, but of this I am certain. We cannot trust anyone else with what we know. We have to find a way to communicate with each other without drawing any attention. Meeting here too often with just arouse suspicion. What do you suggest?"

Jake's countenance changed from dead serious to beaming with pride as he asked Hakeem, "What do you know about secret codes? "

"Not much," Hakeem replied.

Jake smiled from ear to ear and said, "Then leave it up to me to create a code just for us. I will give you a code key to memorize. There will be one key for written notes and one key for spoken messages. This will be a way for you and I to communicate without anyone else knowing that we are up to something."

"Ah, a new language. This is something I will enjoy." Hakeem continued, "We need to keep each other informed of what we learn and this will be the way we shall do it. Let us return to our room by different paths and then get something to eat. No more talk of this for now."

CHAPTER 13

In between the rigorous class schedule and physical activities, Jake worked on creating both a written and verbal code by which he and Hakeem could communicate privately. For the written code, Jake decided to use a modified shifted alphabet code where the shift would coincide with the number of the week in the school semester. This was simple enough, but changed every week based on an agreed upon key. The way it worked was to take the alphabet and shift the number of letters over based on the number of the week. For Week One, the letter A would shift over one letter to become a B; B would shift one letter over and become a C, and so on throughout the alphabet. Z would become an A, as the counting continued back at the beginning of the alphabet.

To develop a starting point for the letter shift, week one would always begin on August 10. Every school year at Winchester began on that date to honor the founding father's birthday, regardless of the day of the week. Each week the shift would advance one more letter. Since the semesters were each thirteen weeks long, the code would start over two times per year to accommodate all twenty-six letters in the alphabet.

Jake always liked to use his name as the example. For week one, Jake Aaronson would be spelled KBLF BBSPOTPO. For Hakeem's benefit, Jake spelled out his name for him to get the hang of the code. Hakeem Baba would be IBLFFN CBCB.

The verbal code would be different, and Jake felt it best to simply create a list of phrases and their translation. He knew this would limit the number of messages they could pass to each other verbally, but it would have to do for now. He decided to start with four simple phrases and then add to them over time.

The first encoded verbal phrases he would teach Hakeem were all related to where they would leave written messages for each. This would make it easier to convey more information in a written note than could be shared through a pass phrase.

Jake knew this would have to be simple in order for it to be effectively used. The first was to be used when they were both in the dorm room, "Do you want some toast?" This would mean there was a note in the breadbox. Once this message had been passed, the recipient could retrieve the message at his convenience without drawing any attention to his activity. What could be more normal than opening a breadbox and making toast?

The second was a pass phrase to be used when in the dining hall and could be used at any meal, "Do we need to pick up some tea for the room?" This would mean there was note in the cupboard in their kitchenette where they kept the tea bags.

Hakeem was fonder of tea than Jake, but there was more in the cupboard than tea.

The third was, "Do you need to go over any Calculus homework?" This would mean there was a note in the other's textbook.

And the final phrase for now would be, "I seem to get thirsty every hour." This would be the signal to meet at the fountain in one hour or whatever time period was inserted.

Between the written code and the pass phrases, Jake was certain he and Hakeem could communicate in private. Why they needed to do this was still unknown along with several other questions that still remained unanswered. Most pressing for Jake what was Building Eighteen all about?

Before Jake sat down at his computer he made a mental note of where the video camera was located and how he could shield his keyboard and monitor from view. Once he figured out how to block out the camera, he keyed in the codes and pass phrases and printed a copy for Hakeem. He placed the document in his calculus book and positioned himself outside of their classroom and waited for Hakeem to arrive. As Hakeem rounded the corner, Jake deliberately stepped in front of him, blocking them both from the camera in the corner of the hallway. Jake had his Calculus book opened to where he had the written instructions. Hakeem saw what Jake was trying to do, took the cue, and pulled his book out and opened it. As if Jake and Hakeem were reviewing some complex formula, Jake slid the paper into Hakeem's book without drawing any undue attention to the pair. Without saying a word, the transfer had taken place.

After lunch Jake returned to their room to dress for martial arts class. On the way he passed Hakeem, who had already been to their room and changed. As Jake passed by, Hakeem said, "You should make sure to drink a cup of tea before you go to class." Jake paused for a moment to process this odd greeting, and then smiled, as he knew his roommate had not only understood the pass phrases, but also improvised them to fit the circumstance.

Upon arriving at their room, Jake put his book bag down and went to the cupboard. There, inside a mug, was a neatly folded note. Jake reached in, palmed the folded paper, and shook his head as if to say he had changed his mind about getting a drink. He immediately went into his bathroom and closed the door. He unfolded the note and there he saw printed: MDNH L XQGHUVWDQG!

Jake wrote underneath these letters the alphabet and began counting. ABCDEFGHIJKLMNOPQRSTUVWXYZ.

First he had to calculate what week they were in from the start of the school year. They were in Week Three of class. Now that he had the starting point, Jake would apply the key and back up three letters.

MDNH L XQGHUVWDQG = JAKE I UNDERSTAND!

Jake smiled as he thought, "Maybe I have underestimated my friend. His language skills do apply to codes."

As Jake dressed for his martial arts class, he took a moment for some personal reflection. In the first three weeks he had encountered no obstacles to his academic success. However, he realized if he were to fully embrace the school's regimen and what lie ahead, he would have to rise to the physical challenge. He took a personal inventory, and made it his goal to improve his physical performance so that he could catch up to Hakeem on the running track. He was already improving, and once he figured out the pattern of the karate moves, he would be able to master them in short order. It was now a priority that when he finished with his four years he would be able to defend himself both academically and physically.

Although he had heard the phrase "Nothing was impossible for the willing" a number of times, it was now a part of his personal mantra. He had come to a crossroads and found within a strength he had never before embraced.

CHAPTER 14

During the first four weeks the school's policy dictated there was to be no direct contact between parents and students. This was designed to give them both the chance to adjust accordingly. Parents could contact the Headmaster via phone or email and would be given regular updates as requested; however, this was not encouraged.

It was now early September. The Jewish New Year, ushering in the biblical Fall Feasts, was soon approaching. Lydia Aaronson wanted Jake to come home to celebrate Rosh Hashanah, the Jewish New Year, and then again, ten days later, for Yom Kippur, The Day of Atonement. She had communicated this both at registration and through follow-up emails to Headmaster Dr. Prescott Reed. Not one to be passive, Lydia persisted until she was given the answer she desired. Norman was ambivalent about the whole thing and left these matters to his wife.

During Jake's first call home, his father asked him the usual questions, and then handed the phone to the more talkative and probing of the two parents. Lydia asked her son if he was eating and how he was getting along with the other boys. Jake knew to give enough information to satisfy her, but too many details would only make the discussion that much longer. The conversation turned to his roommate, and since he had not spoken to his parents since leaving for school, there were many questions about Hakeem. After sharing all he could safely tell without disclosing anything contained in his confidential profile, his mother asked if he thought it would be a good idea to invite Hakeem home for the holidays. Jake thought for a moment and answered, "Mom, he is a Muslim."

Lydia quickly replied, "And when did some-one's race or religion ever stop us from inviting them into our home?"

"I didn't mean it like that!" Jake quickly defended himself. "I only meant that he is not Jewish, and I only know Jewish people who celebrate the holidays we do."

Lydia replied, "There is a bigger world out there than you know, and I have plenty of Christian friends who have been celebrating as well. They have become very interested in the Jewish roots of their faith. I think it would be a good thing for you to invite him since you are referring to him as your new best friend. Let me talk to your father before you say anything. Since that ridiculous silent period has now passed, I can email you and stay in touch with my only son."

After the call, Lydia spoke to her husband about the possibility of inviting Jake's roommate home for the holidays. This was not anticipated and necessitated certain protocols to be followed. Communication went back and forth between the State Department and the Turkish Embassy, since this involved the sons of two prominent members of the diplomatic community. Once approval was given, Jake was free to discuss the invitation with Hakeem. Ultimately it would be Hakeem's decision as to whether or not he would accept.

After receiving an email from his mom clearing the way, Jake approached Hakeem on Sunday morning and said, "I have something I would like to talk with you about." Since they were out in the open and no pass phrase was given, Hakeem expected this to be a rather benign conversation.

Jake began, "Since we have been roommates I have come to recognize that we have much in common, but also many differences. You are a Muslim. I am a Jew. We have never really spoken of what you have been taught regarding Jews. I admit I only know about Muslims from what I read in the paper or hear on the news. In a few weeks my family will be celebrating the Jewish New Year called Rosh Hashanah. I would like to invite you to come home with me and celebrate with us. The food is great and my parents are excited to meet my roommate and get to know you better.

Hakeem smiled and answered, "This is a great honor to be invited into your home. But, please, tell me what this is all about so I might understand it better."

Jake drew upon his Jewish education along with his Bar Mitzvah training and began to tell the story of God calling Abraham. At this

Hakeem interjected, "Yes, Father Abraham, of him I know much. Please continue."

Jake went on, "God called Abraham and told him to take his only son Isaac up on top of the mountain to sacrifice him. Because he was willing to perform this act of faith, God spared Isaac's life and provided a ram instead."

Hakeem was indignant when he proclaimed, "This cannot be so. The son who was to be sacrificed was Ishmael. Where do you get such lies? You do not know much about Islam, but this I do know about the Jews. The Jews have taken everything that belongs to us. Our land, our inheritance, our promises, all was stolen from us. I know this because the Koran and the elders tell me this. I have read it for myself and seen firsthand the pictures of their treatment of the rightful heirs to the land they occupy."

Jake was at first surprised by Hakeem's intensity, but maintained his composure and offered, "We have embraced many of our differences and said we are friends. I have taken nothing from you and you have taken nothing from me. If you will come to visit with me, I will go with you to learn more of your beliefs. You are my best friend here and I want you to come with me. Please Hakeem."

Hakeem stood firm, remembering his father's instruction, and stated, "I will grant this, but I cannot promise how I will sit through such teaching. It will be good to meet your mother and father, and I will show them the proper respect.

Of this you can be sure. Thank you for calling me your best friend. I have found that in you as well. Come now, let us not be late for brunch."

CHAPTER 15

The weeks leading up to the first off-campus trip passed by quickly. The black chauffeur-driven limousine pulled up to the security entrance of the Winchester Academy. In spite of the United States flag and diplomatic plates clearly displayed, the driver was required to stop and show proper identification prior to entering the grounds. After passing through the security gate, he drove up the tree-lined driveway and stopped underneath the portico leading into the school's main offices. After showing his identification for a second time he was then cleared to sign both students out and transport them off the school's property.

Jake and Hakeem waited patiently beside their suitcases as they watched the limo driver check them out. Once everything was properly documented, the driver took their bags and led them to the awaiting car. The average teenager would be excited to be treated this way and driven in a long black limo, but this was routine for the sons of two international diplomats.

Once seated in the back, Jake and Hakeem settled in for the short twenty-minute drive to Jake's home. Hakeem did not know what to expect, and when the gates to the Aaronsons' driveway swung open, he thought they were being taken to another school. Hakeem had come from affluence, but this was not what he was accustomed to either in Turkey or in Iran. He thought to himself, "How greedy these Westerners are. There is only one mother and one father and one son living in such opulence. In my world, families of much larger size live in much smaller accommodations and seem to do just fine."

Lydia was anxiously waiting at the door and ran out to greet Jake and Hakeem. "You look so thin" were the first words out of her mouth as she closely hugged her son. Jake broke the embrace and said, "Mom, this is my roommate and best friend, Hakeem Baba."

Lydia grasped Hakeem's extended hand and pulled him into a motherly embrace and said, "You are most welcome in our home and our family, Thank you for being such a good friend to our son. Come inside now and get something to eat. You boys are so thin."

As they walked inside, Lydia could not help but notice the change in her son. He appeared to have grown at least an inch and looked lean and fit, more like a young man than the boy she had sent off to school just six weeks prior. She liked what she saw and was glad to have her only child home. She did, however, make mental note that Hakeem did not look like she had expected and was much more fair than his name would imply. Her husband had only mentioned the father, and she wondered about his mother. Norman was the diplomat. She was the mother and would ask all kinds of questions that her husband would not dare to ask. He could have his State Department. She had something more powerful—*chutzpah!*

"Boys," Lydia motioned towards the kitchen and continued, "Take your plates and eat in Jake's room. I will have your bags sent up and you can relax until dinnertime. Don't forget we have services tonight and tomorrow morning and you will need to dress for dinner."

As Jake and Hakeem walked up the stairs carrying their plates of food Hakeem looked at Jake and asked, "Do you normally eat dinner without wearing any clothing?"

Jake laughed and said, "Of course not, why do you ask that?"

"Well," Hakeem stated, "your mother said to dress for dinner as if that was something out of the ordinary."

Jake replied, "That's just an expression used to tell us we need to wear a tie tonight." Hakeem's look changed from concern to relief and they continued on to Jake's room.

The first time Hakeem met Jake's father was at the dinner table. The boys had used the time in between lunch and dinner to unpack and take a rare nap. Norman Aaronson was a man of large stature and girth, and to some he looked quite intimidating. After hugging his son and kissing him on the cheek, he extended a meaty hand to Hakeem and welcomed him to his home. Norman shared, "I have had the pleasure of meeting with your father as I thought it would be good to get to know him since our sons were roommates. He told me he looks forward to speaking with you after your visit with us. Please call him when you get back to school."

Hakeem acknowledged with a firm grip and thanked Mr. Aaronson for the message.

"So, boys, tell me, how do you like school so far?" Norman asked.

Jake waited to see if Hakeem would be the first to speak, and when he did not say anything, Jake chimed in, "We both really like school a lot. It has had its challenges, but I think we are doing very well. They require us to excel in all areas, and academically that has been much easier for me than the physical part."

Norman addressed them both as he replied, "If you are both as fit as you look, I would say Winchester has been good for you two. I can't speak for how Hakeem used to look, but, son, you look like you are getting into great shape. Are those muscles?"

"Dad, please," Jake pleaded.

Lydia came to her son's rescue with her own comments, "Well, I think you two are very handsome, and it seems like whatever they are doing over there at that school agrees with both of you. Now, let us begin this New Year by lighting the Holiday Candles. Hakeem, these candles are lit to commemorate the beginning of this holiday, which starts at sundown. These are a reminder of God's first command, 'Let there be light.'"

Lydia stood up and put a doily on her head, struck a match, and reached out to light two candles on the table. She moved her hands over the candles as if she were waiving the light of the candles towards herself and then placed her hands over her eyes and began to pray. She began in Hebrew first with, "*Barukh atah Adonai Eloheinu melekh ha'olam asher kid'shanu b'mitzvotav v'tzivanu l'hadlik ner shel yom tov.*" Then in English, "Blessed are You, Lord our God, Ruler of the Universe, who has sanctified us with commandments, and commanded us to light festival candles."

Hakeem watched and listened intently as he was quite familiar with Hebrew. He spoke the language, but had never seen it used like this in person. He could also tell that Hebrew was a second language to Jake's mother and father and they were quite fluent. He recalled that Jake was born in Israel and that his father had been stationed there on assignment with the US State Department.

As Lydia sat down, Norman stood. All eyes were on him as he lifted a silver cup with wine in it and said in Hebrew, "*Barukh ata Adonai Eloheinu melekh ha'olam borei p'ri hagafen.* He continued in English, "Blessed are You, Lord our God, Ruler of the universe, who creates the fruit of the vine."

He continued, "Hakeem, wine or grape juice is a symbol of joy in Judaism, and tonight we share this cup so that our joy can be shared. Out of respect for your faith, we have filled the cup with grape juice so you may join us in this celebration." After drinking from the cup Norman passed it first to his wife, then his son and finally to Hakeem, who acknowledged the gesture and took a sip.

Norman remained standing as he lifted a plate with the round loaf of bread on it. He reached out and tore a piece from it. He then prayed first in Hebrew, "*Barukh ata Adonai Eloheinu melekh ha'olam hamotzi lehem min ha'aretz.*" Then in English, "Blessed are You, Lord our God, Ruler of the universe, who brings forth bread from the earth."

He then took a bite of the bread and passed it around, explaining, "Hakeem, bread is a symbol in Judaism of God's provision. Please join us as we break bread together as one family." Hakeem participated in this as well.

Norman now pointed to a plate with sliced apples and a small bowl with an amber-colored fluid in it. He took a piece of the apple and dipped it into the liquid and said, "Hakeem, I have taken a slice of apple and dipped it into honey. In Judaism, they are symbolic of the desire to start the New Year with something sweet in hopes it will pave the way for the entire year to be a sweet one. He prayed first in Hebrew, "*Barukh atah Adonai, Elohaynu, melekh ha-olam, borei p'riy ha-eitz.*" And then in English, "Blessed art Thou, Lord, our God, King of the Universe, who creates the fruit of the tree."

Norman then ate the apple dipped in honey and after he finished chewing said in Hebrew,

"*Y'hi ratzon me'elfanekha, Adonai Elohaynu v'elohey avoteynu sh'tichadesh aleinu shanah tovah u-m'tukah.*" And then in English, "May it be Your will, Lord our God and God of our ancestors, that You renew for us a good and sweet year."

Norman looked at Hakeem for the third time and said, "Hakeem will you please join our family in this tradition so that you also may enjoy a sweet New Year?"

Hakeem reached out, took the apple offered to him, and dipped it in the honey as requested. It did taste sweet to his lips.

Norman proclaimed, "Enough praying and blessing. Let's eat already." At that, dinner was served.

Jake enjoyed explaining what all the different foods were. He did not hesitate to point out which ones were his favorites and which ones were not. Hakeem tasted everything out of respect for his hosts and was surprisingly pleased at the variety of flavors. As far as he could tell so far, there was not that much difference between a Jewish feast and a Muslim one. There was plenty of food and laughter, and he enjoyed the dinner meal with the Aaronson family.

After the apple cake and last cup of coffee was finished, Lydia announced, "It's time for us to go to the synagogue."

There would be no chauffeur-driven limousine tonight, and all four piled into the family car. Norman drove, and Lydia asked Hakeem if Jake had explained to him where they were going and what they would be doing. Hakeem answered, "Yes, Mrs. Aaronson, Jake explained much to me. I am interested to hear how Father Abraham is explained. I have been taught and have read for myself a different account than the one Jake told me. Thank you for the wonderful dinner. It was very delicious."

Lydia replied, "After we return from services tonight maybe I will make us all some hot chocolate and we can talk more about your faith and the differences in what we believe. I think that would be very interesting, don't you, Norman?" Her husband nodded in agreement, knowing that was the only acceptable response.

CHAPTER 16

The Aaronsons, along with their guest Hakeem, were greeted immediately upon entering the synagogue and were escorted to a seat right in the front row. Jake leaned over and whispered in Hakeem's ear, "My family traces its ancestry back to the family of Moses' brother Aaron, and they treat us and the others of that lineage like we are something really special. I think it's just because my dad gives them a lot of money."

Hakeem looked around at the well-dressed people and the ornate synagogue. The windows were made of stained glass and depicted scenes from their Bible. He recognized many of them, but not all. It was a lot for Hakeem to take in, and he was not comfortable in such unfamiliar surroundings.

The service was long, and people had to stand up and sit down many times. Hakeem noted that no one lay prostrate as they did in his religion. He also made note of the fact that Jake's father was the first of many to be called up to the scrolls, which Hakeem was told were the books written by Moses.

An older-looking man with a white beard got up to speak and everyone else sat down. He began with a joke that made people laugh, but Hakeem did not understand it. Jake said, "That's

Rabbi Lazar. This is the part where he will talk about Abraham and Isaac."

After the laughter died down, Rabbi Lazar began, "The story of the patriarch Abraham is the subject of many sermons. Our very history and lineage is attributed to the faithfulness of this man. The promises that God made to him and his sons are the very promises we stand on this very night. God promised that our inheritance would be passed down through a specific ancestral line. This lineage was from Abraham to Isaac, from Isaac to Jacob and extending to each and every Jewish man, woman and child born to this bloodline. This was an everlasting and irrevocable covenant that stands even today."

Hakeem began to squirm as he heard these words and could hear his father's voice in his head, "It will not be easy, my son, as you will live with your sworn enemy. You must not allow them to provoke you." He took a deep breath and composed himself as the Rabbi continued.

"Tonight we celebrate the Son of the Promise, Isaac. There is no question as to the faithfulness of Abraham as he followed God's commands to leave his homeland, but what of his son's faithfulness and trust in his father? Let us examine this aspect of the story as we read from Torah. Genesis 22:1-12 reads:

> Some time later God tested Abraham. He said to him, "Abraham!" "Here I am," he replied. 2 Then God said, "Take your son, your only son, Isaac, whom you love,

and go to the region of Moriah. Sacrifice him there as a burnt offering on one of the mountains I will tell you about."

The Rabbi paused for a moment to let the weight of this request from God sink in. He then asked, "What would you do if you were called to make this same sacrifice? Would you be so trusting and faithful to obey what would seem to a merciless command? How could a loving God ask anyone to do such a thing? Let us continue to read more and see how this story unfolds."

3 Early the next morning Abraham got up and saddled his donkey. He took with him two of his servants and his son Isaac. When he had cut enough wood for the burnt offering, he set out for the place God had told him about. 4 On the third day Abraham looked up and saw the place in the distance. 5 He said to his servants, "Stay here with the donkey while I and the boy go over there. We will worship and then we will come back to you."

Again the Rabbi paused to allow these verses to linger a little longer. He then spoke, "How interesting that Abraham would be so bold, knowing what he was being called to do, to say to his servants we, meaning himself and Isaac, would be back. Would you have the same confidence and trust in God that Abraham demonstrated?"

6 Abraham took the wood for the burnt offering and placed it on his son Isaac, and he himself carried the fire and the knife. As the two of them went on together, 7 Isaac spoke up and said to his father Abraham, "Father?" "Yes, my son?" Abraham replied. "The fire and wood are here," Isaac said, "but where is the lamb for the burnt offering?" 8 Abraham answered, "God himself will provide the lamb for the burnt offering, my son."

By now the Rabbi's pause signified a point was about to be made. He looked around the room at each face he could see and said, "The son asked a very insightful question. He realized that there was no sacrifice in sight, yet he knew that he could turn to his father for the answer. Without hesitation, Abraham told Isaac, God himself will provide. He had not seen any evidence of an animal suitable for sacrifice, yet, he boldly spoke in such a confident manner that it satisfied his son."

And the two of them went on together. 9 When they reached the place God had told him about, Abraham built an altar there and arranged the wood on it. He bound his son Isaac and laid him on the altar, on top of the wood. 10 Then he reached out his hand and took the knife to slay his son. 11 But the angel of the Lord called out to him from heaven, "Abraham! Abraham!" "Here I am," he replied. 12 "Do not lay a hand on the boy," he said. "Do not do anything to him. Now I know that you fear God, because you have not withheld from me your son, your only son."

Rabbi Lazar looked out at the crowd and made eye contact with each one on the front row, Hakeem included, and proclaimed, "And as Abraham had assured his son, God himself provided a ram caught in a thicket to be the sacrifice instead of Isaac. What son's trust of his father today could even compare with the trust of Isaac? Surely such an action today on the part of any father would be met with such outrage that it would be difficult to contain. No doubt the police and social services would be involved. The newspapers would run one expose after another demonizing such behavior on the part of a parent. I can not even imagine what would be waiting for him when he came home to tell his wife how he and his son spent the day together!" At this a ripple of laughter swept through the congregation and the tension, for all but one, was broken.

As the laughter died down and the Rabbi added more stories of faithfulness on the part of Abraham and his family, he closed his sermon with this, "Truly, Isaac was the son of the promise, for he was so faithful to trust his father and God's provision that he was willing to be sacrificed. By this selfless act of faith we know that Isaac, Abraham's only son, was whom God had chosen to inherit Israel's blessings. The ram caught in the thicket was sacrificed instead of

Isaac and the blowing of the ram's horn, the sho-far, is our reminder of the promise that stands today for us and all of Israel."

Hakeem could barely contain his outrage, as he knew the Quran spoke of the sacrifice of Ishmael. He had now witnessed firsthand the propaganda and lies of the enemy he had only heard stories of when he was younger. He now understood more clearly that he was chosen as his father reminded him. "Yes," he whispered to himself, "I must learn all I can so that one day I can fulfill my calling to tear the heart out of the very ones who stole all that he knew was sacred."

As the family stood to shake hands and exchange New Year's best wishes to their acquaint-ances, Jake leaned over and asked Hakeem, "You want to get out of here and get something to eat and drink? They have great apple cakes down-stairs." Hakeem nodded without any hesitation, as he would have given anything to run as far as he could from this building.

The crowd was large and Hakeem used the time to compose himself so that his anger would not be perceptible to anyone. By the time they made it downstairs into the fellowship area, he was able to be cordial and engaging to everyone he met. Jake seemed to know everyone, and by the time they made it from the doorway to the dessert table Hakeem was actually hungry. He gratefully accepted a plate filled with little apple and honey cakes from a large woman in a frilly apron. She had a warm smile that softened his attitude even more.

Jake grabbed his arm, pulled him into a corner, and sat him down in the last available chair. The noise in the room was deafening. It seemed each person had to talk louder than the next just to be heard. Hakeem and Jake sat and ate in silence.

"There you boys are," Lydia proclaimed as she approached with a large plate of honey cakes. "You boys need to eat and then we will go home and let Hakeem ask any questions he may have. I know it is a lot to take in." They both enjoyed the honey cakes and needed no encouragement to eat more before they made the return trip to Jake's home.

All during the ride Hakeem's thoughts kept returning to the story he had heard that was so different than what he had been taught. Everyone was so nice, but he could not let this poison his mind.

As they pulled into the garage Lydia spoke to the boys saying, "Boys, go up, change, and join us in front of the fire in a few minutes."

Lydia took Norman's arm and led him into the kitchen. "What did I do?" Norman asked.

Lydia laughed and said, "Nothing dear. Do you think it was a mistake to take Hakeem, a Muslim, to services with us? I am not saying we did something wrong, I am asking because I know their beliefs and ours are not the same. Have we done more harm than good?"

Norman hugged his wife and comforted her saying, "He is the son of a diplomat. He and his father have been exposed to many things and this is just one more to add to his list. I am interested to hear what he has to say about his experience. He seems like a fine young man. Don't worry. I know just how to handle this."

Lydia playfully responded, "Now that worries me!"

As Jake and Hakeem changed clothes, Hakeem spoke, "May I ask you a question?"

Jake said, "Of course."

"You speak of how your family is related to Aaron, Moses' brother. How do you know this for sure?" Hakeem asked.

Jake answered as he opened the door so they could join his parents in the family room. "Our name itself is the biggest clue, but my father can trace his ancestors back many hundreds of years. He is the oldest son in his family and from a very long line of Rabbis dating back at least sixteen generations. You should ask him when we go downstairs."

CHAPTER 17

Norman poked the fire as Lydia served cups of hot chocolate and made sure the boys were comfortable. She began the conversation, "Jake, did you get to introduce to Hakeem to any of your friends?"

Jake replied, "I didn't really see too many people I knew, and the crowd was so big downstairs we could barely find anywhere to sit."

"Well, maybe you will get the chance tomorrow morning when we go back. That is if Hakeem is still interested in joining us," Lydia probed.

Norman jumped in sensing it was time for him to steer the conversation, "Well, before we jump to tomorrow, I would love to get Hakeem's thoughts on what he saw and heard tonight. Hakeem, had you ever been to a synagogue before?"

Hakeem knew how to play this game and was diplomatically engaging as he replied, "No, but it was very beautiful and the people seemed so friendly. I have not seen anything so ornate other than palaces. I was quite impressed to see the scrolls that Moses wrote. I had thought they would fall apart since they are so old."

Jake laughed and Lydia gave him a stern look. Norman spoke saying, "Those scrolls contain the same writings that Moses wrote; however, the scrolls you saw are only 150 years old. What else did you think? I know the sermon was probably different than what you have been taught."

"Yes," Hakeem stated emphatically. "The writing of the Koran and your Bible tell many of the same stories, but it is said that Ishmael was the one Abraham sacrificed, not Isaac. We celebrate a similar Holy Day called Eid al-Adha, The Feast of the Sacrifice. Like your celebration, we wear new clothes and listen to a sermon in the mosque. Where I am from it is a public holiday and celebrated by most in our country. Our calendars are even similar since they are based on the Lunar Cycle and Eid al-Adha is observed around the same time as your New Year. We all agree it was a great test of faith, and I had not thought of how trusting it was of the son to be so willing to obey his father."

"I am glad the message was meaningful for you," Norman continued. "What questions may I answer for you?"

Hakeem paused for a moment to give the impression his question was more contemplative than it really was and then asked, "Jake has told me some of the history and importance of your name. I am interested to know more of your connection to Aaron who the Koran tells us was a prophet and a high priest?"

Norman began, "Our name Aaronson is derived from the ancient tradition of naming a boy by connecting his first name with his father's name. For example your name would be known as Hakeem son of Akram. Since many in the region would know the name of Akram, you would be identified by your father's name. Aaron in the Bible was the first-born son of Amram and would be known as Aaron son of Amram. Once God ordained that Aaron became the first high priest of Israel and Moses performed the miracles before Pharaoh, he became better known as Moses' brother than he did as Amram's son. Our family traces its lineage back at least sixteen generations to the family name Aaronson derived from the historical Jewish name of Aaron's son. Many of the first born sons in our family became Rabbis, and it is believed we are descended from the High Priests of the Bible."

"That is quite interesting. I am indeed interested in the science behind all of this and in particular DNA. I find it quite fascinating and plan to pursue genetics in my university studies," Hakeem shared.

Norman interjected, "How exciting. I have recently heard that there is now a DNA test from a company in Virginia that can tell you if you are of Jewish descent."

Hakeem's next comments clearly hid his real thoughts as he responded, "I find that very intriguing, Mr. Aaronson. You have helped pique my interest even more. Just think how helpful that could be in detecting some illnesses I have read specifically affect people of Jewish descent. Think of all the good that can come from this."

Lydia took back the reins and thought they had enough serious conversation for one evening.

She suggested, "Boys, why don't you head upstairs and get ready for bed." She then asked, "Hakeem, are you still open to joining us in the morning?"

"Yes, of course I am," Hakeem answered. "I am grateful that you would have me as your guest at such a wonderful celebration. Thank you and Goodnight."

The boys stayed up for a while talking, and this gave Hakeem the chance to get to know his roommate even better. They talked well past midnight, and most of the time was spent discussing Jake's love of codes and puzzles. Hakeem was amazed to see the bookcases filled with three-ring binders containing codes Jake had created. He asked Jake if he could show him some of his work.

Jake got out of bed and motioned Hakeem to join him at his desk. They sat close together in front of Jake's Personal Computer with its top-of-the line Pentium Processor and 15" color monitor. Jake typed in commands and showed Hakeem a program he had written. He asked Hakeem if he knew the song Happy Birthday. Hakeem assured him he did and Jake typed the words to the song on the page. "Happy Birthday to you, Happy Birthday to you. Happy Birthday dear Hakeem, Happy Birthday to you."

"Now, watch this." Jake instructed. He pressed a few keys on the keyboard too quickly for Hakeem to see which ones, and when he looked at the screen every letter of the Birthday Song had changed and the new message on the screen

read, "*!'!^"!^"@%' @("!*"@)'*$!'@%' '@)"!%'
'@%', *!'!^"!^"@%' @("!*"@)'*$!'@%' '@)"!%' '@%',
!'!^"!^"@%' @('!"@)'*$!'@%' $%!'!&' *!'!!"%%'!#',
!"!^"!^"@%' @('!"@)'*$!'@%' '@)' "@%'"!%"@!'."

Hakeem was wide-eyed as he saw the screen transform in front of his very eyes. "Is that really Happy Birthday or is it some trick you are playing on me?" Hakeem inquired.

"No trick, my friend. A simple code I created to encrypt a message. If you had the same program on your computer I could send you this message and you could activate the decryption code and decipher it," Jake explained. "It's really quite simple. There are twenty-six letters in the English alphabet and if you gave each letter a value from one to twenty six where an A=1, B=2, C=3, etc. you can have a complete code. Every number on your keyboard has a symbol above the number. By pressing the shift key you type those symbols. For letters that have a value greater than nine you would simply put an apostrophe at the beginning and the end of the number and use the symbol above both the numbers in the letter's value. So Z =26. You would start with an apostrophe and then shift 2=@ and shift 6=^ then close the letter with an apostrophe. You can decipher it manually, but I wrote a program to encode and decode messages so I don't have to press so many keys."

Hakeem put his hand on Jake's shoulder and said, "Truly you are gifted. It is fascinating to me, but more than my tired mind can grasp right now. If you do not mind, I think I want to go to sleep now. I have had many new experiences today and I think I need to rest."

With that he walked over to the twin bed on the opposite wall from Jake's and crawled under the sheets. He reached over, turned off the lamp on the bedside table, and rolled over to face the wall as he said, "Goodnight."

Hakeem had no intention of going to sleep right away as he had much to think about. He could not get the thought out of his head that you could test people's blood to find out if they were Jewish. This he had to share with his father as soon as they spoke.

CHAPTER 18

Jake groggily rolled over and looked at the bedside clock and saw that it was 11:30AM. He could see that Hakeem was still asleep and as quietly as he could slid out from under the sheets onto the carpeted floor. Hakeem rolled over at the sound of Jake's movement and sleepily said, "Is it time to go?"

"I'm not sure what's going on. " Jake continued, "Services started hours ago. I wonder why they did not awaken us."

As the boys began to move around the room there was a quiet knock at the door. Jake opened it to see his father with a huge grin on his face slipping into the room. He looked at the boys and said, "I convinced your mother that you boys needed sleep more than another of the old Rabbis sermons. Boys, I owe you one. You saved me too!"

All three descended the stairs and could smell something wonderful and sweet in the air. "Mom!" Jake almost squealed. "You made my favorite, cinnamon rolls. Hakeem, you will want seconds and thirds I promise."

After breakfast Lydia brought a pot of coffee into the family room and asked Hakeem how he slept and if he had any more thoughts about the night before. He shared again his appreciation for their wonderful hospitality. Lydia then said, "Hakeem, my husband tells me he has met your father and that he works for the Turkish government. He did not mention your mother, and I was hoping I might get the chance to meet her since you boys are roommates."

Hakeem looked Mrs. Aaronson directly into her eyes as he replied, "I have no mother, only a father. She died during childbirth...mine."

Lydia's expression dramatically changed as she said, "How sorry I am to hear this. Please forgive me for asking such a personal question."

Hakeem maintained his directness as he replied, "All is as it should be. There are many things in this life we cannot control or understand and we must accept them for what they are. I cannot miss what I have never had, therefore it is only a fact I share, not a memory."

Lydia moved to sit by Hakeem and said, "You have me now and you are welcome in our home and family anytime."

Hakeem smiled and asked, "Does that include making me cinnamon rolls too?" The four of them laughed and made plans for the rest of their afternoon together before they returned to school in time for dinner.

As they were being dropped off, there were hugs all around, and the last thing Hakeem heard was Norman calling out to Hakeem with a hearty reminder, "Don't forget to call your father. I don't want to cause an international incident."

Hakeem nodded and signaled that he got the message, all the while thinking, "You don't have to worry about that. I have much to share with my father that will be of great interest to him and many others back home."

CHAPTER 19

Jake went straight up to his room as he heard Hakeem calling behind him, "I'm going to call my father before I come up. I'll see you later."

Hakeem went to the payphone booth outside of the dormitory building and followed the instructions his father had given him to contact him on a secure phone. He pressed "0" for the Operator and asked to be connected to the Turkish Embassy in Washington, DC, with a collect call from Hakeem Baba, the son of the Under Secretary to the Ambassador.

Hakeem heard the call going through. After the embassy answered, the operator said, "I have a collect call from Hakeem Baba, son of the Under Secretary to the Ambassador, will you accept the charges?" The voice on the other end confirmed and the call was connected.

Hakeem spoke only a few sentences in Turkish and the call was quickly ended. Not more than thirty seconds after he hung up, the pay phone began to ring. On the fifth ring Hakeem picked up the phone, but did not speak. The voice on the other end gave instructions in Turkish and Hakeem nodded as if the party on the other end could see him. After an extended period of silence, Hakeem heard his father's voice, "We are on a secure line, my son. You are free to speak openly."

"Father, it is good to hear your voice," Hakeem began. "I have much to share with you. I have been to the home of the Aaronson's and they have taken me in as you instructed. I have learned much of the encryption talents of my roommate, and all the reports you have on him are accurate. He is a genius when it comes to codes and cyphers. Everything is going as planned and I am earning more of his trust. I believe he will lead me to Building 18 and I will have the chance to place the package once it is received. I have also learned that there is a DNA test that can identify if someone's blood is Jewish. That means that someone somewhere is collecting such data, and access to this would be invaluable for our cause. I have already indicated my interest in this purely for the purpose of curing disease, and the seed has been planted. Secretary Aaronson was quite willing to share there is a firm in Virginia doing this work. Imagine, father, what we could do if we knew the exact locations of all 14 million."

Akram encouraged his son saying, "You have done well, my son. Do not let their kindness cloud your vision. Do not go back to his home with him on his next visit in ten days. Use that time to look into this DNA testing in the library. Do not use your personal computer for this research as everything you do on your computer is logged. We will speak again in two weeks."

As the phone went silent, Hakeem smiled, feeling good that his father was pleased. Jake was already unpacked from the home visit and was fully absorbed in his studies. Upon hearing Hakeem enter their suit, he quickly acknowledged his presence, and immediately returned to his studies. Hakeem took his bag into his room and closed the door. After unpacking, he too tackled the assignments due in class the following morning.

CHAPTER 20

It had been a week since Hakeem had visited Jake's family and celebrated the Jewish New Year with them. At Lydia's request, Jake asked Hakeem if he would be joining the family for the Day of Atonement services as previously discussed. Hakeem replied, "Jake, please extend my sincere appreciation for your family's invitation, but I think I will stay behind and get caught up on some library work that I have been putting off for far too long. I have a paper due in Physics that requires more research, and I am finding it more conducive to work on such projects in the library than in my room. I hope you will not be offended by my decision."

Jake took it in stride and said, "No problem. I can understand why you would rather study than fast and attend more services. My father will only go to one service and I will accompany my mother to the other ones. I will let them know when I speak with them tonight."

Jake's father said he would have been surprised if Hakeem had wanted to attend. Lydia was more sensitive and inquired if Hakeem was uncomfortable during his last visit. Jake assured them his roommate was perfectly comfortable and felt welcomed into their home and family, but had to catch up on an assignment.

Two days later the black limousine pulled up to the gate and the driver complied with the standard security routine before he could escort Jake off campus. Hakeem watched from the lobby as his roommate pulled away and immediately grabbed his backpack and headed to the library to begin his DNA fact-finding mission. He knew Jake would not be back for two days. With it also being the weekend, he would have much free time to devote to this task.

The walk to the Norton Library Building could have been a direct one, but Hakeem chose the more indirect route that would take him right behind Building 18. The exterior was designed in such a way as to cause anyone to believe it was just a utility building. The noticeable difference was the absence of any windows and a gated, sloping driveway leading down to a rollup door only wide enough for a car. There were no other visible entrances or exits. There were no cameras visible on the outside of the building and no keycard or other access device at the top of the driveway. Since he had been at Winchester, Hakeem had never seen any vehicle enter or exit Building 18.

Hakeem entered the Norton Library and was greeted by an elderly woman perched on a high-back stool. She perched behind a half-round polished mahogany counter. Without lifting her head, she raised her eyebrows, compressed the skin on her forehead, and peered over her glasses at Hakeem. He knew better than to laugh, but could not help but wonder if she had any idea how oddly out of this world she looked.

Without asking for any identification or his name the woman asked, "How may I help you, Mr. Baba?"

Hakeem stifled a chuckle and answered, "I am here to do some research on genetics. Where would you suggest I begin?"

Just as Hakeem finished his answer, he saw a young lady approaching the desk. "Follow me, please Mr. Baba," she said.

Hakeem followed her up the circular marble staircase to the second floor stacks. There she proceeded to quickly walk down the center of the room, past a cluster of tables and chairs, and disappeared into a long row of bookshelves. Hakeem was too busy looking around and had lost sight of his escort. As he took a breath to call out to find her, she appeared from the row she was in, and scolded him saying, "Do not raise your voice in this place, Mr. Baba. If you are to succeed in your endeavors, you must keep up and you must keep quiet." Silently, Hakeem joined her in the stacks and she led him to the section of Genetics. He spent no more than a few seconds looking at the volumes of books and turned to thank her, but found she had already left.

Hakeem searched the extensive list of titles not really certain of exactly what he would find. After thirty minutes of browsing he decided on a strategy. He would begin with building a knowledge base, and once he felt confident he had mastered the fundamentals of the science, he would venture into the more complex material. His first selection was entitled *Molecular Biology of the Cell* published in 1983. He would use this to build on his foundational understanding. Since he was privately schooled prior to coming to Winchester, he had received advanced teaching in the science. He was already on par with college freshmen four years older than himself.

The book he selected was eligible to be checked out of the library. After careful consideration, he did not feel that he would draw any undue attention by taking the book back to his room for studying at his own pace. As he left the stacks and turned to walk back to the circular staircase, the same young lady that had escorted him earlier appeared out of nowhere. At a whisper she simply said, "Follow me."

Hakeem made his way quietly yet swiftly so as not to be left behind again. They descended the circular staircase, and he was deposited back to the elderly woman at the front desk. With raised brow and bended head, she reached out to take the book from his hand. She opened it, removed the card from the pocket inside the front cover, stamped it, and handed the book back to Hakeem saying, "You know the rules. These are rules, not suggestions. Return this book no later than two weeks from today. Don't be late."

Hakeem thanked her and exited as fast as he could. He had barely made it outside before he laughed out loud at the strange woman behind the library counter. There was something about her that reminded him of an alien from another world, and he found himself highly amused.

With his research book tucked under his arm, he returned to his room by the more direct route, bypassing Building 18. That mystery would have to be solved another day.

CHAPTER 21

Since its founding in 1896 the Winchester Academy had occupied the same 200 acres that was originally home to the Winchester Mansion. The Mansion was destroyed by fire in 1936 and had been converted from a family dwelling to classrooms and living quarters for the original students. The first graduates of the academy went on to attend the finest universities in the nation including Harvard, Yale, Dartmouth, Penn, Columbia and Brown. By the time the fire destroyed the original mansion, the reputation and funding of the school had already been well established.

After the fire, all the students, faculty, and staff were relocated to a temporary facility. All classes continued while the new facility was being built. Under the supervision of Spencer Winchester, the founder's son, new plans were drawn up and the original structure was razed. All of the contractors and employees involved with the project were required to sign a non-disclosure agreement. In addition, temporary quarters were constructed on the far side of the property to house all the workers. The contract required that no one leave the project site until it was completed. To ensure full compliance, each would receive an incentive payment on their last day. This insured against anyone violating the confidentiality and travel restrictions.

Once construction began, the first task was to level the existing structure. Much care was taken to leave the foundation intact. What only Spencer, the architect, and the construction foreman knew was there were a series of underground passages that led to all of the outbuildings on the estate. These tunnels and gateways were to be incorporated into the new design. Each of the buildings that the tunnels led to would also be renovated even though the fire had not touched them. The new design would connect what would now become the Administration Building to all the buildings on the campus through a series of tunnels with limited and highly secured access.

Spencer Winchester was not just the son of the founder and sole heir to the Winchester fortune; he was also a graduate of the Naval Academy in Annapolis and served as a Commander in the Office of Naval Intelligence. He envisioned a new era coming and saw the Winchester Academy playing a part in identifying, educating, and training generations of extremely valuable candidates for Intelligence work. Perfectly situated in the hub of the international diplomatic community, Spencer knew he could position Winchester to be the premier College Preparatory Academy attracting students from all over the world. He would use his Naval Intelligence background to take full advantage of the underground network of tunnels to keep his eye on the students, faculty and staff. Thus, there was a high level of secrecy surrounding the rebuilding of the Winchester Academy.

It took four years and a staggering 1 million dollars to complete the full renovation. The campus had the most modern facility available in 1940 and could house 136 students. Modern, furnished three-bedroom apartments were provided for each of the thirty fulltime faculty and their families. The sprawling campus now had seventeen buildings interconnected through a series of underground tunnels; however, there were eighteen tunnels extending from the Administration Building's basement.

In 1965 Spencer Winchester's son, Neville, followed in his father's footsteps and took over the Winchester Foundation and the Academy. This was after his graduation from the Naval Academy and five years service as a Naval Intelligence Officer. Neville had served during the Bay of Pigs invasion, the Cuban Missile Crisis, and the escalation of the Cold War with the Soviet Union. Shortly after taking over he began the design and plans for Building 18. It would be a combination surveillance center and underground bunker in case of a nuclear threat. The area surrounding construction of Building 18 was cordoned off and a twenty-foot-high security fence erected. All material and equipment deliveries were scheduled around mealtimes when all students and faculty were in the dining hall. The sounds of excavation and construction were the only indication of what was going on behind the fence. Nothing was visible even during the well-lit nighttime activities. The proximity to the dorms and faculty apartments was far enough to make the sound unnoticeable.

Neville was an expert in closed circuit video surveillance and designed the intricate network of cables and cameras that would ultimately be transformed into the fiber optic network that exists today. Under his supervision, Building 18 became the intelligence hub of the Winchester Academy. In addition, it served as a fully equipped underground bunker that was stocked with enough provisions to support the Winchester community of over 200 people for as long as one full year. The construction cost of Building 18 alone was $3 million and took two full years to complete. Another $2 million was spent installing cabling and cameras and connecting every building and room on campus into the central hub. A private security firm staffed with cleared ex-military personnel was hired to provide round-the-clock oversight of Building 18. The additional operating costs were reflected in the tuition and passed on to families who would not bat an eye at the increase.

By 1970 the Winchester Academy had upgraded its campus to become the most secure facility of its kind in the United States. The caliber of international students would increase, and Winchester's reputation for exclusivity and security would be secure for many years to come.

CHAPTER 22

Deep in the bowels of Building 18, Team One was on duty. Troy Chapman, Philip Boyer, and, T.L. Houston scanned the monitors that displayed and recorded all movement on campus. They were all Special Ops surveillance experts who had been trained to hone in on changes in the video feeds as opposed to just watching all movement. This enabled them to look past the day-to-day normal activity and identify any anomalies. Audio Specialists Tina Montgomery and Faith Cunningham monitored the audio feeds. From their command center posts, these teams could see and hear all activity on the campus.

There were three weekday teams working eight-hour shifts and two weekend teams working twelve-hour shifts. All were contracted through the security firm JEH and Associates, who only employed top-secret-cleared security experts. Max Hirschberg, who had become a powerful influence in DC politics, headed the firm. He had deep ties into intelligence agencies and had been providing contractors on non-sanctioned operations for many years.

All of the Winchester Academy's students were sons of wealthy business and government families. These highly visible families required the highest level of protection available. JEH and Associates was more than capable of carrying out this assignment for the Academy as well as numerous other clients. Their surveillance and monitoring services allowed them to pass along any actionable intelligence gathered from their client base. This helped to position JEH and Associates as the go to company for these legitimate private security contracts.

JEH's Managing Partners played a role in reviewing students who were being considered for enrollment and completed thorough background checks on the students and their families. It was not uncommon for the Managing Partners to tap into their network to gather more background on students who might be more strategic than others. Each year there were a handful accepted who were placed on the "Watch List" for various reasons. On this year's Watch List were both Hakeem Baba, who had family ties to both Iran and Turkey, and Jake Aaronson, who had savant capabilities in cryptography. One was watched as an enemy, the other as a potential recruit. Having them room together was strategically motivated and influenced by JEH Managing Partner Max Hirschberg. He was to be personally notified of any activity involving any student of the Watch List. He had already been sent the audio transcript of Hakeem's phone call with his father, as well as the details of the codes Jake had developed on his computer.

In their world everything was on a "need to know" basis, and Max Hirschberg had a need to know. He had already shared both packets of information with Jake's father, who had given explicit instructions for all materials regarding his son and his roommate be shared with him first before anything was shared with Winchester Academy's staff. Norman Aaronson was not only influential, he was generous and a source of very lucrative referrals for JEH & Associates. Norman and Max were more than mere business acquaintances. They had been friends for many years and their families were from the same neighborhood.

Max was a trusted advisor and confidant to Norman and was well connected with Washington's elite. He knew firsthand of Jake's gifting and wanted to be credited with recruiting such a valuable asset. He was also keenly aware of the implications surrounding Hakeem's interest in DNA and the genetic identification of Jewish blood. In the wrong hands this could be a means of locating every Jewish person and targeting them for eradication. This was more than a professional interest, it was now personal and he would require regular status reports on Hakeem's activities.

CHAPTER 23

The rigors of the academic and physical curriculum at Winchester made time pass quickly. The end of the first semester was upon them and coincided with the Christmas and New Year's holidays. Jake went home to his family and Hakeem went to stay with his father at his Georgetown home. The holiday visits were uneventful and both boys caught up on much needed sleep and family time.

While Hakeem was at school he had not visited a mosque or prayed five times daily as he did back home. He used this vacation time to join his father at The Islamic Center in Washington on Massachusetts Avenue. This was the most famous mosque in America and was originally opened in 1957 when it was dedicated by then President Dwight D. Eisenhower. Many dignitaries had visited there and it was not uncommon to see non-Muslim visitors.

In his current role as Under Secretary to the Turkish Ambassador, Hakeem's father was in attendance at many of the Center's board meetings chaired by his superior, the Turkish Ambassador. With its large central mosque, along with a library and many classrooms, The Islamic Center was the perfect secure meeting place of many different factions of Islam. The entrances and exits were certainly monitored by the US Intelligence community; however, the interior was swept for listening devices on a daily basis. Not all who entered here were as moderate as they might appear in the public realm.

Amram was proud of his son's interest in the DNA project and had shared this with several key Turkish leaders with strong ties to Iran. This visit to the mosque was not just for the purpose of prayer; it was also to introduce Hakeem to his future handlers.

Hakeem was escorted into a meeting room lined with beautiful handcrafted Persian rugs and ornate artwork from all the Islamic Nations. There was a receiving line of men waiting to greet Hakeem upon his arrival. The moment he walked in the door all eyes fell upon him and the loud talk turned into a whisper as men spoke to each other at low breath. As if on cue, the room broke out into a round of applause as the meeting room door was closed. One by one, each man came and shook Hakeem's hand with a broad smile on their faces. Hakeem was unprepared for such a reception and was thankful his father was by his side to greet each one by name.

After all had greeted and welcomed Hakeem a very distinguished older man with gray hair and beard began to speak. At the sound of his voice the room went silent. All eyes turned to him as he proclaimed, "Tonight stands before us the key to our victory. Our future is in the hands of those who have been raised to put our cause above their own lives. Hakeem, your father has told us of your desire to study this genetic link that ties all of the Jewish Infidels together. This is a most powerful tool, and we will support you until you have discovered all there is to know. It would be the highest victory to annihilate them once and for all. Your education and any resources you need will be provided for you. You will never have to worry about money as long as you remain faithful to this vision. Learn all you can in the coming years. Devote yourself to study and we will see to it you are accepted into the finest universities in the world. Stay close to this Aaronson, but stay closer to us. We are right there when you need us and your father will remain your point of contact until further notice. May Allah watch over you as you bring honor to our cause."

As the older man finished speaking, the door to the meeting room was opened and everyone exited without another word spoken. Amram led his son down the hallway and outside to the waiting car. They rode to Georgetown in total silence as Hakeem weighed what he had heard.

It was not until he and his father were settled in the townhouse that anyone spoke. Amram broke the silence, "My son. I am more than proud of you and the Elders feel the same. If you have any questions, now will be the time to ask."

Hakeem spoke, "No, Father, I have no questions. This is my destiny and I will do what I must to see our vision fulfilled. I am honored to be the one so charged with this responsibility."

Amram reached out to hug his son saying, "Sleep well, my son. There is much work to be done. Goodnight."

CHAPTER 24

With the holidays and winter break behind them, the students arrived back at Winchester refreshed and ready to tackle another semester of hard work. Hakeem and Jake returned to their normal routine with little change. Jake had kept up his physical conditioning and worked out and ran every day during the break, but did not share that with Hakeem. He was on a personal mission to catch up to his roommate and surprise him on the track. It had been over four months since Hakeem first blew past him, and Jake was committed to not letting that happen again.

While most of the other students groaned at the first day back in class, Jake was excited for the afternoon martial arts classes to resume. He had already advanced to an Orange Belt and still had a long way to go to catch his Black Belt roommate. Although there was a long way to go, he was still quite proud of his achievement. As the boys hit the track, Jake immediately positioned himself next to Hakeem. It was his goal to keep up with him no matter what.

Hakeem did not pay much attention to Jake starting out by his side, as this was not unusual. What he did notice was that by their fifth time around the track Jake was still keeping up stride for stride. Hakeem decided to kick it up a notch and increased his stride, but Jake held his position. With three more laps to go, Hakeem kicked it into high gear and had a point to make. He fully expected Jake to be left behind and was stunned to see his roommate keeping pace. Like two Olympians finishing the last leg of a Gold Medal race, they charged to the finish line. Jake had kept up with his roommate. As he fell to the ground gasping for air, he had the biggest smile on his face. He had made his point and would never be embarrassed again.

The videotape of this race was copied and sent directly to Max Hirschberg, along with the video of Hakeem's visit to the Islamic Center in Washington over winter break. He would analyze them both and make sure that Norman was briefed on his son's accomplishment. Of more concern was Hakeem's meeting at the Center and the list of attendees that he was sure to have met.

CHAPTER 25

The next three months were a blur and as the semester was about to draw to a close, Lydia Aaronson asked Jake if he would like to have Hakeem come home with him for the holiday break. Norman had learned that Hakeem's father would be out of the country and would not be able to see his son during the Spring Break. Unbeknownst to the Aaronsons, Amram had sent a message to Hakeem to go with the Aaronsons.

Jake was pleased Hakeem accepted the invitation and would be staying with him over the break. Upon arrival at the Aaronson home, Hakeem was welcomed as if he were a family member. Lydia again took notice of Jake's physical stature and this time made no mention of how thin the boys were. In fact, she was quite impressed at their physiques and how fit they both looked.

Jake had not mentioned Passover to Hakeem before the visit, but thought he should prepare him for what he would experience on this visit. "Hakeem," Jake began, "are you familiar with the Exodus?"

Hakeem replied, "I am quite familiar with the Exodus. The Koran speaks of the Pharaoh and of Moses and Aaron. Why do you ask?"

"The last time you visited we celebrated a special holiday." Jake continued, "This visit falls on

Passover when we celebrate the Exodus. I hope you do not mind joining us for this."

Hakeem allayed his friend's fear when he said, "Jake, your family has welcomed me and I am delighted to learn all I can of your customs. I hope you will join me one day to learn of our celebrations."

Jake replied, "I know so little about Islam. I must admit I have only learned of my own Jewish background. I know very little about Christianity and before I met you, everything I knew about Islam was reported in the news. Now that we are friends, I no longer believe what the reporters have to say. I would like to learn more from you."

Hakeem had a serious look on his face when he asked, "Do we dress for this occasion or is this when we do not wear clothes?"

Both laughed so loud that Lydia knocked and asked what was so funny. When they shared it with her she joined their laughter and all three enjoyed the joke.

"I am glad Jake told you about our dinner tonight," Lydia began. "It is called a Seder, which means Order. We tell the story of the Exodus in the order in which it happened so that each of us can share in the experience as if we were also there. Tomorrow night we will go to services and Rabbi Lazar will speak about the significance of this event and our life in the desert after the Exodus. I think you will find it quite interesting to learn about Moses and Aaron."

"Mom," Jake interjected. "Hakeem has studied the Koran and knows a lot about Moses and Aaron and the Exodus."

"Then he should enjoy the Seder since he will know what's going on. Be downstairs in an hour so we can get started on time," Lydia answered.

The boys joined Norman and Lydia at the dining table along with Max Hirschberg, his wife Naomi, and their twin twenty-two-year-old daughters, Sadie and Molly. Norman sat at one end of the table and Lydia at the other. The twins sat on the side with their mother and Max sat on the side with the boys. Norman felt it best to seat them this way to respect Hakeem's customs as best he could by keeping the men and women separate.

The table setting was quite unique and in the middle of the table was a round plate with a variety of items, each nestled into its own compartment. In front of each person was a booklet, and Norman explained this was called a Hagaddah, which meant The Telling. He then went on to explain the Hebrew names for each of the items on the center plate and their significance to the story of the Exodus.

Max Hirschberg thought to himself, "Impressive. Hakeem has not let on that he speaks and reads Hebrew and Jake, has not slipped by saying that he knows about it."

As the night progressed, Hakeem participated in the tasting of each item and listened respectfully to the telling of the story of the Exodus and the plagues. During the dinner break conversation, Lydia asked Hakeem to share what he had been taught about the Exodus.

"I have been taught much of what I have heard here tonight," Hakeem replied. "The Koran tells of the arrogance of Pharaoh and only speaks of five of the ten plagues you have mentioned here tonight. The symbolism of these items on the table has given me a better understanding of the suffering of your people. This we have in common as our history has been filled with much suffering as well. The Koran teaches us that both Moses and Aaron were Prophets of God and worked miracles to prove that God existed. I am honored to be in the presence of their descendants."

Norman laughed and said, "Don't be too impressed with our family tree. I have some relatives that are more closely related to apes than we care to discuss."

Everyone at the table laughed and Hakeem was grateful that he could now be finished sharing his knowledge. After coffee and dessert, the last part of the Seder was completed. As the caterers began to clear the table, the men headed to the den. Lydia wanted some time to catch up with Naomi and the girls, so they joined her in the living room.

Max Hirschberg opened the conversation by commenting on how physically fit both Jake and Hakeem looked. They shared their training regimen and Max listened intently, even though he knew precisely what they were doing each and every day. Although Norman and Max were best friends, he had not shared the details of his assignments or his knowledge of all the boys' activities.

The night ended with a series of hugs and handshake and the reminder they would all see each other again at services the next evening. Both Jake and Hakeem were ready for the night to be over and catch up on some much needed sleep. They said their goodnights and turned in without much dialogue.

CHAPTER 26

I t was well past noon when the smell of cinnamon rolls finally made its way into Jake's room. It seemed like both boys caught the scent at the same time, as they almost simultaneously swung their feet out of their beds and onto the floor. Still competitive, they sprung to their feet and headed towards the door in a mini foot race and laughed as they ran down the stairs following the enticing aroma. Lydia smiled as she heard the rumbling of teenage feet bounding down the stairs and racing into the kitchen. The reward waiting for them was a pile of freshly glazed cinnamon rolls. Lydia waited for them to take the first bite to see if they even noticed these were made without yeast, as it was Passover. Neither boy noticed anything as they devoured the entire contents of their plates without so much as a word spoken. Based on their actions, Lydia no longer felt the need to say anything about the unleavened rolls. As soon as they were done they thanked her, ran upstairs, climbed into their beds, and fell back to sleep.

Around 4:30PM Norman poked his head into Jake's room and roused the boys saying, "Time to get up, showered, and dressed for dinner. See you in an hour."

After dinner, the Aaronson's and Hakeem rode to the synagogue. The conversation was light and everyone, including Norman, was looking forward to the evening service. Upon arrival they immediately searched for Max Hirschberg and his family and found them in the usual spot on the front row. Norman and Lydia stopped to exchange pleasantries as they made their way to the Hirschbergs. Jake and Hakeem went ahead and took their seats. Soon after Jake's parents joined them and the service began. Hakeem watched with great interest as Norman was again called forward to pray over the open scrolls.

After the reading from the scrolls Rabbi Lazar approached the podium and began to speak, "Tonight, we celebrate the miraculous deliverance of our people after 400 years of bondage to Pharaoh. From the time our children are very small we teach them of the role Moses played in demonstrating the mighty power of the God of Israel to Pharaoh. Who can forget the movie The Ten Commandments where Charlton Heston plays the mighty role of Moses standing before Yul Brenner as Pharaoh? How many of you remember who played Aaron in the movie or, for that matter, what role Aaron played in the Bible? Certainly we all have read and recounted the passages of Torah from Exodus Chapter 4, but can we really discern what role each plays in our history? No Jewish scholar would discount in any way the role Moses played in the history of our people. This celebration, Passover, commemorates his numerous confrontations and pleadings to let our people go. Much of what we focus on in this story is the deliverance of our people from the bondage of slavery. But before Pharaoh was to be convinced that the God of Abraham, Isaac, and Jacob was the one true God, our people had to be convinced. He used Aaron for that purpose as we read the rest of the story not often told from Exodus Chapter 4, Verses 27-31:

> The Lord said to Aaron, "Go into the desert to meet Moses." So he met Moses at the mountain of God and kissed him. 28 Then Moses told Aaron everything the Lord had sent him to say, and also about all the miraculous signs he had commanded him to perform. 29 Moses and Aaron brought together all the elders of the Israelites, 30 and Aaron told them everything the Lord had said to Moses. He also performed the signs before the people, 31 and they believed. And when they heard that the Lord was concerned about them and had seen their misery, they bowed down and worshiped."

Rabbi Lazar peered over his reading glasses and paused for a moment to let the emphasis he had placed on these four verses sink in. He then began to speak again saying, "Few remember that Aaron was the first to perform the miracles of God. Israel had to be convinced before they would be able to endure what was in store for them. Aaron was entrusted with performing the miracles for Israel. He was told everything that Moses had heard on the mountain. Moses was to perform the signs for Pharaoh, but after their release from bondage, God appointed Aaron as the High Priest. His role was to be secured forever as a sign to Israel of the power of God. It was Aaron's descendants that would be the heirs to the Priesthood. It was Aaron's descendants who would minister in the Temple with specific responsibilities for all the generations to come. What God promises, He fulfills. "

He continued, "Make no mistake. I am in no way diminishing the role that Moses played in the deliverance of our people. I am only reminding you of the hope we have in the rebuilding of the Temple in Jerusalem and the restoration of the High Priesthood that began with Aaron and lives today through his bloodline. This is our hope and prayer for our ultimate deliverance."

The service soon ended and the buzz could be heard throughout the sanctuary. Hakeem shared in the enthusiasm for the message's content, but for different reasons than anyone else in the congregation.

Jake led Hakeem downstairs again so he could taste the variety of unleavened treats. The room was filled to capacity, and there were many engaged in discussions about tonight's sermon. A large group had gathered around Rabbi Lazar who seemed to be making his way to the side of the room where Jake and Hakeem sat eating their macaroons and drinking their grape juice. Jake was surprised when Rabbi Lazar emerged from the crowd surrounding him and extended his hand to Jake.

After shaking hands, Rabbi Lazar spoke directly to Jake, "Jacob, your father tells me how well you are doing. It is good to see you back here again. How did you like hearing of your rich ancestry tonight?"

Jake spoke, "Rabbi, the message was great tonight. I would like to introduce you to my roommate and best friend, Hakeem Baba. He is a Muslim, but has very much enjoyed hearing you speak. This is his second visit, and I was hoping to introduce you to him."

Rabbi Lazar looked at Hakeem and greeted him in Hebrew with "Shabbat Shalom. It is my pleasure to meet you young man."

In perfect Hebrew Hakeem answered, "Shabbat Shalom. Chag Pesach Sameach."

Rabbi Lazar was pleased at Hakeem's Happy Passover greeting and the Rabbi answered him with more Hebrew to see how much this friend of Jake's really knew. Hakeem followed along flawlessly, and the two of them engaged in a five-minute conversation in Hebrew. Jake could only pick out a few words here and there, but there was no mistaking how much Rabbi Lazar seemed to be enjoying the conversation. Soon the group that had gathered around the Rabbi reappeared and watched and listened to the conversation taking place. Max and Naomi Hirschberg stood shoulder to shoulder with Norman and Lydia Aaronson as they tried to listen in on the dialogue. By the time it was done Rabbi Lazar and Hakeem embraced and separated with huge smiles on their faces. No one dare ask the Rabbi what they had talked about, but the room ignited with many side conversations.

Norman, Lydia, and Naomi stood there with their mouths wide open in amazement, while Jake and Max feigned a look of wonder. Both knew of Hakeem's linguistic mastery, but neither could let the others in on their secret. Jake and Max exchanged a knowing glance and then joined in the fuss being made over Hakeem.

Hakeem handled the attention well and was astounded that so few could understand the conversation that had just taken place. He had not really considered that speaking Hebrew and being Jewish were not synonymous. This was the same reaction he had when he had met American Muslims who could not speak Arabic, but had memorized the prayers. He could see firsthand the impact the West had had on assimilation and how liberal these Westerners had become.

CHAPTER 27

It was after 10:30PM by the time they arrived back home and all agreed to call it a night. Jake and Hakeem made their way up to Jake's room and agreed it was fine for the old folks to turn in, but they had no intention of going to bed so early. They had slept most of the day and still had a full weekend of vacation left. They made their way back to the kitchen, stacked more macaroons on a plate, poured two glasses of milk, and made their way to the den to watch some late night TV. Just as they got comfortable, Jake's father walked in carrying his own plate of cookies and a glass of milk and smiled as he sat down in his favorite chair. "Mind if I join you?" he asked.

The boys just nodded and Norman sat quietly as the boys searched for something to watch. Hakeem broke the silence and said, "Mr. Aaronson, I was wondering if I might ask you some questions about what I heard tonight."

Norman encouraged Jake to turn off the TV so they could all talk and listened as Hakeem began to ask him questions.

Hakeem spoke directly, "Forgive me if I am asking something that I should know, but I have not heard about there being a High Priest anymore in your religion."

Norman answered him, "That is a very good question, Hakeem. I have not had this discussion even with Jake. The heir to the Priesthood was the first born in the bloodline of Aaron. Since his first two sons died, his son Eleazar became the High Priest. His son Phineas became the next High Priest, and this continued up until the destruction of the Second Temple in 70AD. From about 160 Bc there were High Priests who were appointed by the rulers over Israel who were not in the bloodline. Most remember Caiaphas who was called the High Priest, at the time of Jesus, but was appointed to the position and was not in the bloodline. The High Priest also served as the head of the Sanhedrin, the ruling body over all things political, economic, and religious."

Hakeem thought for a minute and then asked, "May I ask who is this High Priest today?"

Norman replied, "That was the very point of the Rabbi's message. Until there is a third temple built in Jerusalem we do not have a High Priest."

Hakeem then asked, "How is that possible if the High Priest is from a bloodline and you are a part of that bloodline? Are you or Jake the High Priest?"

Norman tried his best not to laugh at the prospect of being the High Priest and answered, "No, Hakeem, we are not. The last High Priest from the bloodline we have on record was Zadok who was High Priest during King David's reign and in the First Temple until its destruction. After it was destroyed the High Priest was appointed. The Prophet Ezekiel wrote about the Third Temple and the return of the High Priest."

Norman paused for a minute and turned to Jake saying, "Son, please hand me your mom's Bible from the bookshelf."

He thanked his son and turned to Hakeem and said, "I hope I am not boring you with so much information. To be honest you have taken me to the end of my knowledge."

Hakeem was wide-eyed and replied, "No, this is fascinating to me. I have only heard pieces of this before, but you are painting the whole picture for me now. Please continue."

Norman opened the Bible to the Book of Ezekiel and seemed to be searching for something. He stopped with his finger on the page and said, "Yes, here it is beginning in Chapter 40 and continuing through Chapter 48. This clearly refers to a future time and how the priestly system will be restored. You boys have access to this on your own time so you can read it for yourselves. The bottom line is a prophecy here that says the Temple will be rebuilt and the High Priest will take his place again as the one who can stand in the Holy of Holies and make offerings on behalf of the people according to biblical instructions. According to tradition when the Messiah comes to take up His seat on the throne of Israel, he will be the sin offering and no offering for sin will be required for those who accept Him as the final sacrifice. Since God had promised Aaron that it would always be one of his descendants to minister in the Temple then the High Priest of the Third Temple will have to be one of our relatives. "

Hakeem looked in wonder and said, "I am humbled to be sitting among such greatness."

Norman looked directly at Hakeem and replied, "The way things are going, Hakeem, it will be a long time before this could happen. The place they say the Temple will be built now has the al-Aqsa Mosque sitting on it. Your father and I have sat in many similar meetings discussing the fate of Jerusalem and Israel. I am sure he can tell you that no one is volunteering to move the Dome of the Rock to make room for the Third Temple. Middle East politics is too big a discussion to have tonight. I hope I have answered some of your questions. I am going to call it a night, boys. Don't stay up too late. If you are still interested tomorrow I will tell you some of the legends surrounding the High Priest and our family."

Hakeem stood to thank Mr. Aaronson for his insight, but he had already left the room and was headed up to bed. Hakeem took note of the Bible sitting on his chair and asked Jake if he thought his father would mind if he read some of it. Jake assured him he would not mind. Hakeem picked the Bible up and told Jake he was going to read a little before falling asleep. Jake said he would be up later and wanted to watch TV.

Hakeem had many thoughts about what he had learned that night, but decided to focus on reading what this Prophet Ezekiel had to say. He was familiar with his name as he had read "Qisas Al-Anbiya" or "Stories of the Prophets" in his schooling. He knew he was a Prophet, but did not know many details. He opened the Bible and found the Book of Ezekiel and began to read. By the time he had finished Chapter 48, Jake had already returned to the room and fallen asleep.

"If this prophecy were true then The Dome of the Rock would be gone and Israel restored," Hakeem thought to himself.

Hakeem lay awake for over an hour trying to process all he had learned and could not wait to hear of the legends Mr. Aaronson mentioned. Sleep finally came around 3:00AM, but it was not a restful one, as his dreams were more like nightmares.

CHAPTER 28

Morning came with the usual smell of cinnamon rolls wafting through the air. Both boys bounded down the steps and found only Norman there to meet them in the kitchen. Lydia had left a tray full of warm cinnamon rolls with strict instructions that Norman was to leave them all for Jake and Hakeem. Norman read the note and carefully placed it back in its original place as if he had not seen it. Plausible deniability was the watchword of the State Department, and today it applied to cinnamon rolls.

It was a chilly April morning and Norman had a fire already blazing. He invited the boys to grab their plates, join him in the den, and he would finish where he had left off the night before.

Hakeem and Jake looked at each other and simultaneously grabbed their plates and followed Norman. With mouths filled with their favorite morning treat they listened as Norman shared the story that was passed down in his family for as far back as anyone could remember.

Norman began, "I don't represent myself as any kind of scholar, and my wife can tell you I am much more secular than religious. I can only share with you what was told to me by my grandfather who was told the same story by his grandfather. As far as we know this story has stood for many generations. Moses' successor was Joshua and many of the Jewish scholars base their traditions and teachings on the belief that Moses shared everything with Joshua that he shared with Aaron. They have taught that he transmitted this knowledge to his successors in an unbroken chain, even to this day. They attribute the Oral Law and the writings of the Talmud and Mishnah to these instructions passed through that lineage."

Norman paused to see if the boys were able to keep up and Hakeem reassured him that he was keenly interested in what he was saying. Jake had heard it before and was familiar with the story.

Norman continued, "The Aaronsons' version of this is different than the traditional storyline. Rabbi Lazar read the very passage of the Torah last night that stated Moses told Aaron everything he heard on Mount Sinai and that Aaron then performed the miracles as a sign to Israel of God's power. Although Joshua prayed and God made the sun stand still, there were no recorded miracles attributed to Joshua's successors. In fact, it was God who appointed Aaron as the first High Priest of Israel and ordered that certain garments be made exclusively for the High Priest. The legend has it, that before Aaron was to die and pass the robe to his son Eleazar, he wrote down secrets revealed to him when he was alone with God in the Holy of Holies. It is rumored that this document was sewn into the lining of the robe, and God would give each successive High Priest instructions as to how to translate and protect this secret. In addition to making sure these scrolls were secure, the High Priest was to keep an ongoing record of miracles that were being performed and prophecies regarding the Messiah. In many circles, the contents of these scrolls are considered as important as the Ark of the Covenant. The last known descendant of Aaron's bloodline that served as High Priest was Zadok, and to date no one has been able to locate his robe. There is a group in Jerusalem called The Temple Institute that plans to recreate the priestly garments, including the robe. Some have rumored they are in possession of the scrolls, but this is only a rumor."

Jake had a look of wonder on his face when he asked, "Dad, now that I hear you telling this again I can't help but wonder. Do you think there is some hidden code in the breastplate or robe?"

Norman laughed and replied, "Jake, I know you would be much more interested in this if there was a legend of hidden codes, but no one has ever implied that to me. Maybe that is something your genius can uncover and solve and bring about world peace."

Hakeem inquired, "Mr. Aaronson, do you really believe that such a scroll exists today?"

Norman answered, "It seems far fetched, but archeology has come a long way since they started digging all over Israel. Before they found the Dead Sea Scrolls few would have believed such a document could survive for over 2000 years, but they did. I would not be surprised if it were true."

Hakeem pressed further, "Do you think that someone alive today could be in possession of such a scroll?"

"When they found the Dead Sea Scrolls they were discovered by a shepherd boy looking for his lost goat. The scrolls passed through a number of hands before they were finally purchased and it took years for them to be authenticated." Norman continued, "If someone alive today has possession of them, it would most likely be someone in the direct line of Aaron who would be the rightful heir to the High Priesthood. I think it is highly unlikely, but we Aaronsons like to hold on to our legends, so, of course, I think it is possible. Enough of the family stories, how about we get dressed and catch a movie before you head back to school tomorrow?"

Hakeem did not want to press Norman any further and gave Jake the signal he was all for going to a movie. They dressed and headed out. Norman made sure to leave a note for Lydia so she would know they were all safe and sound.

CHAPTER 29

The next semester seemed to speed by as Jake and Hakeem were fully acclimated to life at Winchester. With the improvement in the weather, more classes were being moved outside, and there seemed to be a more relaxed atmosphere on campus. Afternoons, weather permitting, were spent on the outdoor track, and martial arts training was combined with a rigorous obstacle course. The competition between the boys increased and Jake advanced in his mastery of Karate. Hakeem was now becoming more adept at handling a variety of weapons as a part of his training. The foot race around the track increasingly became more zealous, and by summer's end they were both leading the pack. They grew in knowledge, physical maturity, and depth of understanding. They were becoming multi-dimensional and balanced. The friendship between Jake and Hakeem grew, and they made each other better by challenging one another on many levels.

In early August, Hakeem and his father were called away for a family emergency back in Turkey that would cause him to miss the start of the new school year. This was the first time Jake was on campus without his roommate. Since they were only just now becoming sophomores they had no role in mentoring or escorting the incoming class, so Hakeem would not really be missing anything special, other than the start of classes. With his scholastic aptitude, he would catch up in no time at all.

The assembly went like Jake had remembered from his first day at Winchester exactly one year before. The only difference was he could not remember seeing Max Hirschberg being in attendance at his orientation. Max caught Jake's eye and gave him an acknowledging nod. After the assembly, Jake was not surprised to see Max headed in his direction. They greeted each other and shook hands. Max then said, "Jake, I know you have an open schedule this afternoon, would you mind spending a little time with me? There is something I would like to show you."

Jake accepted the invitation without a second thought, as this was his father's closet friend. They left Meanly Hall and began what Jake thought was a leisurely stroll on one of the tree-lined sidewalks that meandered through the campus. It wasn't until a few minutes into their walk that Jake realized they were on a direct route to Building 18.

Jake was well schooled in when to ask questions and when to be silent. This was one of those silent times when he knew answers would soon come. What he didn't understand yet was what role Uncle Max played and why he was taking Jake in the direction of Building 18. They arrived at the top of the singular driveway ramping down to the roll up door and no sooner had they arrived, than the gate swung open and the roll up door lurched upwards on its track. Jake had spent a year trying to figure out what was housed inside and now a family friend, so close he called him uncle, was escorting him inside.

This had to be the most exhilarating moment of his Winchester existence. Jake was nervous and excited at the same time and tried to register every sight into his photographic memory for recall at a later time.

The sound of the roll-up door closing behind them startled Jake. As he turned around to look at it, he noticed a significant drop in temperature. They were in a cooled zone, and Jake had an idea they were in some sort of data center, but he was unsure why he would be there. They walked down a sloping ramp and came to a stop some 200 feet from the entrance. Both he and Uncle Max walked though what appeared to be a scanning machine of some type, but way more complex than anything he had seen or read about in use at airports or other government installations. He looked, but could not see into the room where the operator was reviewing each of their scans. A green light was illuminated as they continued their downward journey on an ever-narrowing passageway, now too small for even a car to pass. Jake noticed they had come to a Y and veered to their left along their journey. He made note that the wider of the two paths followed the right side.

Uncle Max still had said nothing more than a "follow me" as they began their journey. Jake was ready to explode with so many questions building up inside him. As if he could read Jake's very thoughts Uncle Max said, "Relax, Jake. You will have all your answers in a few minutes."

They rounded another bend and came to a metal doorway with a box protruding from the wall. Uncle Max inserted his entire hand into to the box and a green light illuminated at the same time the sound of a locking mechanism disengaging could be heard. A door swung open inwardly. No sooner had they stepped through it and into the hallway, than it closed automatically.

The hallway was well lit and not very long. The same process was repeated and they were now in an open room surrounded by glass windows. Inside one room were three men looking at what appeared to be video monitors surrounded by racks of recording devices. In the other room were two people with their backs turned looking at audio panels and wearing headphones. No one stopped their activities to acknowledge their presence. In a third room were rows and rows of cabinets that Jake assumed housed computers and mass data storage equipment. That would explain the cool temperature and them being underground. There was still another door leading somewhere that was not visible from their location.

Uncle Max walked over to a keypad on the wall next to the mystery door and punched in a series of numbers. He looked up into a camera and the door swung open. Jake was now standing in the underground bunker that would house students and faculty to protect them from any threat.

All Jake could do was stand there and take in the enormity of what was in front of his eyes. There were many rooms all along the outer walls. In the center were various living areas, each with a specific function. Jake could not even estimate how large this facility was, but knew it could house many people.

Uncle Max walked over to a sitting area and invited Jake to take a seat across from him. It was then he finally spoke, "Jake, we know you have had many questions about Building 18. We trusted you would quickly notice the map's deliberate error in not even showing its existence. In every way possible you have lived up to our expectations. Your father and I knew, even when you were a small child, you had gifts that would make you a valuable asset to your country. We didn't know how well you would adapt to the rigors of physical training, but you have far surpassed our every hope. You have demonstrated your trustworthiness and loyalty through the various tests we have placed in your path. By now, I am sure you have figured out that all is not as it seems here at Winchester. You have observed the cameras, microphones, and rigid standards of conduct. You have risen to every challenge and distinguished yourself as someone who can be trusted. Your father and I are very proud of you."

Jake could only muster a short "Thank You" as his mind was focusing on what Uncle Max was really talking about.

Max Hirschberg continued, "Jake, let me ask you a question. If you had a chance to make a difference in the world and could save many lives, would you be willing to take that chance?"

Max paused a long time, allowing the question to marinate inside Jake's mind. He didn't have to wait too long until Jake answered, "Yes, I would."

Max continued, "Neither your father nor I see you going off to some college after Winchester to pursue some career in gaming technology. We see you using your gifts in cryptography to see patterns and assist us with our efforts to thwart the terrorists who want to destroy The United States and our Jewish people. Does this sound like what you want to do with your life?"

Jake thought for a moment and answered, "I never knew exactly where I fit in. I knew I wasn't like my friends growing up and we never shared the same interests. My father's position kept me from becoming too nerdy otherwise I would not fit in at all into his world, but I have no interest in doing what he does. I had figured I could go get a PhD and teach, but that didn't exactly thrill me either. What you are describing sounds very interesting and maybe even a little dangerous. Yes, I do think I would be very interested."

"Your father and I are thrilled, Jake; however, if you accept this from me, you will not be able to share your activities even with him. Is that clear?" Max asked emphatically.

"Yes, I understand," Jake replied. "What is it you want me to do?"

"What I am proposing is officially unofficial," Max explained. "We have reason to believe your roommate Hakeem Baba is not exactly who you think he is. Our intelligence proves he and his father are connected to radical Islam and are operating here in the United States under the cover of the Turkish Embassy. We have every reason to believe they are planning something here at Winchester and will attempt to plant something in or around this building. You are to keep a close eye on him and from time to time make certain information available to him. I will be the conduit for such information. When you graduate Winchester you will have a job waiting for you as a JEH Security Consultant on assignment at the NSA. You are already more qualified to monitor and decipher Internet chatter than anyone they have over there now. Do you have any questions?"

"Can you take me on a tour now of all the rooms here in Building 18?" Jake asked.

"Seriously, that's really the only question you have?" Max remarked.

"Uncle Max," Jake replied, "why does that surprise you? I thought you said you knew me!"

Max laughed and pointed the way to the first room and they spent the next four hours touring all the underground facility known as Building

18. Each room was more impressive than the next, and Jake was fascinated to see the high level of security employed at Winchester. He had not really grasped what Uncle Max did for a living, but now he had firsthand knowledge. He thought to himself, "If he is doing this extensive work at a College Preparatory School for the sons of the wealthy and influential, what must he be doing for corporations or governments?" All he kept saying out loud, over and over was, "WOW."

They departed Building 18 in the same manner they entered and Jake no longer wondered how they could time it where no one else would be around. He knew, now, of the power housed in Building 18 and the people behind it. Now he was one of them, and he liked that feeling.

CHAPTER 30

Hakeem returned from his emergency family trip and never offered to share any details with Jake. It was business as usual and they were right back to life at Winchester. This year Jake and Hakeem shared a surprising number of classes and, with the exception of their respective martial arts training, they seemed to always be together. Jake had advanced to a Brown Belt and was taking his training very seriously.

There had only been casual discussion about another home visit to celebrate the Jewish New Year. This year's calendar had the holiday fall in early October, and it would be celebrated Thursday night and Friday, yielding a four-day visit. With Hakeem having missed the first two weeks of classes, he felt he needed the time to catch up. He asked Jake to explain this to his mother and make sure that his family understood the circumstances surrounding his decision. Jake assured him he would make sure no one's feelings were hurt. He was hoping this would give him a chance to see Max Hirschberg again and maybe even receive his first "assignment."

While Jake was heading home for Rosh Hashanah, Hakeem was working on more than just his school assignments. It had been prearranged for Hakeem to also be gone that weekend, but to return early enough so that his absence would be undetectable to his roommate. Unbeknownst to Hakeem, Jake would be made aware of this and much more on his visit home.

The limousine driver escorted Jake to the awaiting car and as Jake slid into the backseat he was surprised to see Max Hirschberg sitting there waiting. Max sat motionless as Jake entered and the door was closed behind him. It wasn't until they left the grounds of Winchester that Max addressed Jake, "I'm sure you are surprised to see me, Jake. I apologize if I startled you."

Jake smiled and said, "Not that surprised, I was hoping to see you on this visit and hear more about my assignment."

Max took the cue and said, "I am glad to hear that. I didn't want to draw any attention at services or at the house. I thought it best to use this time to fill you in. Hakeem went to Turkey as he told you, but once there, they flew on to Tehran and spent time there meeting with some very influential people. They also spent several days meeting at the National Research Center for Genetic Engineering and Biotechnology. You can imagine what those discussions were about. Our sources tell us Hakeem had the welcome mat rolled out for him. He will enroll there as soon as he completes his studies here. He will enter into advanced genetic training under the most brilliant scientists from all over the world. There are many nations who have maintained relationships with Iran and are supplying the intellectual capital to finance major breakthroughs in genetic engineering. We also know he and his father are meeting with a delegation from Turkey this weekend. That is why he is not joining you for the holiday."

Jake took it all in and then asked, "Although I am surprised you did warn me that he was not exactly who he appeared to be. What can I do to help?"

"We have reason to believe Hakeem will have a device in his possession that can tap into the audio and video feeds at Building 18. Now that you have seen the operation, you know we are able to gather a broader spectrum of intelligence than just to provide security for the students and faculty. We want you to bring Hakeem along the next time I visit you on campus and have him join us for a mini tour of Building 18. This will give him the opportunity to plant the bug. We will relocate his device and use it to locate those who are monitoring the transmissions. What they see and hear will be under our control. Do you understand?"

Jake questioned, "Exactly how do I bring him along? Won't that seem odd?"

Max replied, "Here is the plan, and it will seem harmless enough. You are to let it slip that I am taking you to Building 18 and put me in a position where I would look like the bad guy if I declined to take him along with us. You will have to play your part well to pull this off. If my guess is right, Hakeem will ask to go to the restroom or change clothes before we go. That way he will have a chance to get the device. We must be certain to give him time to plant it where he thinks it will not be detected. Do not be concerned, that is a virtual impossibility."

"Got it," Jake confirmed.

"One more thing," Max continued. "Make no mention of our relationship to anyone at any time. I will brief your father when I feel the timing is right. Are you ok with that?"

Jake nodded affirmatively and said, "You're the boss."

The limo pulled up in front of Jake's house. The driver carried Jake's suitcase and escorted him to the door. Max sat quietly behind the tinted windows to shield his visibility. No one other than Jake knew he was even in the car.

Lydia opened the door and embraced her son. She stepped back from him, looked him up and down and said, "Jake, you look so good. I think this is the best you have ever looked in your life. Whatever you are doing at that school keep it up, it agrees with you. I think the girls at the synagogue are going to stand up and take notice. I am sorry Hakeem could not join us."

"Thanks, Mom," Jake continued, "Hakeem was away from school for two weeks and has fallen a little behind. He said to thank you for your invitation and to let you know he will miss your cinnamon rolls and company. He wanted to be sure you knew he had no choice but to stay and get caught up."

Lydia answered, "I understand. Let's be sure and send him a little care package to let him know we missed him."

"Good idea, Mom," Jake confirmed.

"Dinner is almost ready and we can't be late for services," Lydia instructed. "Get a shower, change and be down in forty-five minutes. Your father will be home soon."

Jake did as he was told, the whole time replaying the conversation with Max Hirschberg over and over in his head. He was beginning to appreciate more and more the life his father led and the complexities of diplomacy. He felt more a part of his father's life now than ever before. He wanted to be sure to spend some quality time with his dad this trip and even stay home with him and miss the morning service. His mom would just have to understand.

Norman was standing at the bottom of the staircase talking with Lydia when Jake came bounding down the steps. He watched as his son seemed to take each step with a new confidence he had not seen before. Jake stopped and hugged his father, both realizing at the same time they were now the same height. Norman felt Jake's strength in his embrace and knew his boy was now a man. As they broke the embrace Jake said, "I love you, Dad."

Norman smiled and said, "I love you too, son. You look great. I'm glad to have you home. Let's make sure we spend some real father-son time together on this visit."

Lydia looked on and smiled as her vision for her family was being fulfilled right in front of her own eyes. She turned toward the dining room wiping away a tear of joy, as she knew this was going to be a sweet New Year.

After dinner they rode to the synagogue and met up with the Hirschbergs. Together they walked down the center aisle to their places on the front row. As Lydia had predicted, many eyes were on her strikingly handsome son, Jake. She didn't turn to look, but smiled knowing she was right.

Either the Rabbi was extraordinarily brief or Jake was preoccupied with his new assignment, as the service seemed to be over rather quickly. Norman told Lydia he did not want to stay for the meet and greet. He would rather head home to spend more time with Jake. She did not put up any resistance and they left to go home.

The next morning Lydia slipped out to give Jake and Norman some well deserved rest. Upon hearing her leave, Norman went in to check on Jake and he was already awake.

"Coffee?" Norman asked.

Jake swung his feet out of the bed and followed his father downstairs where he knew what was awaiting them. This time there was no note.

Norman and Jake took their places at the table and enjoyed the quiet, sipping their coffee and eating their cinnamon rolls. Norman broke the silence and asked, "Did you and Max have a good visit?

Jake knew what his instructions were and kept his answers short saying, "Yes, I did. It was very interesting. He told me he would share the discussion with you. Have you spoken with him about it?"

"I have," Norman began. "We are both very proud of you and I support you 100%. I have been told not to ask you for any details and I would never do anything to jeopardize that trust. I had always hoped you would want to use your gifts for your country. I just never knew how. I am excited and nervous at the same time, but that goes with being a dad. I don't need to remind you this stays between us. Your mother would not share the same enthusiasm we have. Understood?"

"Understood," Jake replied.

"How about you and I take a ride over to my office and I show you around? There are some things I think you will find interesting. Now that you are a part of the team you have clearance. Interested?" Norman asked.

"Wow, I have clearance, I had no idea. Am I Interested? That is an understatement." Jake said as he was on his way to get ready. Norman just smiled, left the dishes on the table and went up to ready himself.

It was Friday and Washington was busy. Norman decided to drive himself, parked in his reserved spot, and entered the Main State Building. They passed through security and rode the elevator to the Fifth Floor, Executive Suite, where they exited. Jake only had fleeting memories of visiting before when he was much younger. After entering Norman's office, Jake sat across from his father and watched as Norman unlocked a polished mahogany cabinet and took out a wooden box with a worn leather handle.

He came around to the same side of the desk and took a seat next to his son, handed the box to him and said, "I have waited for the right time to give this to you and I believe that time is now."

Jake carefully unlatched the box and lifted the cover and immediately recognized what his father had handed him. Jake was holding in his hands an Enigma Machine like the one used to decode encrypted messages during World War II.

Norman looked at his son as his eyes were filled with wonder and heard the emotion in Jake's voice when he could barely get the words "Thank You" out of his mouth. They would spend the rest of the weekend together discussing the Enigma Machine and many other areas of encryption technology.

This might have been Jake's best weekend ever, and there was more in store for him once he returned to school. He could hardly contain his excitement.

As Norman and Lydia dropped Jake off, they knew more than ever before that their son would make a significant contribution to the world. They just didn't yet know what it would be.

CHAPTER 31

Hakeem had prepared for Jake's return, and when he heard the door open he immediately said to Jake, "How was your visit home? I hope you conveyed my best wishes to your family and they understood why I could not join them. While you were gone I realized I was thirsty every hour. I don't think it is too serious, but I need to have it looked into."

The two roommates had perfected their encoded communications their first year and it had become a routine way of life for them. Both seemed to enjoy leaving encrypted messages for the other, and every now and then would simply leave a joke or some other inane playful message. Up until Jake's meeting with Max Hirschberg, Jake had never suspected Hakeem of being anything more than a friend. Now that Jake had been briefed on Hakeem's activities and intentions, he found himself suspicious of his friend. He wondered, "Why does Hakeem want to meet me at the fountain in an hour?"

Jake unpacked and waited until he heard the door to the apartment close, signaling Hakeem had already left for the rendezvous at the fountain. Jake would wait five minutes and take a different route and meet up with him at the appointed time.

Jake arrived at the fountain just in time to see the shadow of another person heading away from where Hakeem was standing. It was immediately apparent to Jake that Hakeem had been speaking to the man prior to Jake's arrival and his exit was timed so that Jake would not be able to see who it was.

Hakeem greeted Jake saying, "My friend, I wanted to tell you in private that I will not be returning to Winchester after this semester ends. My father is being transferred back to Ankara in preparation for a promotion. He has decided I should finish my education elsewhere. I did not want to discuss this where others could hear since his appointment has not yet been announced publicly. I was given permission to tell you as I value our friendship. I know our paths were brought together for a reason and this is not the end for us. We still have two months together, but I felt you should be the first to know."

Jake looked at his friend and said, "I will miss you. We have become best friends and have shared much. I hope we don't lose touch with each other. Let's make the best of the time we have together. Thanks for giving me the head's up on what is going on. Let me know what I can do to help."

As they walked off together to return to their room Jake thought, "I will need to notify Max of this right away. Whatever Hakeem is planning will have to take place before he leaves in December."

As they rounded the corner to walk into their dormitory one of the Winchester Campus Security Officers was standing there. He motioned to Jake to join him on the far side of the entryway. Jake looked at Hakeem and shrugged his shoulders as he joined the officer. The officer positioned himself so that Hakeem could not see or hear what he was saying to Jake.

Officer Haralson spoke to Jake saying, "I have a message for you from Mr. Hirschberg. All I want you to do is nod your head and not speak. Ok?"

Jake nodded in affirmation that he understood what he was to do during their conversation.

Officer Haralson continued, "Tomorrow afternoon, after you run your laps, you are to pretend to have pulled a muscle and ask to go to the infirmary to have it checked. Understood? When Hakeem asks you what I wanted to speak with you about, tell him you failed to sign in upon your return to campus."

Jake nodded his head in acknowledgement, and Officer Haralson walked straight past Jake and headed off to finish his rounds. Jake stood for a moment before he rejoined Hakeem, who asked, "What was that all about?"

Jake gave his prepared, albeit untrue, answer, "When I got dropped off earlier I did not sign back in. There was no one at the desk and I didn't feel like waiting around. He was sent to make sure I was back and to tell me not to let it happen again."

Hakeem lightly punched Jake in the arm laughing at him bucking the system. They raced up the stairs to their room and prepared for another week of classes.

CHAPTER 32

All throughout the morning classes Jake struggled to keep his mind from wandering. The afternoon could not come soon enough, and Jake wrestled with himself to keep his focus sharp. Since he and Hakeem shared the same classes, any change in Jake's behavior would be noticed.

The afternoon finally arrived and, as planned, Jake grabbed his leg and fell during the last lap around the track. Hakeem along with Jake's Karate instructor rushed to his side to check on him. Once they were able to assess that he had probably just pulled something and was able to walk unassisted, they sent him to the infirmary to get checked out.

Instead of the nurse sitting at the desk inside the infirmary, it was Max Hirschberg. Jake was not surprised and shook his hand and took the seat next to him. Max spoke quietly, "Jake, we have learned that Akram Baba has been called back to Ankara and will be taking Hakeem back with him. Is that what he told you last night at the fountain?"

Jake no longer was surprised at what Max knew or wondered how he knew it and confirmed that Hakeem would be leaving at the end of this semester. He asked Max, "Does this change anything or is he still planning on planting something in Building 18?"

Max answered, "No, this only moves up the plans. We now know what timeframe we are working within. They will want him to plant it right before he leaves so that if it were to be discovered he would be far out of reach. There is a scheduled Campus Security Briefing for all students and faculty next Thursday. I will be present for that. It is scheduled for the afternoon and is in lieu of the regular afternoon Physical Education activities. It is only an hour long, and the students will be given free time afterwards. We will use this time for our special tour of Building 18. Make sure you keep Hakeem close by after the briefing. I will come over to say hello, mention the special tour, and let him overhear it. Follow my lead and when I invite you, make a point to ask if Hakeem can join us. It will appear impromptu and I will reluctantly agree to make it appear totally unrehearsed. I will tell him you and I will meet him there so he will have time to retrieve the device. We have already located it and checked to be sure it is not dangerous. It is very well designed and contains synthetic polymer materials that will not trip our scanners. We have already prepared a place for him to plant it and have set up where we will relocate it to accomplish our purpose."

Jake replied, "It sounds like everything is in place. I will do my part."

As Max opened the door to the infirmary to leave, Head Nurse Sylvia poked her head out of the examination room and called out, "I'll be finished in here in a minute. Take a seat and I will get to you next."

After just a few minutes, Jake was escorted into the examination room. His vital signs were checked and Nurse Sylvia asked what was wrong. Jake played along with the plan and described the pain in his thigh after running laps. Nurse Sylvia checked his range of motion and his level of discomfort and told him to take it easy for a few days and take ibuprophen for the inflammation and pain. If it didn't feel better after three days of rest, he was to return for a recheck. She gave him a note and released him.

Hakeem was waiting outside the infirmary and Jake wondered how long he had been there and whether he had seen Max Hirschberg leave. He was relieved when Hakeem said, "Are you ok? I just got here and they said you were still inside. What did they tell you?"

"They said it was just a pulled muscle and to take it easy for a few days. Nothing life threatening," Jake replied.

Hakeem said, "I am thankful for that. We have the afternoon free and not much homework. This would be a good time for you to show me that machine you brought back that your father gave you. I am quite interested in it."

Jake smiled and replied, "Sounds great. I haven't had much of a chance to really look at it myself. Let's stop by the library and see if they have a book on it that can tell us more."

Their trip to the library was a success and they checked out a book entitled *The Enigma War: The Inside Story of the German Enigma Codes and How the Allies Broke Them* by Jozef Garlinski. With the book in hand, and a free afternoon to examine the gift Norman Aaronson had given his son, Jake and Hakeem returned to their room.

After a few hours Jake was still enamored with the Enigma Machine and its capability to generate billions of different codes. This was Jake's passion, but Hakeem's enthusiasm had worn off. Once it was determined the code was broken because of human error and carelessness, Hakeem had enough and went to his room to rest.

Jake was still studying the machine when Hakeem came back out to go to the dining hall. He pried Jake away to join him. On the way Jake said to Hakeem, "You know, Hakeem, the day may come when you will find a use for our messaging system. It may even help you solve something in the pattern and code in DNA. You have said many times, 'Nothing happens by chance.' There must be a reason you and I have spent the last year and a half together. Maybe one day we will know the real reason."

Hakeem pondered Jake's statements and wondered the same thing.

CHAPTER 33

On Wednesday night it was announced there would be a mandatory security briefing for all students and faculty on Thursday afternoon immediately after lunch. The briefing would take approximately one hour and the rest of the afternoon would be free time. After the first part of the announcement was met with some sounds of disapproval, the free time portion was cheered.

The Thursday afternoon briefing arrived and Jake and Hakeem took their seats next to each other in Meanly Hall. It was an annual event; a review of security measures and any changes from the prior year. Nothing much had changed, other than the announcement that there were new cameras installed around the fountain and added lighting along some of the walkways.

Both Jake and Hakeem took note of the new cameras around the fountain. The meeting ended after one hour and everyone was dismissed for an afternoon of free time. Jake took his time exiting, giving Max Hirschberg enough time to make his way to where the boys were standing.

Max extended his hand to both Jake and Hakeem and addressed them, "I was hoping I would run into you before I left. Jake, what are your plans for this afternoon?"

"I don't really have anything going on," Jake replied.

Max offered, "In that case why don't you join me? I have to make a visit to one of our installations here on campus."

Jake inquired, "Can Hakeem come too?"

Looking at Hakeem he said, "You want to come, right?"

Hakeem nodded and Max interjected, "Well, I don't see why he can't join us. You must keep everything you see and hear confidential. Jake, come with me while I notify the Headmaster that Hakeem will be joining us. Hakeem, how about if you meet us in thirty minutes at the gate to the unmarked building at the back of the campus?"

Hakeem agreed and headed back to his room to get ready for the visit to Building 18. Along the way he spoke out loud, "Allah be praised for giving me this opportunity to complete my assignment."

Max and Jake walked slowly looking back to see Hakeem headed straight to his room as expected. Max broke the silence saying, "Well done, Jake. I don't think he suspects a thing. Once we enter, I will look for the right opportunity to leave Hakeem alone long enough to plant the device. You will just have to follow my lead."

Jake nodded in affirmation and walked along side of Max as they conversed about family vacation plans. By the time they arrived at the gate to Building 18, Hakeem was there waiting for them.

Hakeem watched as Max followed the same procedures as he had with Jake to gain access into the interior of Building 18. Once inside, Max said he was thirsty and to follow him to the break room to get some drinks. He handed each a can of soda and they sat at a round table to talk.

Max explained that Building 18 was managed by his company JEH & Associates and was the central monitoring hub for all security activities on campus. He briefly explained some of the technology being used and the reasons for each one. He stayed away from too much detail, as that would have been inappropriate. He told them to pick up their drinks and to follow him.

They walked down several different corridors until they came to the largest room in the facility. This was the underground bunker and he showed them the storehouse of food and medicines. They left the bunker and Max told them their next stop would be the data center where the brains of the entire operation were housed. Just as they were about to enter the data center the guard reminded Max that no beverages were allowed in that room. Max laughed and apologized and said to Jake, "Take Hakeem's drink and follow me so we can toss them out. Hakeem, wait inside for us. Feel free to look around until we get back. When we return I will answer any questions you have about what you see."

Max instructed the guard to make sure Hakeem was not disturbed until they returned, and since Max was his boss he did not question but obeyed.

Hakeem looked around the sealed room and inspected every corner for video cameras.

He knew he only had a few short minutes to locate the cabinet where he was told to plant the device. He walked up and down the rows until he saw the cabinet with the number 271 on it. He looked in both directions before he pushed the button that released the handle. He opened the cabinet, found the slot marked TC124, and slowly reached behind the board in that slot and clipped a small transmitter to the cable connecting that circuit board to the main panel. Quickly he closed the door and made his way back to the center of the room, then headed in the opposite direction to the far side of the room. At the sound of his name being called, Hakeem poked his head out and made his location known. Jake and Max joined him and the tour started.

After the Data Center tour they briefly looked in on the audio and video monitoring stations, but did not go inside. Max spoke briefly to each of the managers while Jake and Hakeem looked on.

Their visit now over, Max escorted the boys back out of the building and deposited them at the top of the driveway outside the gate. "I hope you enjoyed that little afternoon tour. Not many here have ever seen what you have, and I would appreciate it if you keep this just between us. Everyone knows this building is here and we like to keep the mystery going. We are responsible for the security and safety of all here at Winchester, but it is best to keep security centers secure. Jake I will see you during the break. Hakeem, are you going to spend the break with Jake this year?"

Hakeem replied, "No sir, I am afraid this is my last semester here at Winchester. My father has received a new assignment and we will return to Turkey. I will finish my schooling somewhere in Europe or the Middle East. My father has not informed me yet where I will attend. I thank you for taking me on this tour and I hope to see you again."

Max replied, "Good luck to you, Hakeem. I am sure our paths will cross again. It was good to spend time with you."

As they departed Building 18, the crew was already relocating the transmitter Hakeem had placed to its new location. There it would be fed data containing encryption that would identify where the information was going and all the routes it took to its final destination. It would also deposit monitoring code along the route that would install a backdoor granting secure access to each of the computers involved.

JEH & Associates would provide this to both the NSA and CIA as a part of their contract with each of the agencies. In addition, each agency would notify JEH & Associates of activity related to any of their clients. This was just one of the many benefits of providing high-level security and surveillance to the sons of dignitaries from all over the world.

CHAPTER 34

akeem's departure from Winchester left Jake with a sense of loss, combined with a deep desire to grab hold of his destiny. He used the next two-and-a-half years to focus his attention on mastering cyber technology in preparation for the position awaiting him at JEH & Associates. No longer did he need the competitive motivation of a Hakeem to hone his martial arts skills. Jake had found a personal vision as his greatest motivator. He set the bar high, and upon graduation from the Winchester Academy he received his Black Belt in Karate. Jake's confidence had been bolstered by finally seeing where he fit in the world, and it energized him to excel.

He was not satisfied to leave his education unfinished. With the help of his academic advisor, they found a university program that allowed for online classes. During his four years at Winchester, Jake simultaneously accumulated enough online credits to receive a Bachelor's Degree from the University of Cincinnati. Both his high school and college diplomas carried the same month and year, June 1999. It was still his intention to complete a doctoral program, and he found an online university for that as well. His goal was to have his PhD in Computer Science within his first year out of school. He would find a way to balance his new job with his online classes.

Max Hirschberg agreed to give Jake the summer off to travel with the family before he started his new assignment with JEH & Associates. This summer would be his first return to his birthplace since leaving Israel and moving back to the states. His parents had arranged for him to spend the first two weeks on a tour with them and the next two weeks staying with friends of the family.

Norman and Lydia would remain in Jerusalem on official business for the State Department, while Jake made new friends in Netanya. He would enjoy the beach and the nightlife of Tel Aviv more than hanging out in a hotel room with his parents. Max had also made some plans of his own for Jake to meet some of his Israeli associates.

Although Jake had dual citizenship in the United States and Israel, he would be traveling with his US Diplomat Passport. This was required by the State Department, since he was accompanying his father on a dual-purpose trip involving some portion of official business. Norman had filed his itinerary well in advance so that the proper security agencies in Israel would be aware of his plans. The State Department would coordinate with the Israel Ministry of Foreign Affairs as proper notification of official visits had to be documented and coordinated between both governments. Even though a portion of the trip was a family vacation, both the CIA and the Israel Security Agency (ISA) would be keenly aware of security measures. Once inside the borders of Israel, the Aaronson family would be under the watchful eye of the Protective Security Department of the ISA.

Travel was routine for Jake, but this trip started off different than all the rest. It wasn't the packing or preparation. It wasn't the transportation to the airport. It was Jake's heightened awareness of security. He was acutely aware of video cameras, uniformed and plain-clothes personnel, baggage inspectors, drug- and bomb-sniffing dogs. His watchful eyes scanned back and forth from the moment they exited the car until they arrived at their gate. His mind took inventory of the order of things so that he could discern what was out of order.

In spite of traveling with Diplomatic Passports, Jake and his family were still subjected to the standard three questions asked of every passenger. The agent at the First Class counter robotically asked, "Did you pack your own bag? Have your bags been in your possession since you packed them? Has anyone asked you to bring anything with you?"

The agent barely listened to the answer, but Jake watched carefully as a well dressed supervisor behind the counter turned his head when the agent asked, "Are you checking these bags straight through to your final destination of Tel-Aviv?" Norman answered in the affirmative, which seemed to activate a certain protocol. The supervisor took his place beside the agent and asked to see the passports. After taking notice of the words DIPLOMATIC stamped in gold across the front, he seemed to relax and thanked the Aaronsons for flying with them. They were issued their boarding passes and made their way to the security check-in lines.

Jake observed the people in line waiting to have their bags x-rayed. Dulles was filled with every ethnicity from around the world, and the security area was where they all converged into one moving herd of humanity. As the line moved, Jake took notice of the security personnel strategically positioned along the outer perimeter of the baggage screening area. They communicated regularly via walkie-talkie to each other passing some sort of information between them.

Jake took his place behind his mother in line as the agent inspected their boarding passes and passports and compared their photos to their faces. Everything was routine and seemingly automatic as thousands of people passed through these same checkpoints all day long. One last check of the boarding pass before boarding the aircraft and the Aaronsons were on their way to JFK to catch their long flight to Tel Aviv.

Things were much more hectic at JFK than Jake had anticipated. They had to transfer from one concourse to another. After that, they passed through another gatehouse where there was an even more extensive review of their documents and baggage. Norman explained this was normal for international travel. What he did not explain was the heightened security surrounding all travel into and out of Israel. Upon entering the El-Al Airlines boarding area, Jake began to notice something he had not seen anywhere else. There he was greeted with another set of scanners and security personnel. Instead of friendly faces, he took note of a "No Nonsense" presence. Everyone was pleasant, but there was a total level of seriousness he had not previously observed. Jake scanned the boarding area and caught the eye of no less than five individuals who made no attempt to avert their eyes from meeting his straight on. There was no question in his mind these individuals were well trained and armed. He watched carefully as seemingly random individuals were asked to bring their carry-on bags and follow an airline representative to one of several rooms off to the side of the boarding area.

As the Aaronsons passed through the screening area, Jake listened carefully as his father was being questioned about the purpose of his visit. Upon hearing that he would only be accompanying his son for part of the trip, the security agent motioned for Jake to come forward. Jake took his place beside his father and was immediately escorted to one of the rooms.

One male and one female security agent entered the room, closed the door, and asked Jake to take a seat across the table from them. The female spoke first, asking Jake for his passport and boarding pass. After she flipped through every page examining all his visa stamps, she handed it to her counterpart. He performed the same review and returned it back to her.

Jake maintained his composure during the extended silence in the room. He did not speak, knowing signs of discomfort would only draw more attention. After a few minutes the male agent spoke, "What is the purpose of your trip to Israel?"

Jake did not hesitate to answer, "I have just graduated and my parents are taking me on a tour of where I was born."

The agent looked up and said, "You are Israeli? Where is your Israeli passport?"

Jake replied, "I am traveling with my father who is with the State Department and will be working during the second half of our trip. We are required to travel with these passports while on official business."

The agent did not seem happy when he said, "I asked you where is your Israeli passport. Why did you not answer my question?"

Jake thought for a moment and realized his error. "I am sorry. You are correct; I did not answer your question. My Israeli passport is at home."

"Whom will you be meeting with during your trip?" the female agent inquired.

"I do not know the names of everyone I will be meeting with during my visit, but I will be staying with Chaim Levy and his family in Netanya after our tour. I will also be meeting with friends of Max Hirschberg."

Jake listened as the two agents spoke to each other in Hebrew and knew he had triggered something when he mentioned Max Hirschberg's name.

The male agent looked at Jake and said, "Did you understand what I just said to my partner?"

Jake said, "No, I do not speak Hebrew."

The male agent admonished Jake saying, "An Israeli who does not speak Hebrew can do little to help his own people." With that, the agents escorted Jake back to his anxiously awaiting parents. Lydia hugged her son asking, "What did they say?"

Jake looked at his mother and then at his father and replied, "They said I needed to learn Hebrew."

Throughout the flight Jake listened carefully to all the announcements made in English and Hebrew. He heard conversations all around him in the language of his birthplace, but could only pick out a few random words. Jake thought back to the long list of languages that his old roommate Hakeem Baba had mastered and it began to ignite something inside.

During the over twelve-hour flight, while most slept, Jake stayed awake and laid out a plan to learn Hebrew and Arabic. He knew he would be more effective in the long term if he accomplished this before he embarked on his PhD. He would let Max know he wanted his support in this effort. Reading, writing and speaking Hebrew and Arabic would enhance his value and effectiveness in identifying the patterns that Jake innately saw in everything.

With a new clarity and vision for his future, Jake was fully embracing it. He would channel his gifting into a multi-language capability that would exponentially increase his effectiveness. With Jake's aptitude for seeing patterns he knew he could master these languages, but he would need to immerse himself in them. Even before landing he knew he would not be making the return trip back home for some time.

CHAPTER 35

The arrival concourse at Ben Gurion Airport in Tel Aviv led straight to the Passport Control Counter. Almost immediately upon presenting their Diplomatic Passports, the Aaronsons were escorted to the baggage claim area by a well-dressed Israeli government official named Samuel. He welcomed the family to Israel and spoke perfect English. He handed their baggage claim tickets to a young lady carrying a two-way radio, who located their luggage for them. After all their bags were collected, they followed the representatives to an awaiting car where they were introduced to Ariel, their driver and guide for their two-week tour of Israel.

For the first time Jake heard both his parents speaking to their guide in fluent Hebrew. It had never really occurred to him that both his parents would be fluent, even though they had been stationed in Israel for a number of years before returning to the States. The conversation soon reverted back to English as Ariel explained they would check in at their hotel in Tel Aviv and then meet for dinner to discuss the itinerary.

Jake noticed a heightened sense of security everywhere they drove. He had not seen this kind of presence back home and questioned Ariel about it.

Ariel explained, "Since our creation as the Jewish State in May of 1948 we have come under attack many times by our enemies. There are many Islamic terrorist organizations, funded by neighboring countries, which oppose our very existence. They do not hide their agenda. One such group is named Hamas. This word Hamas in Hebrew means violence. Another you may have heard of is Hezbollah, who are also Shi'ite Muslims. They operate out of Southern Lebanon and are funded by Syria and Iran. These groups claim they have the right to this land and trace their inheritance back to Abraham through Ishmael. They refute the historical accuracy of the Torah, yet claim those parts of it that support their position. Judaism is more than 3,000 years old. Islam is 1,400 years old. There were no Muslims when God made his promises to Abraham, and there were no Muslims on Mount Sinai when the Torah was given to Moses. It is true there were Arabs living in Israel at the time the United Nations voted to establish the Jewish State. However, most people fail to realize that being an Arab does not prohibit you from being a citizen and living in Israel. In fact, over 15% of the population is Arab Muslims. Since the bombing outside the Great Synagogue in August 1998 took 21 lives, more armed soldiers are visible throughout the city. It is not uncommon to see small groups of Israel Defense Force (IDF) soldiers carrying machine guns walking throughout the city. Military service is mandatory for all boys 18-25 and girls at age 17-20. That is why you may think these soldiers look so young. Do not be misled by their youthful appearance. IDF soldiers are the best-trained soldiers in the world. I am still serving in the Reserves as a Captain and will remain on active reserve until I am 55 years old."

Jake inquired further, "Are all citizens of Israel required to serve?"

Ariel answered, "Yes. There are certain exemptions granted, but it is a right and a privilege for every citizen to serve."

Jake replied, "I was born here and have dual citizenship. Would I be eligible to serve?"

Lydia quickly jumped in, "Jake, what would possess you to ask such a question? We are barely here one hour and you are asking about becoming a soldier? That's some way to start a family vacation."

Norman jumped to Jake's defense, "He is just asking a question, dear. I don't blame him for being interested in his heritage and where he was born. That was one of the reasons we wanted to make this trip. Remember?"

"No one said anything about enlisting when we made these plans," Lydia replied sternly.

Just as she made her feelings known they arrived at their hotel, the Dan Tel Aviv. As they pulled into the secure parking area, a distinguished-looking gray-haired man dressed in a tailor-made suit approached the car. Ariel shook his hand and then introduced the Aaronsons to Baruch Mordecai, the hotel manager.

Baruch shook hands with the family and invited them into a small hospitality room where he had beverages and fresh fruit waiting for them. Shortly after sitting down to have a bite, two men entered the room and introduced themselves as representatives from the Israeli Government. They offered their services to the family and gave them their business cards containing their personal contact information. No sooner had the first two men left, than in walked two more official-looking gentlemen. This time there were no introductions made as Norman and Lydia jumped to their feet in excitement and ran to embrace them both. After some very loud and excited chatter in Hebrew, they brought the two visitors over to where Jake was standing.

"Is this really that baby we said goodbye to almost eighteen years ago?" asked the older of the two. "It doesn't seem possible," he continued.

"Yes, this is our son Jake," Norman stated. "The last time you saw him you were carrying him to the plane sending us back home."

The older of the two men spoke first, "Jake, I am Ezra Weiss and I served here under your father in the embassy. He taught me everything I know and I was there with him waiting for you to be born. I had always hoped I would get the chance to see you again. Please take my card and let me know if I can help you in any way. Your parents have told me so much about you and they are very proud of you. I am very pleased you have come to visit your true home."

Jake replied, "Thank you, sir. I must be honest I don't remember you, but it is a pleasure to meet you."

Ezra laughed and introduced Jake to the younger man accompanying him, "And this is Ethan Hirschberg. Max's oldest son."

Jake looked a little astonished and said, "Ethan, it is nice to meet you. I didn't know Max had an older son, especially one living in Israel."

"Yes," Ethan replied, "I came here when I was just about your age and decided to stay and serve in the IDF. I have since joined the security community here heading up JEH & Associates' Israeli operations. I will be your contact during the second part of your trip. My father has already briefed me about you and your visit."

Jake said, "It is very nice to meet you. I am sure we will have a lot to talk about."

Jake knew this was going to be a contact worth having and one he could ask all his questions to without his mother overhearing him. They had only been in Israel a few hours and Jake could already start to see how things would fit together.

After unpacking and getting settled in their adjoining rooms, Norman knocked on Jake's door. He motioned Jake to sit and discuss what he hoped to experience over the next four weeks.

Jake was very forthcoming as he knew his father would not respond emotionally like his mother would. "Dad," he began, "ever since you talked about our lineage and the legend of the scrolls, I have not been able to shake the feeling that somehow I am going to play a part in that. I don't know how, but just landing here made me feel like I was home. I can't really explain it, but it is very clear to me that I want to see and learn everything I can related to who we are. I want to see the museums and the archeological digs. I want to learn about the Temple and its history and the role of the High Priest. I want you to use your influence to get us into places others can't go. Something in me tells me this is where I belong. I don't think it is long term, but I do think I need to consider learning Hebrew and Arabic. I am physically fit and I would much rather serve in the IDF than consider anything in the military back home in the United States. I can be of more long-term use to Max Hirschberg and whatever agencies he plans to connect me with if I have Middle East experience. If I didn't know any better, I would say you planned this with Max to get me here and build your case with Mom. I know you can't confirm or deny anything, but I am the family genius when it comes to solving puzzles. I want you to show me what I need to see in order to learn who I really am and what plans are being made by our enemies."

Norman put his hand on Jake's shoulders and said, "I am very proud of you and know if you search hard enough the answers will come. Leave Mom up to me. We will see the sights and spend the two weeks enjoying each other. The following two weeks will help you see clearly what you are being called to do. No matter what you do, son, I love you."

CHAPTER 36

Sitting in his office in Ankara, Turkey, Akram Baba read with great interest the Al Jazeera story of the US Under Secretary of State's visit to Israel. The article stated the family would be in Israel for one month on both personal and State business. Specifically mentioned in the story was a short bio on Jake and his recent graduation from both the Winchester Academy and the University of Cincinnati.

Akram immediately sent a message to his son Hakeem, who was in Iran at the Tehran University of Medical Sciences. He also sent a confidential message to his well-placed resources in Hamas to keep a watchful eye on the movement of this family. He gave specific instructions to personally notify him of any meetings taking place outside the normal scope of diplomacy. They were to report to him daily where the family was at all times.

Upon receiving his father's message, Hakeem immediately went to the library on campus to read the article for himself. As he read of Jake's dual graduation he smiled at his friend's accomplishment. He took note of Jake's picture and how physically well developed he had become. He wondered what Jake would think if he knew that Hakeem would soon be the youngest graduate of the medical school and was about to join the team at the National Research Center for Genetic Engineering and Biotechnology in Tehran.

During Hakeem's two-and-a-half years in Tehran he had devoted himself to study and prayer. His once moderate persona was no longer necessary to appease the Westerners he had to live among. He could now embrace the fullness of his calling to take his place among those who furthered the cause of Radical Islam and the commands of the Koran for the annihilation of all infidels.

His appearance had also changed during the years since he had roomed with Jake. He no longer wore the Brooks Brothers shirts and khaki pants of the over-indulgent and self-serving capitalists. He was proud to have his head covered with a skullcap and his beard grown long. He faithfully wore his thobe at all times, maintaining the highest regard for the teachings of the Koran. In order for him to fulfill his destiny his conduct as both a religious man, and as a scholar, had to be above reproach. He was faithful to pray with the men of the community five times daily and live a life of spiritual cleanliness. He would find a way to take his place among those who were at the forefront of a new form of Jihad, one that would change the very face of humanity forever.

Hakeem did not allow the rigorous schedule of prayer and study keep him from further honing his martial arts skills. He regularly trained with an elite group of special ops personnel from the Islamic Revolutionary Guard Corps (IRGC). Hakeem's favor extended into the highest levels of government, and he was being groomed and financed by those closest to Ayatollah Seyed Ali Khamenei. One day he hoped to sit in the presence of the one he knew as the Grand Ayatollah.

In a few short weeks he would transition to his new laboratory at the National Research Center, where he would begin his work on DNA. There he would work with some of the greatest geneticists from around the globe. His laboratory was being funded and would be equipped with the latest equipment. He knew how difficult it was to obtain scientific equipment from certain countries and marveled at the intricacies of international trade and the ingenuity of his benefactors. He had already begun to wonder what circuitous route these instruments would have to take in order to cross into the borders of Iran. The West had tried to cutoff trade with Iran, but they had many friends who were ever too willing to keep open the lines of commerce with this oil-rich country. Not everyone was as enamored with America as America was with itself. As the Arabian Proverb states, "The enemy of my enemy is my friend."

CHAPTER 37

Jake's first few days in Tel Aviv were filled with visits to one museum after another. He was fascinated with the rich cultural and historical contributions that made up his heritage. He was certainly worldly enough to know that Israel was not one country completely immersed in religiously observant Judaism, but he was not prepared for the cosmopolitan lifestyle of Israel's second largest city. He had expected to hear Hebrew, Arabic and English spoken, but was surprised at how many spoke Russian and Yiddish. The style of dress ranged from very conservative to what he saw back home in his own neighborhood. Arabs walked and worked among Jews and all seemed calm. There was a visible military and police presence on the streets. It was not unusual for stores to employ security guards to inspect backpacks, bags, and purses upon entering. This was significantly different than anything he had experienced back home.

Dinners were in the hotel each of the three nights they stayed in Tel Aviv. Norman and Lydia made it a point to invite old neighbors and friends to join them. It was great to renew old friendships and introduce Jake to them all. After dinner each night the sons and daughters of their old friends escorted Jake to check out Tel Aviv's nightlife. This gave him a break and afforded

Norman and Lydia some uninterrupted time to catch up with old friends.

His first walk along the beach of the Mediterranean took place in Tel Aviv. As he walked along his new friends chattered away, describing the plans to turn Tel Aviv into more of a world-class city with new nightclubs and restaurants lining the streets. As they walked along, Jake noticed that two men seemed to be keeping pace with them, but at a distance. He made no mention of it, but remained alert to see if they would remain outside the coffee shop they were about to enter. He made sure to ask his friends to get a table by the window so he could watch people as they passed by. While they were sitting and talking, Jake saw the two men standing opposite the coffee shop. Like a scene out of a spy movie, two men appeared out of nowhere and pushed the ones following Jake into an awaiting vehicle. For the rest of the evening, Jake did not see anyone else following them.

From Tel Aviv they travelled by plane to Eilat and spent several days enjoying this resort city on the border of Jordan in the most southern portion of the Negev Desert. Norman had a surprise waiting for Jake and had scheduled his first tandem parachute jump. From up above Eilat you could see into both Egypt and Jordan. The skies were always clear and the visibility perfect. Norman would accompany Jake on this adventure while Lydia took advantage of the spa treatments.

Jake took note of how friendly everyone was, but more especially how overly attentive and interested the manager seemed to be about their daily activities. It was as if he needed to know where the family would be at all times. On the way to the local skydiving facility Jake mentioned this to his father, asking, "Dad, have you noticed anything unusual about the manager's behavior? Is it me, or does he seem to be asking a lot of questions about everything we are doing?"

Norman replied, "I hadn't really noticed, but now that you mention it, I haven't noticed him interacting with others the way he has with us. Don't mention this to your mother. You know how she worries. I will make a call to Uncle Max and see what he can find out. I promised I would check in with him before we made our way up to Jerusalem. He is seven hours behind us so I can call him when we get back from our adventure. Are you excited about skydiving for the first time?"

Jake could not contain his excitement as he blurted out a very loud, "Yes!"

After the safety presentation and basic instructions about their tandem dive, both instructors, along with the pilot, ushered Norman and Jake on board the single engine plane. Once onboard, they climbed to 12,000 feet and after linking up, they exited the plane for their 45-second free fall. Once the chutes were deployed, they descended for another 4 ½ minutes. Jake took in the topography and mentally recorded everything he saw.

From this vantage point Jake had a perspective of aerial surveillance. This was also something he knew that he would add to his list of skills to acquire that would be useful to him at a future date.

Norman and Jake compared experiences on the ride back to the hotel and agreed this would rank high on their list of highlights. Norman was thankful to have had this bonding experience with his son and felt they had grown closer since the trip began.

Lydia was waiting anxiously for their return and hugged them both as if they had been reunited after an extended absence. Her eyes filled with tears as she kissed them and told them she loved them. She was already finished with her spa treatments and was ready to enjoy the rest of the day by the pool. She sent them up to change and went out to secure three chairs and an umbrella.

Immediately the manager made his way to Norman and Jake and inquired, "Mr. Aaronson, how was your skydiving adventure?"

"Invigorating!" replied Norman.

"And, what are your plans for the rest of your stay here in Eilat?" he further inquired.

Norman stated what the manager already knew, "We depart tomorrow."

The manager smiled and said, "If I can be of any assistance, please do not hesitate to call me directly. Enjoy the rest of your day."

On the elevator ride up Norman looked at Jake and said, "I will call Uncle Max as soon as we get into the room."

"Dad, there is something else you need to mention to him," Jake replied.

"What?" Norman asked.

Jake answered, "I think I was being followed in Tel Aviv. I noticed two men who seemed to be watching me as we went from place to place. I didn't say anything because I saw two other men approach them and they all went off together. I think it's worth mentioning."

"Next time, tell me when these things happen," Norman admonished.

"I'm sorry, Dad. I will in the future," Jake assured.

Norman picked up the hotel phone and placed it back in its cradle. He looked at Jake and said, "If we suspect anyone of watching us, maybe I should make this call from my secure mobile phone. Let's change into our swimsuits and I will make the call from poolside. They are less likely to have listening devices near the water."

Lydia was peacefully asleep in her lounge chair when Jake and Norman arrived poolside. They dropped their towels, walked to an unoccupied area and called Max Hirschberg's mobile phone number. Max answered right away and listened carefully as Norman described the manager's zealous interest in the family's whereabouts and Jake's observations in Tel Aviv.

After hearing what Norman had to say, Max replied, "Tell Jake his observations were spot on and the two men were following him. My men had been advised to intercept them if they persisted in their surveillance a second night. The manager is another story and I know he has connections with several less friendly factions within the Arab world. Let me do a little checking and see if we can connect him with any specific groups. There is no cause for concern as you are also under the watchful eye of the ISA. I will call you when you arrive back in Tel Aviv and give you my full report then."

By the time they returned to their chaise lounges, Lydia had opened her eyes and said, "What took you boys so long?'

"Just guy stuff," Norman joked.

"Well, it's family time now," Lydia chided. "I think we should enjoy this resort and have some drinks to celebrate Jake's graduation. He is of legal age here in Israel."

Norman was not one to oppose his wife on matters of this nature and ordered three glasses of champagne to toast his family and Jake's accomplishments. They all rested in the warmth of the afternoon sun at this beautiful resort, but Jake still kept a roving eye out looking for anything out of place.

Dinner was quiet and there were no visitors to entertain on this leg of the journey. As a trained guide, Ariel knew when to make his presence and his services known and when to blend into the background. He was close by throughout their stay in Eilat, but not too close. Bedtime came early again as they would be flying back to Tel Aviv in the morning.

After landing at Ben Gurion on the flight from Eilat, they drove to Netanya just thirty minutes north of Tel Aviv. They would spend one night there introducing Jake to the families he would be staying with during his two weeks on his own.

Norman's mobile phone rang. He knew it was Max, but did not want to talk to him in front of Lydia or Ariel. He quickly answered and said, "We are in the car on the way to the hotel in Netanya. I will call you after we arrive."

"Who was that, dear?" Lydia asked.

"Max," Norman replied. "He must be lonesome for us. I'll call him back later."

CHAPTER 38

As they poured into the lobby of their hotel in Netanya, Ethan Hirschberg greeted them, "Welcome back to your birthplace, Jake."

"Ethan," Lydia cheerfully called out. "This is such a nice surprise."

"Yes, it is great to see you again. I hope your stay in Eilat was enjoyable. My father asked me to meet with Norman and Jake for just a few minutes," he replied. "Would you mind if I stole them away for just a moment?"

"Not at all, I will go get settled in the room while you boys talk," Lydia responded.

After Lydia departed and Ariel was parking the car, Norman asked, "Ethan, what is this all about?"

Ethan sat down and leaned in, saying, "My father called me after he spoke with you and asked me to look into who may be following you. It appears that some suspected members of Hamas have been watching you. We intercepted some instructions to observe and report your whereabouts to Akram Baba in Turkey. This, as you know, is Dr. Hakeem Baba's father."

Jake quickly blurted out, "Dr. Hakeem Baba?"

"Yes," Ethan explained, "Dr. Hakeem Baba graduated from Tehran University of Medical Sciences and will be heading up a DNA research team at the National Research Center for Genetic

Engineering and Biotechnology. He is one of the youngest graduates of the medical school and is funded by some of the most influential people in Iran."

Norman asked, "Why would Hamas have any interest in our activities?"

Ethan replied, "We are uncertain at this point exactly what they are interested in. All we know is who they are. It seems their intentions are purely to observe and report, and neither my people nor ISA have intercepted anything that would indicate otherwise. We have doubled your security detail and have the full cooperation of the ISA. You are not only VIP's, you are family."

Norman thanked Ethan for the briefing, and as he shook his hand goodbye Ethan asked, "Might I have a moment alone with Jake?"

Norman nodded and said to Jake, "I will be upstairs with your mother. Come on up when you are finished talking with Ethan and let us know when you are in your room."

Ethan looked at Jake and said, "I have been looking forward to your visit ever since my father told me you were coming. He is very fond of you and has high hopes for your contribution to our efforts to stay several steps ahead of those who have made their hatred of us known. You seemed unsettled when I mentioned the name Dr. Hakeem Baba."

Jake paused for a moment and then spoke, "I was not expecting that, but I am not really that surprised either. I am sure your father told you that he and I were roommates at the Winchester Academy. I brought him home for the Jewish holidays and ever since he visited my family and heard about DNA markers he became driven to know more. He left school suddenly and said he was returning to Turkey. Hearing that he actually went to Tehran and graduated medical school means he is still on that path."

Ethan responded to Jake, "My father has told me he has a place waiting for you when you return, but he wanted me to tell you he is not expecting that to be right away. Do you know what he means by this?"

Jake laughed, "You know your father better than I. He seems to know a lot of things long before most. I have decided I want to stay here in Israel and serve in the Israel Defense Forces. I believe I can be more valuable if I learn Hebrew and Arabic and the mind of the Middle East. I can study it or experience it. I have made my decision to experience it. I do not want to go on any more tours with my parents. I can see all I need to see by living here and serving here. Ethan, can you help me with this?"

Ethan smiled and said, "Yes, I know my father very well. He is on the phone right now with your mother and father explaining your desires to remain here in Israel. He has already couriered your Israeli Passport to me and given me instructions on how and where to assist you in activating your status. We agree with your decision."

Jake looked at Ethan and began shaking his head back and forth saying, "So, this was the plan all along? How did I not see this? Tell me, were my parents in on this from the start?"

Ethan nodded, saying, "Yes. My father thought your mother would be reluctant to go along with the plan, but she was more on board than your father. She hopes it will ignite more of your Jewish identity and you will take more after her in that regard than your father. She has known for some time your gifts would be used in the intelligence community. She and your father have been in agreement on that all along. You will stay with me for the first six months and I will have you tutored in Hebrew and Arabic. With your aptitude, you will have no problem whatsoever. I will make all the arrangements for you to enter into Officer Training since you already have your college degree. Your parents are waiting for us upstairs. Are you ready to fill them in on your decision?"

Jake stood up, signaling his readiness. Together they rode the elevator to the top floor. Jake was not surprised to find his mother and father waiting for them when the doors opened. Jake's journey in Israel began in July, 1999.

CHAPTER 39

On September 11, 2001, the United States was attacked by the Islamist terrorist group al-Qaeda. Masterminded by Osama bin Laden, they commandeered four passenger planes and flew them into the World Trade Center, and the Pentagon. The plane targeting the White House crashed into a field in Pennsylvania. Their justification for these actions was the United States' support of Israel. This was a coordinated attack from highly trained terrorist cells located outside and inside American borders.

The formation of the Department of Homeland Security transformed security all across America. In support of this effort, JEH & Associates was being called upon to increase its staff of consultants. Something had to be done to break the ability of these terrorists to communicate with each other and coordinate activities. American intelligence had greatly underestimated the vast network of the Taliban, Al-Qaeda, The Muslim Brotherhood, Hamas, Hezbollah, and other organizations with an anti-American or anti-Israel agenda.

Although there were isolated terrorist attacks across the US over the course of the next ten years, nothing so far compared to the attack on 9/11. The more urgent threats seemed to be coming out of Iran as they developed and perfected their nuclear capabilities. Tensions between the US and Iran were at an all-time high. Peace was fleeting in the struggle within Israel between the Jewish State and the Palestinian opposition. Terrorism there was on the increase and thousands of rockets were being launched regardless of cease-fire treaties. There was trouble in North Korea, Afghanistan, Iraq, Somalia, and many areas around the globe. China and Russia were still on the radar of every member of the intelligence community.

Ethan Hirschberg headed up Middle East operations for JEH & Associates and had been a liaison between internal and external agencies within the Middle East. His contacts included local CIA, MI6, Mossad, and other operatives from a number of countries. His staff acted as an intermediary for secure communications across multiple intelligence organizations. He held regular briefings within the community and became a key resource as one who was always in the know. His base within Israel also kept him connected with one of their key encryption experts, Jake Aaronson. Demand for Jake's skills stateside was increasing as more terrorist acts took place around the world and Iran was heating up as a formidable enemy.

Jake had quickly made a name for himself within the IDF and had been useful on many assignments to the Shin Bet, Israel's Internal Intelligence Agency. His ability to break the encryption schemes of intercepted communiqués using his own gifts, along with his mastery of computer technology and algorithm development, often times surpassed the capabilities of computers alone. He became the missing link that made the difference.

On more than one occasion, Max had sent consultants working for him at various intelligence agencies in the states to train along side Jake in encryption technologies. It may have appeared to Jake that he was doing Max a favor by sharing his gifts, but it was more than he was led to believe. These contractors were also assessing Jake and his readiness to return to the US and join JEH & Associates team in DC.

As a distinguished member of the IDF, Jake had been involved in the elimination of numerous Hamas cell groups. He had also been involved in breaking encrypted messages that led to the seizure of ships laden with weapons destined to take innocent Israeli lives. His skills were in high demand and he was proud to serve where needed.

Increasingly Ethan had to exert political clout in order to keep the Shin Bet from recruiting Jake into their ranks. Year after year they pursued him, and Ethan knew there was change in the air. After almost ten years of fighting this battle, it was time to send Jake back home to the States to begin his assignment at NSA Headquarters at Ft. Meade. The reports from those who had been sent to assess Jake had been stellar.

Ethan called Jake into his office and gave him his new assignment. They both knew this day was coming and Jake had readied himself to step down from his role as a Colonel in the IDF. This was carefully timed to coincide with his service renewal period. Everything Jake had hoped to accomplish during his years in the Middle East had been obtained, and he had mastered multiple languages and trained with the finest military in the world. He had experienced archeological digs, biblical studies, traveled extensively and knew who he was. He left with honor and a renewed sense of his calling to fight against those who would destroy Israel.

Lydia and Norman were delighted to have their son coming back home to stay. Ft. Meade was commutable from Bethesda, and they hoped Jake would choose to come home to live for a while before he ventured out on his own. Their son was a grown man with a wealth of experiences under his belt since they made that trip to Israel ten years prior.

Since that time, Norman had retired from the State Department after serving his country for over thirty years. He was proud of his record of service. Retiring to Norman did not mean he no longer worked. He, too, was employed by JEH & Associates and worked alongside Max Hirschberg in the complex world of intelligence contracting. One of his personal dreams was about to come true as he and his son would be working together. Norman had been hard at work preparing for Jake's arrival at NSA headquarters. They knew of his outstanding work in Israel, but were about to have firsthand experience with his God-given gifts. The timing could not be better. With the holiday season coming, there would be more reason to celebrate this year than in years past while Jake had lived in Israel.

CHAPTER 40

Dr. Hakeem Baba's laboratory at the National Research Center for Genetic Engineering and Biotechnology in Tehran was equipped with everything he needed. An entire wing was devoted to his work and contained DNA synthesizers, a DNA extractor, chromatographic systems, a protein sequencer, orbital shakers, incubators, a PCR machine, incubator shakers, a lyophilizer (freeze-dryer), fermenters, centrifuges, a culture propagation system, microfuges, a spectrophotometer, a gel-scanning system, an ultracentrifuge, instruments for DNA sequence spectroscopy, a spectroscope, a high performance liquid chromatography (HPLC) electrophorus, and -C 70° and -C 20° freezers.

In his hands, these instruments became his weapons in the campaign to rid the world of the sworn enemy of Islam, the Jews. He devoted as many hours to studying the work of other geneticists as he did overseeing the operation of his own lab. He had read study after study about genetic markers, and cell mutations in specific nationalities. His most exciting discovery was the breakthrough study out of Haifa in 1997 entitled "Y Chromosomes of Jewish Priests." He had never forgotten the statement Norman Aaronson had made so many years before about the possibility of a DNA link specific to not only Jewish people, but to the line of Aaron.

After finding this study and the lengthy lists of related research, Hakeem reached out to his contacts in the Ministry of Intelligence and National Security of the Islamic Republic of Iran (MISIRI). His request to meet with the Director was granted and a car was sent to drive Hakeem to the meeting. What he thought would be a private meeting was anything but that.

Upon arrival at the North Tehran headquarters, Hakeem was welcomed first by uniformed guards who escorted him into the secure facility. After his credentials had been matched in their database, he passed through a series of detectors searching for metals and polymers not permitted within the facility. The armed guards escorted him to a secure elevator, inserted a key, and deposited Hakeem into the elevator. There were no buttons to push and no floor indicators. The elevator was so well designed that Hakeem could not tell if he was going up or down.

The elevator stopped, the doors opened, and Hakeem was now facing a large conference table. Seated there were distinguished leaders ranging from leading clerics to generals. Seated at one end of the table was the President of Iran. To his right sat the Ayatollah.

Hakeem was directed to sit at the end of the table closest to the door and opposite the President. He knew protocol and he would not say anything until he was instructed to do so.

The President was the first to address the group, "I have put up with most of you for some time, but I see we have a distinguished guest in our presence. Dr. Baba. Your reputation precedes you and we are anxious to hear of your latest breakthroughs in our war against our enemies."

"I am honored and humbled to be in the midst of such men of greatness, " Hakeem began. "I had simply requested a meeting with the Security Agency to request assistance in securing research and actual samples in support of my hypothesis."

"And what hypothesis would that be, Dr.?" asked General Abdul El-Amim.

"I was not prepared to share the details at this meeting. I was simply making a request through my regular channels for assistance," Hakeem replied.

The General barked, "Prepare yourself now."

"My apologies," Hakeem offered. "I would not want to offend. My research has uncovered more than just a DNA marker that links all people of Jewish descent. We have replicated, as best we can, experiments into a marker that identifies those in the lineage of the ancient high priest Aaron. My request was to obtain the original research being done. I have a list prepared of where this can be obtained. How it is acquired is not my concern."

The General seemed even more irked when he snapped at Hakeem, "Enough of your scientific ramblings. What is this hypothesis you refer to in no specific terms? Either explain what it is you are working on, or leave. Do not waste any-more of our time."

Hakeem's posture changed as he sat upright in his chair and then, breaking protocol, stood to his feet and began, "The Jewish hope is for the Third Temple to be built on the site of the al-Aqsa Mosque in Jerusalem. In order for this to happen they must have a High Priest in the bloodline of Aaron. If I can identify the exact genetic makeup of this person, we can determine who it is and eliminate his entire family. I will need more than just research for this. I will need blood samples from bones unearthed from archeological digs from the past 100 years. Many of these samples are securely housed in museums and laboratories in Israel."

The General's tone softened, "Is there more to your theory, Dr. Baba? What about this legend of the scrolls you have been heard discussing with members of my staff?"

"With all due respect, General," Hakeem began. "I had hoped to limit my discussions here to the science."

Harshly the General barked, "Are you refus-ing to answer my question, Dr. Baba?"

Hakeem paused briefly before answering, "I mean no disrespect. There is more to the story than we have been able to confirm; however, I have been conducting secondary research into this legend and can only offer unconfirmed find-ings. It appears that throughout history there have been records kept of all the miracles and prophecies that have occurred since the days of Moses and Aaron. It is rumored; these documents have been in the possession of the High Priest since being passed from Aaron to his son. According to this legend, these scrolls are the most sacred and secret writings of all Judaism. If they were to make it into our hands we would strike a double deathblow to Israel by destroying their High Priest and their most secret and prized possession. I need a sample of the blood of the one named Zadok. If I have that, I can find his direct descendant today. That will be my greatest contribution to the destruction of our enemy and the victory for all Islam."

There was silence in the room as every one present weighed what they had just heard. The only voice in the room was that of the Ayatollah as he proclaimed, "Allah does not need the hand of help from one so naïve as to believe that our victory rests on your shoulders. We will continue to fund your research, but will hear no more of this legend. Leave us now."

After Hakeem left the room, the General addressed the remaining leaders, "Watch this one carefully. I am certain he has a great mind, but his zeal may be misplaced. He is quite head-strong and still has connections to the West. If his research is successful, we will have a database of every Jewish person in the world. It will prove quite valuable when the time comes."

Hakeem knew right away that he would have to devise his own way to obtain the samples he needed. Over the course of the past twenty years Hakeem had stayed in touch with his four child-hood friends, Numair, Mahfuz, Jafar, and Farooq.

Numair lived in France, where he operated an import/export business. Mahfuz was in London and had become a wealthy financial advisor. Jafar was the only married one of the five, but he married into an oil-rich family and lived in Greece most of the year. Farooq had become a wealthy diamond merchant operating out of Antwerp.

After many faithful years of service, each of their fathers returned to Tehran to finish out their lives in comfort. Farooq's father was the first to pass, and Hakeem had mixed emotions of grief and excitement. The Five were about to be reunited for the first time in two decades.

CHAPTER 41

Jake's homecoming was cause for a big celebration. Norman and Lydia had invited the Hirschbergs and several other friends to join in the festivities. This was also an informal opportunity for Jake to meet some of the staff he would be working with on assignment at the new NSA facility. Jake had only heard rumors of the extensive monitoring systems that were driven by the world's most sophisticated and powerful super computers.

Max made it a point to gather the new team together for a short introduction. Technically, Jake would be an employee of JEH & Associates assigned as a civilian contractor to the NSA. In this capacity, Max had the ability to assign Jake to any other projects requiring his particular skill set without setting off any internal alarms. Max's specialty was assembling Black Ops teams supporting Black Ops organizations. His associates had no direct ties to the organizations he supported, and Max liked it like that. They had full access, yet remained under his direct control. He and all his associates held Top Secret clearance, and no distinction was made in their respective work environments between who was a direct employee and who was a contractor.

Jake was escorted around the room and given a brief introduction to each team member. Their names and resumes were recited from memory, and each had experience in the Middle East while in uniform or on special assignment. Many had worked for the NSA or CIA directly, before being referred to Max by their respective agencies. All had expertise in programming, encryption, surveillance, martial arts, and a variety of other skills. He was impressed with the balance of men and women and looked forward to serving on such an impressive team. They all seemed to be as enthusiastic to work with him as he was with them.

After the introductions were finished, they joined the others to celebrate. Jake took note of how his new team melded with everyone else and fit right into the party atmosphere. They really were professionals. Unless you knew their particular backgrounds in Special Ops, you would never suspect their professions. Even the academics in the group did not fit the stereotype of thick glasses, pocket protectors, and a lack of social skills.

The party broke up around 9:00PM to give everyone a chance to get home and rested before the workweek began. Norman, Lydia, and Jake sat together in the upstairs sitting room to stay out of the way while the staff cleaned up from the party. Lydia beamed with joy as she cooed over her son, "Jake, you were quite the hit at the party. I think everyone was very impressed with your stories of life in Israel and the political tensions in the Middle East. How did you feel about your new team?"

Jake replied, "I am excited to be back home and had a great time. Thank you for inviting everyone. It was good to meet the team in an informal environment, and it is clear Uncle Max has assembled quite a diverse group of experts. "

Norman interjected, "They are the ones who should be impressed. You have a gift that none of them have. I am anxious to see what that uncovers. In the meantime, your mother and I have a gift for you. You are going to need your own transportation now that you are back home. Here are the keys to your new car. You need to be able to come and go at anytime and we understand you have new responsibilities. You can stay here as long as you like, but we know the time will come when you will want your own place. We are glad to have you home for however long. Get some rest. You need to get an early start for your first day. Max left a briefing for you to read before your first day. Goodnight, son."

Jake stood, hugged his parents, and headed off to read the briefing.

The envelope was secured with a tamper-proof security seal. Jake saw that it was intact and opened the envelope and pulled out the contents. Included were a four-page typed briefing, a photo identification card, and a leather card case containing several keycards. Jake read the briefing explaining each of the items in the envelope and his arrival instructions. His name was already on the active roster and would be verified by the security guards at the main gate. He would need each of the keycards to gain access to the main level, elevators, secure floors and ultimately the panopticon, where he would be working. The keycards were color-coded, encrypted and the order changed daily. He was to memorize his personalized sequencing and then destroy the briefing package. The instructions were clear: any card used out of order would render all other cards useless and all access would be denied.

Jake read the briefing a second time. After being certain he had committed all the information to memory, he walked downstairs, placed all the papers in the fireplace and watched until the last one turned to ash. He stirred the fire to be certain no trace was left and returned to his room.

Jake lay awake for sometime as the excitement about his new role played out in his head. He knew he was about to enter a facility unlike any he had ever seen. He had only heard rumors about the panopticon, and no photographs had ever been released. He would be provided with every resource and tool he would need to uncover patterns, plots, and terrorist movement. Tomorrow he would not only see it, but would be a part of the largest surveillance system in the world.

It was after midnight by the time Jake finally drifted off to sleep.

CHAPTER 42

Hakeem was anxious to meet with his old friends. Since they had each been planted in their own communities, they had all obtained the status necessary to finally use their wealth to effect real change. Over the past nineteen years The Five had corresponded, but only via courier and never in person or by phone. Unless you were at the very highest echelon within the Iranian Islamic leadership, you would never be able to connect them to each other.

He was the only one to return to Iran in an official capacity. The other four channeled funds through legitimate businesses in support of radical Islam and garnered power in their respective countries through their success in business. All were held in the highest regard in their professions, and no one would have suspected they had been hand selected by the Ayatollah. They represented the newest breed of terrorist that would take over traditional leadership roles in major areas of commerce and seize control for the purposes of Islam. This strategy had been in place and had gone undetected in the US and across Europe for many decades.

After a suitable time of consolation for the loss of Farooq's father, Hakeem met with the other four and laid out his plans. "My brothers," he began, "my heart has longed for this day for many years. We were chosen to change the face of Islam, and we have all made significant contributions in our respective fields. The plans made for us when we were very young have been fulfilled, yet the victories we have seen pale in comparison to what we can achieve if we now work together. Allah has blessed each of you with wealth and influence. I am no longer interested in suicide bombings and creating an atmosphere of fear that lasts for a few days or weeks. What I am about to propose to you will change the face of the world forever. It will not require one bomb to explode or one more precious Muslim life to be lost. Instead, it will tear the heart out of every one of our enemies and destroy Israel forever. Others have only dreamed of the complete annihilation of our enemies, but none could ever achieve it. The last to even come close came within days of destroying all the Jews, and a woman named Esther defeated him. Others tried and only managed to exterminate half of them. We can no longer leave the plans for the destruction of our enemy in the hands of amateurs and military minds. The destruction of our enemy must be done in such a way that their hope is destroyed. I have a plan that will require each of you to commit your financial resources and influence in order for it to succeed. Before I share the details of the plan with you I need to know if you are ready to fulfill your destinies along side of me.

Farooq was the first to speak. "My father died without seeing our dreams fulfilled. I will do whatever it takes to insure that another son does not bear the sadness I feel for my father. He devoted his life to the fulfillment of our cause and never saw our enemy defeated. I have hidden away a fortune in diamonds that will finance any operation that you propose. We have been chosen for this, and I will do my part."

Numair was next to voice his support. "As you know, I have at my disposal goods and services from all over the world. I have built my fortune by obtaining the unobtainable for those who are willing to pay my price. I can ship into and out of any country without question and have at my disposal well-placed custom's officials in every port. I pledge my support to this operation and to our cause."

Mahfuz echoed the support of both Farooq and Numair and added, "I have been fortunate to have at my command the portfolios of some of the wealthiest families throughout Europe. My legal team can set up a corporation to channel funds that will yield enough of a return to keep even the most diligent eyes from looking past the profits. Capitalists are blinded by high-yield investments and really do not want to know many details as long as they are getting paid handsomely. Once you tell us the details I will set up the company that will fund your enterprise."

Jafar was the last to speak, "My fortune has been made, and I will do all I can to insure that my children do not suffer like Farooq has in burying his father without seeing our victory."

Hakeem further explained, "I will not bore you with the science, but I have made my appeal to the highest levels of government for funding and they rejected my request for support. I have no choice but to pursue this through our own channels. I will lay out a comprehensive plan and will need you to put together a team of trusted associates to carry it out. We will need to set up a foundation and get permits to conduct archeological digs. I will also need you to use your resources to acquire research from multiple laboratories around the world. I will leave the details to you, as all I am interested in are the samples themselves. Nothing must connect me to any of your activities. I will need to build a duplicate laboratory in one of your secure locations to conduct testing. Anything I do here in Tehran will be tracked and linked to the specific work I am doing here. I am free to travel as needed and will cover my tracks with your help. For the time being, I will need each of you to make a significant contribution designated to support my work here at the National Research Center with the condition that you will receive in person progress reports from me. This will be our cover and keep prying eyes and ears from suspecting anything. Over the course of the next few days I will meet with each one of you separately. You will only know your particular assignments so that no one other than myself knows the entirety of the plan. Should anyone of you be questioned you will not be in a position to divulge anything more than your part. This is for the protection of us all. Are we all in agreement?"

The Five agreed and made arrangements to meet one at a time to be given the specifics of their role. Each would arrange for the funds to be donated before they returned to their respective homes. This would provide Hakeem with the latitude he needed to pursue his research without regards to costs.

For the first time they had a shared hope and confidence they could strike the deathblow to the enemy, even though they did not know the details of the plan just yet. The very idea that your enemy could be defeated and no Muslim blood had to be shed was very intriguing. This must have been the vision of the Ayatollah when he chose The Five.

CHAPTER 43

Jake found an available parking space and entered the headquarters of the world's largest intelligence-gathering operation. He followed the security check in procedures as outlined in his information packet and was greeted by an Administrative Assistant assigned to show him around. He was overwhelmed by the sheer magnitude of the facility and immediately recognized the power wielded there. He had visited the National Cryptologic Museum adjacent to the NSA Headquarters and was fascinated by its history, but now he was actually standing within the very walls that housed the code makers and the code breakers. Jake would be a part of the inner workings of both the NSA and the Central Security Service (CSS) and his work would be both developmental and applied.

After being shown his modest office he was taken into the panopticon that had only been seen by very few civilians and not that many more government employees. It had only been rumored to actually exist, and now he was standing in the middle of it. As he was being introduced to the other analysts, he noticed that there was a common attitude permeating the team. He couldn't pinpoint exactly what it was, but it was finally revealed to him upon his last introduction to the most senior analyst on the team, Trevor Carlson.

As Jake reached out his hand to shake Trevor's he was greeted with, "So, this is the mysterious codist who sees patterns that our most sophisticated programs can't see. Let's see how gifted you are with these files filled with code that our systems say are pure gibberish. I say it's a waste of time, but the higher ups seems to think there is something hidden here that only you can see. For the life of me I can't imagine how one person can see what our super-computers can't. Have at it, Rain Man!"

With that remark, Jake now knew why there was such an air of resentment hovering over the room. He took the files into his office and began leafing through the pages containing rows of numbers and spaces. All the dates of the communications they harvested seemed random, and any identifying information contained had already been run through every automated filter available. They may have been ridiculing Jake, but this was exactly what he had hoped he would find in this new role. It wasn't so much the code itself that he loved. It was the challenge. He had been called a lot of names before, but this one seemed to fit, "The Codist."

He had not just joined an organization devoted to spying. He had joined an organization charged with defeating an enemy by cracking their internal communications methods to reveal their plans before they took innocent lives. He was part of an elite group of proactive professionals who connected the dots and were devoted to staying steps ahead of their enemies. Jake loved the puzzle and would pass their test and prove his value. They were no different than Jake. He, too, had to have things proven before he would believe them.

He spread the printouts on top of his work-table looking for something that would give him a hint. What was it about the string of numbers? He reviewed the computer analysis that applied every known coding and encryption scheme and found no common alpha or numeric sequencing. It could only be one of two possibilities. This code was either too new or sophisticated for their current technology, or it was so rudimentary that it was dismissed as being gibberish.

Once he was able to organize the files into groups, he did begin to see a pattern to one group in particular. There was nothing really noteworthy about the postings, but they were sequentially dated and spanned a period of five days. It had been Jake's experience that sequentially posted codes usually pointed to a future event and contained a series of clues meant to reveal the location of the event. If the puzzle was not solved the incident would still take place, but any number of radical organizations would scramble to take credit for it, only frustrating the real perpetrator. It was not uncommon to read of several fringe radical groups taking credit for the same bombing or attack.

Jake began to look at the sequencing of the numbers, and he thought they might correlate to the alpha numeric values assigned on touch-tone phones where 1 had no alpha assignment, 2=ABC, 3=DEF, 4=GHI, 5=JKL, 6=MNO, 7=PQRS, 8=TUV, 9=WXYZ. It was a long shot, but one worth taking if he was going to prove his ability to see patterns others had missed. He ran multiple permutations applying each letter to the numbers and still came up with the same gibberish the other analysts did. He even tried dialing the numbers to see if they connected to some international phone. Still he had no success. What he did notice was something familiar to him, and that was the sound the touchtone phone emitted when each number was pressed.

Jake requested a few pieces of sound recording equipment, and after completing the appropriate requisition forms his request was granted. He heard the rumblings of a wobbly wheel approaching, and an older gentleman dressed in a gray wool cardigan sweater rolled the old cart into Jake's office. He held out a clipboard and spoke only two words while pointing a crooked index finger to the line on the form and said, "Sign here." Jake signed and the older man left Jake to unload the equipment. He wondered what he was supposed to do with the cart. Treating it like a room service tray, he placed it outside his office door and pulled the door shut.

Jake set the recording equipment up and the touchtone pad and began pressing the numbers on the pad and recording the tones generated by each press of the button. He was careful to press each one in order and paused when a new line of numbers was on the page. After punching in all the numbers, Jake began playing the tape to see if he could recognize any pattern, and after playing and rewinding the tape at various speeds he finally heard a familiar sound.

13691369
13693132
332112996
3693221

When the numbers were played in sequence it played the song, "When the Saints Go Marching In."

The next set of numbers were keyed in just like the first set.

84446
848
91439#

This time it took him a little longer to get the cadence down, but finally he recognized the song "Auld Lang Syne."

Jake was starting to see a pattern. Something was going to happen in New Orleans on New Year's Eve, but where. The last set of numbers would have to contain the final clue.

55754
45085
55754
45085

These numbers did not register with Jake no matter what speed he tried to play them. He was tired, frustrated and ready to give up when in walked the older gentleman in the gray cardigan sweater. He looked at Jake and asked if he was done with the equipment yet. Jake was just playing the tones again when the older man said, "Funky Town!"

"What did you just say?"

The man in the gray sweater looked Jake up and down and then blurted out, "FUNKY TOWN. Those are the notes to Funky Town. I know what these other folks do around here, but I have never seen one yet doing what you are doing. My name is Harper. What's yours?"

Jake extended his hand and introduced himself.

Harper shook his hand and said, "Now you listen to me, Aaronson. I may not be some whiz kid like the rest of you, but I'm the one you all come to when you need something. Treat me right and I'll look out for you. Got it?"

"Got it," Jake replied. "You might not realize this, but you just helped me break a code."

"Code, you say? What kind of code?" Harper asked.

"I'm trying to figure out what someone is planning to do in New Orleans on New Year's Eve at Midnight at Funky Town."

"You ever been to New Orleans?" Harper asked.

"Never," Jake answered.

"Well, I've spent a few nights there. Some I remember better than others. Funky Town is a private party place that people rent for special occasions."

Jake smiled at Harper and said, "You are much more valuable than you think. You have helped me again. We are going to become good friends, Harper. Mind if I ask what kind of name is Harper?'

"It's my last name," he replied. "My first name is Jerome. No one here has ever asked me that before. Just call me Harper like everyone else."

Jake thanked Harper and documented everything before calling Max with the news he had made progress on the gibberish that the computer analysts said had no value.

"Max," Jake began, "I have spent the past three days examining the first file and have solid evidence there is going to be an attack of some kind on New Year's Eve at a venue called Funky Town in the New Orleans area. Can you have one of your analysts search for any significant guests or see who is hosting this event to determine why this would be a target?"

Max replied, "Good work Jake. I will get one of my people on this right away and will get back to you as soon as possible. In the meantime, there is one more file those computer jockeys could not crack that I need you to focus on. I have my suspicions there is a new faction gaining power, and I am not sure who is at the helm. They seem to be well financed and there have been a number of sizeable purchases made that lead me to believe we have a new enemy much smarter than the usual terrorist groups. A special courier will deliver this file to you and no one there knows you will be working it. You will have to continue your other work there and take on this special project. You ok with that?"

"This is what I came back to do and I am up for any challenge you assign to me." Jake added, "It's not like I have a personal life...but I have started to think about that since coming back stateside."

Max kidded Jake saying, "Then maybe you should go on one of those online sites and create a profile all in code. If there is a girl out there who can break it, then she wins a date with you."

Jake laughed and said, "Maybe I'll do just that. Imagine my wife and me and our seven children all with the ability to communicate in code. What a wonderful world that would be!"

Max quickly answered, "Now you are scaring me. Get back to work. I'll let you know about New Orleans. Goodbye for now."

Jake hung up the phone, gathered all his notes, and put them into a folder he labeled "New Orleans." He placed the file into the secure cabinet in his office and decided it was time to take an unescorted walk through the facility. He thought it best to notify the Administrative Assistant of his whereabouts and dialed the number she had pointed out to him on the list of extensions. He noticed that there were no first names listed, only initials and a last name. He dialed her extension and when she answered she simply answered with her last name. Jake asked, "Miss Breakstone, may I ask your first name?"

"Everyone here goes by their last name. It's less personal and that's how they like it. What may I do for you, sir?" she replied.

Jake got the point and said, "Well, Breakstone, I was just calling to let you know I was planning to look around on my own."

Breakstone was firm when she said, "Sir, your whereabouts within these walls are monitored, and access to any other part of the facility is controlled. You are free to go wherever your access cards allow. I am here to support your administrative needs. If you have no administrative needs at this time then I will return to my duties. Is that all, sir?"

"Yes," Jake answered. Before he could get the short answer out of his mouth the call was ended.

Just as he was about to leave his office the phone rang. In NSA form he answered, "Aaronson."

"Jake, it's Max. I already have news for you on New Orleans."

"That didn't take long," Jake replied.

Max quipped, "All you had to do was a quick search for yourself and you would have seen it all over the web. The Governor of Louisiana is planning to announce his candidacy for President at a fundraiser on New Year's Eve. In true contrarian fashion he decided to do it at Funky Town. It's a $10,000-per-plate event for 200 of the state's most influential donors. He has lots of wealthy friends, but a few powerful enemies as well."

Jake inquired, "Do you have any idea who hates him enough to plan an assassination attempt?"

Max's tone became very serious as he explained, "Jake, his biggest supporters represent off-shore oil-drilling interests. He is a strong advocate for oil independence, and if he were to be elected it would ultimately cost the Middle East billions in oil revenues. Imagine the economic devastation and panic if the heads of the major US oil companies were all killed at one time. Their stocks would plummet and oil prices from the Middle East would skyrocket. It would represent a financial windfall for Islamic interests funded with their own enemy's money. It's a perfect storm."

Jake responded, "What do I need to do?"

Max ordered, "I want you in the panopticon. Put together every searchable keyword you can think of and I will get the analysts to load them. Head up the team and find out who is behind this and what they are planning to do. We have two weeks before the event. Welcome home, Jake!"

"I'm on it," Jake replied.

For the next sixteen straight hours Jake sat behind his computer accessing one database after another until he had compiled every combination of keywords, phrases, and names he could find. In addition, he created a comprehensive list of organizations and aliases of known enemies capable of pulling this off. His new team was about to get to know him very well in a very short period of time.

CHAPTER 44

Jake stood at the opening to his office and called out the names of the four Team Leaders on the floor: Hutchison, Goldberg, Smith, and Thompson and the Group Leader, Trevor Carlson. All five came forward, and Jake ushered them into his office and closed the door. Before anyone could utter even a single syllable Jake made it clear he was in charge. "I am sure you all have questions, but save them until the end of the briefing. You will find out quickly I do not repeat myself so pay close attention to everything I say. If you have not been given my background, all you need to know is I have just finished a ten-year assignment with Israel's most elite intelligence team. If we work as a team with one heart, one goal, and watch out for each other we can make the world a better place. If you have a problem with the new guy heading up this project, either resign or change your attitude, because I'm not going anywhere. Are we clear?"

All four nodded in agreement.

Jake continued, "That gibberish you handed off to the newbie to see if it had any value at all turned out to contain three very specific clues to an attack being planned at a gathering in New Orleans on New Year's Eve. There are 200 targets, including the Governor of Louisiana, who plans to announce his candidacy for President at this event. Oil interests in the Middle East have the most to gain, but this could also be the play by any number of domestic or foreign terrorists trying to make a name for themselves. I have put together a briefing packet for each of you containing search strings and potential organizations we need to tap into to see what is being planned. We have less than two weeks to get this accomplished, and failure is not an option. All holiday time off requests are being rescinded until we have our answers. This is a Priority One case and daily briefings will be held in my office every morning at 8:00AM. I was just kidding when I said you could ask questions at the end of the briefing. Until you have read your packets, any questions would be a waste of time. You are dismissed."

Jake waited thirty minutes before he poked his head out of his office to see how the team was responding to his instructions. He was impressed at what he saw. All four Team Leaders were meeting with their teams parsing the contents of the briefing packet and assigning various tasks based on areas of expertise. Almost in unison, the team meetings broke and each member returned to their command post to begin executing their assignments. No one returned to Jake with any questions and all were focused on the task at hand. Now Jake would witness firsthand the power that would search every email, text message, video, selfie, upload, download, and hard drive contents on over 1 billion computers and smart phones from around the world. No one was immune and no server was safe from the prying eyes of the NSA. It was programmed to mine data from every known source and process it simultaneously with more computing power in one room than most nations had combined.

Jake's personal estimate was that he would have a list of suspects to review within the first twenty-four hours. He had his own guesses, but wanted to see if the powerful supercomputer would come up with the same answers. In the meantime he anxiously awaited the courier to show up with the briefing Max was sending his way. Jake could never have enough simultaneous puzzles to solve. That's what made it exciting.

He did not have to wait long for the courier's arrival. What surprised him was the apparent volume of material being delivered. Boxes were marked Purchase Orders, Bills of Lading, Wire Transfers, Emails, etc. The boxes had to be filled with paper, and Jake was surprised at the old-school approach. As the courier unloaded the dolly, Jake bent over to pick up a file box, prepared to lift a heavy object, and laughed out loud upon feeling its emptiness and hearing the rattle of a small object inside. He opened the box to find a flash card inside the otherwise empty box. Taped to the inside of the lid was a handwritten note from Max that simply said, "LIGHTEN UP!"

He opened each box to find a similar flash card containing information related to the project. After downloading them onto his personal laptop, he placed the original flash cards into the vault for safekeeping. He would examine the files on his own time, but for now, he needed to focus his attention on the plot brewing in New Orleans.

He packed up his laptop, left his office, and stopped to tell Breakstone he was headed home and to contact him with any updates. Without turning her head away from the computer screen she simply nodded her acknowledgement. That was confirmation enough.

During the short commute home, he played out the last twenty-four hour's activity and found a combination of feelings. He had grown accustomed to the daily imminent threat of attack in Israel and had learned to live on high alert. Here he was surrounded by cyber threats and plans that may or may not directly affect him and his family, but they were still threats nonetheless. He did not feel the adrenaline rush, but did feel quite stimulated to apply everything he had learned while with Israeli Intelligence and make a real impact here at the NSA. For the first time he allowed himself to feel tired and hungry. He would eat, sleep, and then look at the files Max sent over.

CHAPTER 45

It was not the alarm, but Jake's ringing cell phone that jolted him out of the first deep sleep he had since being back home. Trevor Carlson's voice had a certain urgency to it as he spoke, "This is no time to be sleeping, we have some leads about New Orleans. I'll have a briefing ready for you as soon as you get here. Max Hirschberg and some others will be joining us at 9:00AM sharp! I'll only say this once. You made sense out of that gibberish and I respect that."

The next sound Jake heard was silence as Trevor hung up. It was then that Jake noticed the time was 5:30AM. He knew Trevor had taken his findings seriously and had the team work through the night, just as Jake had the night before. It was early, but not too early to delight, just a little, in standing up to the challenge of man versus computer.

Max's files would have to wait as they were one day closer to New Year's Eve and there was much work to be done. Jake showered, dressed and headed downstairs wondering where he could get a strong cup of coffee. He should not have been surprised to find his mother and father already at the table waiting for him with his coffee in a stainless steel travel mug. After a few rushed comments, Jake was out the door and on his way back to the office ready to hear the day's briefing.

Breakstone was already at her desk, and Jake knew his "Good Morning" would go unacknowledged, but greeted her in spite of her lack of response. He was already learning pleasantries were not in her job description, but took comfort in the knowledge that she was already at her post ready to support him in her assigned duties.

Trevor met Jake at his door as he arrived, and his entire demeanor had visibly changed since their first meeting. He spoke to Jake as a trusted peer and said, "I wanted to give you a chance to review this before I presented it to the team at 9:00AM. I would appreciate you adding anything you think it needs to fill in some blanks we still have. One day soon, maybe you can tell me what made you think of touchtone notes. I never saw that and neither did any of our systems. I already have a team coding new programs to run numbers through a tone generator. This won't happen again."

Jake was all business when he said, "Give me a few minutes to look through this. I'll have my comments to you as soon as possible."

The briefing was thick and already bound with tabs and indexes. He would come to recognize Breakstone's signature work and attention to detail. What she lacked in social graces, she made up for in extraordinary efficiency and professionalism.

As Jake read the Executive Summary, one fact jumped out at him that caught him by surprise. The Organization of the Petroleum Exporting

Countries (OPEC) received close to $1 trillion in oil purchases from the United States alone. What was even more shocking was which twelve nations made up OPEC. Jake, like many others, assumed it was an oil cartel of Middle Eastern countries. However, the list was actually Algeria, Angola, Ecuador, Iran, Iraq, Kuwait, Libya, Nigeria, Qatar, Saudi Arabia, United Arab Emirates, and Venezuela. Of this list, the United States had either strained or severed diplomatic relations with a number of them, and one common thread was their overwhelming tie to Islam. The OPEC nations were over 85% Muslim, and the United States had little or no input into how these nations spent America's oil money.

As Jake continued to read the rest of the Executive Summary he became increasingly aware of the magnitude of global terrorism and the financial resources of the world's most powerful enemy to democracy. The label that once belonged to communism had now transferred to an enemy funded by the very ones they wished to destroy.

As Jake dug into the detailed findings, he studied the list of invitees already confirmed to be at the Governor's New Year's Eve Gala. It was, as suspected, a who's who of oil industry leaders with a vested interest in offshore drilling in the Gulf of Mexico and proponents of American oil independence from all over the nation. It was all fascinating reading, but Jake had little time for education on the world's oil dependence and needed to get to the possible list of suspects and scenarios. The thoroughness of the research was overwhelming and almost too much to process. Jake called Breakstone and asked her to gather Trevor and the other Team Leads in his office right away.

Within three minutes all were gathered in Jake's office where he addressed them all, saying, "I appreciate the degree of detail and resources committed to this briefing. All of you have worked very hard, but right now what I need is a bottom line summation of who you think is behind this and why you think that way."

Trevor spoke first, "We have run all the searches you requested plus added many more from our own programs. We have cross-referenced travel plans of both domestic and international groups who have the most to gain from this. We have run the backgrounds on every employee of all the vendors involved. We believe we have ruled out a bomb as the perimeter has already been established and a 200-yard radius has been under video surveillance since the venue was picked many months ago. We have monitored satellite feeds and tracked any activity even remotely near the targeted location and find no record of any activity."

Jake was quick to comment, "I am already impressed with what you and the machines are capable of ruling out, but what I want is what you think, not what the computer thinks."

Trevor stared at Jake before he answered, "We are the NSA. We are not in the business of giving opinions."

"Your brain is the most powerful computer on the face of the earth. It is the one God made. All the rest are man made. I can read a print-out just as well as you can, but what I want is your collective opinions as to how this is going to take place."

Before Trevor could answer, Jake reached over and pressed the intercom button, and as soon as it was answered he told Breakstone, "Get Harper in here right away."

As if he knew he would be needed, Harper knocked on the Jake's door and walked into the room. Jake looked at him and asked, "Harper, if you want to kill 200 people all at the same time in the same place, and you weren't going to blow them up or shoot them, how would you kill them?"

Harper did not hesitate to answer with one word, "Poison."

Jake looked at Trevor and the team and said, "There is your answer. Run a scenario through the system before the briefing and present all the probabilities and possibilities for how and who would have access to this venue to poison everyone there."

As they all left Jake's office, Max entered and said, "Think you might have been a little hard on them?"

"Maybe," Jake began. "But they were so arrogant and full of themselves and their technology that they seemed to have lost any sense of intuition and logic. We have got to strike a balance and work in tandem with all of this or we stand the chance that our arrogance will cost the lives of many. We are dealing with a human condition, not a computer virus. Isn't that what you brought me in here to do?"

Max replied, "Yes, that is exactly why you are here. You have given them a lot to work on and the briefing is in one hour. Let's see what they come up with. In the meantime, have you had a chance to look at any of the files I sent over?"

"Not yet," Jake replied. "I uploaded them, but haven't had a chance to even open the first one. Want to fill me in or wait until I look at them?"

Max used the time to fill Jake in just enough to tease him, "It seems there is some new movement underway, and there are some common connections I think you will find most interesting. I would hate to spoil the surprise and give it all away, but there are a number of very interesting puzzle pieces that I want you to connect. It is activity we have not seen before, and the group that is forming seems to have unlimited resources. That alone poses a formidable threat. This war we are in has moved to a level of sophistication that redefines itself almost daily. Technology is being introduced faster than we can keep up with it, and the threats that were so obvious a decade ago have escalated far beyond missile attacks. Our moral code has eroded so far that we are protecting the very ones who would destroy us. It has got to be so confusing for the generations being raised in this culture. We have been lulled into such a false sense of security that we have lost sight of our enemy and they are now reading our emails and stealing our identities. We give out our photographs, announce our travel plans, and broadcast to the world where we are every minute and then wonder why our identities are being stolen. I'm in the business and it's confusing to me. Enough of my ramblings, let's get some coffee and head over to the briefing."

CHAPTER 46

The briefing room was filled with as many representatives from other agencies as there were NSA employees. Jake was surprised to see the Deputy Director taking charge of the meeting and introducing the various CIA, FBI, Homeland Security, other visitors and key members of the staff. He gave a brief situation summary and turned the meeting over to Trevor Carlson.

Trevor was a seasoned professional, and his ability to deliver a situational analysis was one of his gifts. He highlighted several of the methodologies used and explained Jake's role in discovering the plot. Most there had heard of Jake's arrival and had read his file. They gave him an acknowledging nod as Trevor pointed him out. What he did not expect was the level of candor Trevor used in his presentation. He began, "Our team had queried all of our systems and came up with four of the highest probability scenarios. We cross-referenced and profiled suspects and narrowed the list to two Middle Eastern factions and one Chinese. An advance copy of the briefing was delivered to Jake Aaronson for his review. At approximately one hour and thirty minutes before this meeting he discounted all of our findings and applied a hybrid analytical system previously unused by this agency. He narrowed the scope of our investigation to one method only and had us focus 100% of our resources in this area. I am pleased to report our team has confirmed the attempted method to be used at the Governor's Gala was poison. We have traced purchase orders for spices placed by the caterer for this event to a company with previously identified ties to other smaller incidences of poisoning not on American soil. They have clear ties to several terrorist organizations operating out of the Middle East. Our game plan is to intercept the order, substitute uncontaminated spices, and sound no alarms of any kind. We believe those who are behind this will make their identities known when they learn their plan failed and they deal with those along the way who did not deliver as promised. We will let our enemy do the dirty work for us and help us cross more names off our list. Once they have completed cleaning up their own internal problems, we will have enough evidence to pass along to Interpol and have them taken out of circulation. This is the only scenario that works, and we have confirmed it within our own technology. Thanks to the work of Jake Aaronson, we have applied several patches to our programming that will incorporate more of his innovative thinking to our risk assessments. If there are no questions, that concludes today's briefing."

The only response from those gathered was a round of applause and handshakes all around. Trevor looked across the room at Jake and slightly lowered his head as a sign of respect. Jake returned the gesture and was encouraged that he had won over the very skeptical Trevor Carlson.

Max had motioned for Jake to join him on the far side of the room where several others were gathered. He introduced Jake to Colonel Richard Condon of the CIA, Special Agent Daniel Magnus of the FBI and Dr. Samuel Flint of Homeland Security. All had been briefed about Jake's experience and he felt a little off balance not knowing as much about them as they did about him. There was the usual small talk, and Max sensed Jake's uneasiness and graciously extracted him from the group and out of the briefing room. On their way back to Jake's office Max encouraged Jake, "It appears that you are getting settled in and already figured out the lay of the land. Trevor can be a real pain, but he is a top-notch cyber expert and a good ally to have. Tell me how you were able to figure out the poison angle."

Jake smiled and said, I simply applied the Harper Method and the answer became quite clear."

Max queried, "The Harper Method? I'm not sure I am familiar with that approach."

Jake stated, "If you follow me, I will introduce you to the author of the method. Interested?"

Max had no idea where Jake was going with this, but thought it best to play along. They walked down the hall by Breakstone's desk and asked her to summon Harper. She placed a call and within a few minutes Harper showed up.

Jake said, "Max Hirschberg, meet Jerome Harper, the creator of the Harper Method."

"The Harper Method you say?" quipped Harper.

Max looked at them both and said, "I have no idea what you are talking about."

Harper chimed in and said, "That makes two of us."

Jake said, "Let's get a cup of coffee and I will explain it to you both."

Jake proceeded to share with both Max and Harper the events leading up to the question Jake posed to Harper about how he would kill 200 people at a dinner event. Jake explained its logic and simplicity was something that he had found was often overlooked. It was Jake's belief that analysis should begin with the simplest solution and migrate to the complex if the simple does not yield a plausible answer.

Max surprised Jake when he told him, "I'm not surprised Harper would be the one to come up with the answer. He has been with us for almost thirty years and was one of my very brightest and best operatives. He chose to come inside because of a commitment he made to his family. Otherwise he would still be in the field working for me."

Jake said, "Seriously! I want him on my team. I need a right hand that I can trust to give me straight talk and who knows his way around this place. Can you get him assigned to me?"

Both Harper and Jake just smiled as Max said, "What makes you think we hadn't already done that before you arrived? The old man still has a few surprises up his sleeve, so don't think too highly of yourself. The Harper Method was being used before you were born. Now, about those files I sent over. I want your analysis in one week. You can collaborate with Harper, and he is already briefed. Outside of the three of us no one else is to be involved. Are we clear?"

Jake and Harper nodded in the affirmative and Max left the two alone. Jake looked at Harper and said, "No wonder Trevor didn't raise an eyebrow at your theory. You two must have some history together."

Harper simply said, "If someone has been here more than a few years, I have history with them. I'm happy to be a part of your team and look forward to writing history with you."

As they arose to leave Jake stopped and extended his hand to Harper and said, "I'm honored to serve with you. I will start reviewing the files Max sent over right away. Let's meet tomorrow afternoon to compare notes."

Harper confirmed, "I have already begun my review and will be prepared to share it with you. If you can see clear to meet at 3:00PM tomorrow, I can get home in time to take care of what I need to do. I only need a few hours in the morning and at night to tend to it, but other than those few times I am available seven days a week. I think it best to let you know these things up front so we get off on the right foot. Max has been very accommodating and I don't like the idea of taking advantage of anybody. If I have enough advance notice I can make other arrangements, but the more notice I have, the better. I don't like to mix business with my personal life, but since Max trusted you enough to share, I felt I should at least let you know this much."

Jake was very respectful when he said, "How about if we make it 2:30PM just to give you plenty of time?"

Harper smiled and said, "Thanks. I'll see you then. I appreciate your understanding. We can use the extra time for you to tell me your story since we are going to be working side by side."

CHAPTER 47

Jake pulled up the files that Max had given him. He had placed the contents of each of the flash drives into folders on his laptop for easier retrieval. He opened each one, took mental note of the names of the files, and created his own mental compartments for future access. It took over an hour just to tab through each of the folders and the file names. He then began the task of opening each file and scanning the contents. What would be tedium for the average person was exhilarating for Jake. It was like an archeologist putting his shovel into virgin ground knowing there was something lying beneath the surface that no one had seen before.

Jake logged key names and numbers into his brain as he searched each file for clues and patterns. At first glance, he was able to piece together numerous transactions and purchases of medical and scientific equipment, none of which indicated anything relevant to bomb making or biological weaponry. The items that made up the consolidated list of acquisitions were more geared to human genome research than any other science. Other than the fact that it was well funded from a seemingly disconnected number of sources, there was no initial red flag that piqued Jake's interest. The money's final destination, regardless of the routing, was Geneva, Switzerland. Certainly this was not a hotbed of terrorist activity.

Jake knew there was something missing. There had to be a connection to some nefarious activity that seemed to be eluding him. It wasn't until he began to dig into the official Swiss documents associated with the formation of the International Centre for Genetic Research that he began to connect the dots. This non-profit organization was created for the purpose of promoting a global collaboration to identify and develop cures for genetic diseases. What seemed to be a noble enough cause was not of concern to Jake. Hidden within the funding sources were names of individuals who had been loosely linked to the financing of terrorist activities. Four of the names listed represented over 80% of the funding, and all were originally from Tehran. On the surface that was the only connection they seemed to have. Jake would probe deeper into this when he met with Harper and would target those four to see how they were linked together.

After another few hours of poring over the files, Jake had processed all he could in one sitting. He packed up his laptop and glanced at the clock. He remembered the last time he had noted the time it was 12:30PM. It was no wonder he was tired and hungry. It was now after 10:00PM and he had not taken a break in 9 ½ hours.

By the time he made it into his car and made the trip home, it was too late to think about fixing something to eat. He would just head to bed and grab something in the morning. As he entered from the garage into the kitchen there was a plate with a note stuck to it that simply said, "Heat and Eat, Love Mom." Jake placed the plate in the microwave, waited the two minutes for it to heat, and then took the plate and headed to his room. He ate quickly, brushed his teeth and crawled into the bed. As soon as the lights went out Jake's mind went into overdrive. All he could think about was why Max would be interested in some non-profit human genome research center when there were so many other more imminent threats looming. What was the connection, and why was Jake handed this assignment? Why was this a project he couldn't share with the rest of the team? The questions began to pile one on top of the other as Jake struggled to make sense of it all.

Sleep came, but rest did not. There were more questions than before, and Jake would not rest until he had his answers.

CHAPTER 48

Jake needed answers before he could even think about briefing Harper. Something was amiss, and he didn't like it when he had to solve for multiple missing puzzle pieces. Either Max had not been forthcoming in disclosing all of the details, or he was stringing Jake along for some other reason. He called Max from the car on his way to get coffee hoping he could meet with him before going into the office. There were no pleasantries exchanged as Max simply answered his phone by saying, "Meet me at Sylvia's for coffee and a piece of that Danish that my wife won't ever let me eat. I can be there in fifteen minutes."

It no longer unnerved Jake when Max responded like that. It only confirmed there was more to this investigation than he had revealed and was expecting the call. Jake, too, liked the Danish at Sylvia's and knew it was a secure location where they could speak freely. Sylvia was actually Jonathan Sylvan, a former CIA Agent who was shot in the line of duty and used his payout to open a diner. With the kind of friends he had, his reputation for keeping a safe meeting place was well known in certain circles. The public was unaware of the bulletproof glass windows, the trap doors, the armed wait staff, and the electronic sweeps that were made searching for listening devices as a part of their open and closing routine.

They arrived at the same time and took a booth along the back wall. Max ordered a cherry Danish and a black coffee, and Jake had his usual cinnamon Danish with a chai tea. There was no small talk and Jake got right to the point, "Ok, I looked over the files you sent. What did you leave out and what aren't you telling me?

Max was all business when he answered, "Look buddy, if every case were easy to piece together I would just feed it to those computer jockeys and let the system spit out answers. There is something brewing, and it is not a classic case of terrorists acting like terrorists. That's why I need you leading this one. Something doesn't add up and I need you to tell me what it is."

Jake fired back, "How can I do it with just Harper and myself? I need access to the panopticon and have all that data run through a series of permutations that will identify the anomalies. I can identify multiple missing pieces of a puzzle, but I first need to assemble a straw man of what we already know in order to search for the unknowns."

Max lowered his voice when he said, "I know what you need, and if this was a sanctioned project, you would have it. With no clearly identifiable threat to national security, I can't get the Agency to fund the machine time and the manpower. Covert operations conducted inside a covert organization are nearly impossible to pull off."

Jake leaned across the table and looked Max squarely in the eye and said, "What aren't you telling me?"

Max leaned back and paused before he answered. "Jake, I have told you everything I know about this. I have some speculations, but I am not going to share them regardless of how many times you ask me. Harper knows the ropes and can help you accomplish what you need to, but I can't be of much help on this one until you can bring me some solid links. You are off to a good start with Carlson. Talk to Harper, and if he thinks it's safe to pull Carlson in on this you have my approval. Inside the Agency anything linked to bio-terrorism gets carte blanche. If you can find a way to even loosely connect this to a biological threat you will not be scrutinized and I can cover for you. Are we clear on how this works?"

Jake replied, "Clear enough that you pay the check and leave the tip."

Jake rose to leave and Max reached out and took his arm and said, "When this all comes into the light, we have to be prepared to do what we must regardless of our personal feelings. I know you are here for a bigger reason than we can realize. I will be right there by your side making sure you are protected. Let me know what you and Harper decide."

Jake left even more confused than he was when he arrived. He thought, "What could any of this have to do with me? I didn't see any Israeli connection or even an American one. There is more than one blank that needs to be filled to connect this group with a real threat, but what or who can it be? Why isn't this sanctioned research? Who wants the answers if it's not the CIA, FBI, DOD, or Homeland Security? I've got to talk to Harper before our scheduled 2:30PM meeting. I'm almost at the office, I'll just track him down once I get there."

Jake walked by Breakstone's desk to offer up his usual unacknowledged "Good Morning," but she was not there. As he rounded the corner to his office he saw her standing there with Harper.

"Good Morning, Breakstone," said Jake. "Good Morning, Harper."

Breakstone responded first, "I have the resource, systems, and Analysts' scheduled per your request. Will there be anything else you need this morning before your meeting with Harper?"

Jake looked at Harper while answering Breakstone, "No, thank you. I believe that is all I need for this morning's meeting."

Breakstone turned to leave, and while walking away she said, "As instructed, I will hold your calls until noon. If you need longer, just let me know."

Harper just smiled and followed Jake into his office. After closing the door he looked at Jake and said, "Max knew you wouldn't call. He filled me in on your coffee talk and I moved our meeting up so we could get right on this. I have set up an Accounting Code in the system assigned to the Geneva Project and set it up as a Special Access Program (SAP) requiring your specific sign off on anyone being able to access the files. No one in the Agency, even with Top Secret clearance, is permitted to see what is going on. I have requisitioned Random Access Code Generators that changes the Access Code to the project files every two hours. Until otherwise instructed, only two have been programmed. There is one for you and one for me. All files coded Geneva Project will be encrypted and cannot be accessed or decrypted without the code and a retina scan. I have secured the Identity Room for you and me to have our scans done and linked to this project. I have also had Breakstone secure a Situation Room with a biometric hand scanner as a secondary security access device. It will be set up while we are in the Identity Room. A special keycard will also be required, and it will automatically apply the proper account code to any facilities we use. There is no reason for you to know anything more about how our project is being funded. Have I left anything out?"

Jake sat down and replied, "Harper, you are one smooth operator! I appreciate your handling all the logistics and maneuvering through the system. I know nothing about any of that stuff. What I do know is I have more questions than answers as to who is behind this Human Genome Center and what possible link there is to terrorism other than the money source. I need to be able to load all this data into our supercomputer and run a series of queries linking all the parties and cross-referencing everything from birth to present including commonalities in family ties, education, finances, travel, and associations with known or suspected terrorist organizations or individuals. These donors are from the four corners of the world and on the surface share nothing in common. Once we find the link, we can start to identify what other dots we need to connect to get to the bottom of this. Harper, on a side note, do you have any idea why Max would imply that I might have some personal connection to all this?"

Harper shook his head and answered, "Max has shared nothing more than to make sure you make your way around here without raising too many eyebrows."

Jake also inquired, "What are your thoughts about bringing Carlson in on this team? He's got more of a command of the panopticon than I do right now and could be instrumental in getting me up to speed."

Harper replied, "I trust him. He won't let you in the command capsule until he trains you himself, so we might as well bring him in from the start."

Jake responded, "All right, let's brief him and get these ID things out of the way. Then we can get the Situation Room ready. I will leave the schedules up to you out of respect for your time."

"Thank you," Harper said. "Follow me and we will get started."

Jake and Harper stopped to talk to Carlson on their way. He listened to what they had to say and did not hesitate to commit to the team. Together they made their way to the Identity Room and began the process of retina and biometric scans and the creation of access keycards to secure the Situation Room. They would requisition one more Random Access Code Generators for Carlson's use.

For those who worked there it was just another day and another new project to protect America and the rest of the world from its myriad enemies. Business as usual at the NSA.

CHAPTER 49

Once inside the Situation Room, Carlson was brought up to speed on what they had pieced together so far. On the surface everything appeared to be legitimate, but there were too many unknowns and questions that drove them to dig deeper. Jake was still perplexed as to why Max had implied there was some personal connection to all of this.

Carlson was the technical lead on the team and would load all the data into the supercomputer. He would run all standard protocols to search out even the most miniscule of connections. He had already figured out Jake's personality and knew it would be easier to show him how everything worked so he could apply his special skills to the solving of this puzzle. Carlson had already figured out Jake would make a much better friend than an adversary and together they could take the team to a higher level of effectiveness.

Once the data was loaded and the routines started running they would have to begin the process of analyzing the system outputs. Harper would pull together all the summaries and work with Breakstone to create briefing packets. After the initial review was completed they would begin the process of connecting the dots.

Jake and Trevor made their way to the panopticon and along the way discussed how the command capsule operated. The capsule itself was set up similar to a helicopter. It was surrounded by a glass enclosure and was connected to a hydraulic arm capable of lifting and extending the capsule to access all the monitors in the entire room. The joystick controlled all the movements. The windshield was a display panel that allowed for fingertip control of the monitors. At the swipe of a finger, monitors could be relocated anywhere the operator designated, thereby linking outputs into a more user-defined configuration.

On any given day there were multiple search routines running through the system looking through emails, cell phone logs, text messages, social media postings, and general Internet chatter. The information displayed on the monitors was controlled by each of the eight agents assigned to that particular section of the panopticon. Each had a set of assignments and was under the direction of the Deputy Director. The data displayed could only be reconfigured by the command module currently operated by Trevor Carlson. Each of the eight other analysts had been trained as a backup only. After Jake's training he would be the only other primary operator and would have equal access to the command capsule as Carlson.

Due to the sensitive nature and SAP security clearance, all non-cleared personnel had to leave the panopticon any time the data connected to that project was displayed. After clearing the room, Jake and Trevor entered the command capsule while Harper pulled up the system file and populated the displays with the outputs from the search protocols. The entire room seemed to flash as the monitors refreshed with all the new data. The sheer size of the room and the amount of data being displayed was overwhelming to the untrained eye. It was as exhilarating for Jake as it was for underwater divers to discover treasures from centuries-old shipwrecks.

Jake looked at Trevor and said, "Once around the block, please." Without hesitation the command capsule lifted off its platform at the gentle nudging of the joystick and Jake's journey began. His eyes darted back and forth across the monitors blinking like a camera shutter capturing the images into his brain for later reference and retrieval. After the first round trip he asked Trevor to pause mid air as he took his first in-depth look at the monitors within his line of sight.

"How do I rearrange the monitors?" Jake asked.

"Your hands do all the work for you," Trevor began. "The windshield is interactive and you simply point to the monitor you want to move, drag it through the air and move it where you want. Try moving one now. It won't take long to get the hang of it and you can't break anything."

Jake reached out and before long was rearranging the wall of monitors at lightning speed. Trevor did not say a word as Jake intuitively reached for the joystick and began moving the capsule through the air around the room, rearranging the data monitors. After almost an hour

Jake broke the silence saying, "There. Can you see it?"

Trevor looked and saw the pattern Jake had assembled. The four financial backers of the human genome research center in Geneva were connected in many more ways than originally thought. They shared a commonality that sent a shiver through Jake's body. All four were from Tehran and had European mothers who died at childbirth. The name Jake knew, but was not found anywhere else in the data they had mined, was his old roommate Hakeem Baba. Could it possibly be a coincidence that he, too, had a European mother that died at childbirth? It was now apparent why Max had said what he did, but what was the connection and how was Hakeem involved?

Somewhat shaken, Jake pressed on in his examination of the data and saw what appeared to be several inconsistencies. He began to make a mental checklist that he would draw upon during his debrief with Max and his two teammates. The data clearly showed that the only time all four of the financial backers were together was in Tehran attending the funeral of one of their fathers. Jake needed to know who else was there at that time and what was their connection to Hakeem. Another anomaly was the number of purchases of bone fragments from museums across the Middle East, including Israel. There were no other records of purchases of bones from any other regions of the world. There was also a significant investment in several groups that appeared to be involved in archeological exploration, also confined to the Middle East.

Jake made eye contact with Harper as he spoke to him through his headset and gave the following set of instructions, "Harper, I want you to run a search on Hakeem Nisralla Baba, date of birth: September 11, 1980. I need that data right away."

Harper gave him the thumbs-up signal and began typing away at his workstation. In just a few seconds the monitors directly in front of Jake began refreshing with new data. Jake learned all he needed to know about Hakeem and his whereabouts during the past fifteen years. He saw the clear connection between Hakeem and the four others, but Jake added another big question to his debrief checklist. "If Hakeem was heading up a fully equipped and established DNA laboratory and research center in Tehran, why would he need a duplicate one in Geneva?"

The more he learned the more questions he had. It was time to call Max and schedule the debrief.

CHAPTER 50

For the first time in a long time, Jake made time in his usually overloaded schedule and joined his parents for dinner. What was normally a lively platform for discussions of a variety of subjects was thick with silence. Every time Norman would look like he was about to say something, Lydia shook her head to stop him. Finally, Jake broke the silence, without breaching any classified information, and shared what he had learned about Hakeem and his years since he left the Winchester Academy.

Jake began, "Once Hakeem left he did not go to Turkey as indicated. He went to Tehran and was fast tracked through their academic system and entered the Medical University there. He was one of, if not the youngest graduate in the university's history. He gained the respect of the scientific community in his breakthrough doctorate thesis at Tehran University of Medical Sciences. From there he went directly to the National Research Center for Genetic Engineering and Biotechnology in Tehran. He never married and he travels extensively throughout Europe and the Middle East collaborating with some of the world's greatest scientists. He has devoted himself to both testing and developing cures at the cellular level for diseases."

Jake's parents knew not to press the subject and understood exactly what Jake was not telling them. It was clear Hakeem was on the NSA's radar and there was much more to the story than Jake could reveal. Max had never mentioned Hakeem to Norman in any of their conversations, and that in itself was all Norman needed to confirm the sensitive nature of this matter.

Lydia, ever the diplomat's wife, immediately changed the subject. She invited Jake to join them at one of the many social and charity functions they would be attending in hopes of him meeting a suitable young lady. As usual, Jake declined and was more interested in solving his latest case than he was in being social. She was not surprised at his response, but was concerned that this new case would become personal due to Hakeem's name being mentioned. He was a grown man and a trained intelligence operative, but, nevertheless, he was still her son. She and Norman had their share of heartache during their years of diplomatic service, and she never wanted Jake to know that lifestyle. She had never asked him what he had to do during his ten years in Israel and wasn't going to start prying now.

Norman looked across the table at his son and admired how much this geeky little boy of his had grown into such a skilled strategic and tactical man of valor. He took no credit for it, and that made him even more proud. The only comfort he could offer him now was to tell him how proud he was to be his father and leave it at that. As dinner ended, Norman walked over to Jake and hugged his son, saying, "You make me proud to be your father. I love you, son."

Jake hugged him back and said, "I love you too, Dad." He looked at his mom and thanked her for dinner and told her that he loved her. "Don't wait up or expect to see much of me for the next week or two. I'm not sure, but I expect I will be making a few trips in the near future. I will let you know what I can, when I can."

After Jake left to head back to the panopticon, Norman held Lydia close and assured her Jake would be ok. She knew in her heart that something wasn't right.

CHAPTER 51

Jake called Max on his way into the office and set a time for them to meet to debrief. Max let it be known he had additional information to share with the team and it would be best for them to all meet in the morning at 10:00AM. Jake texted Harper and Carlson to put it on their calendars. He knew that if he waited until after he entered the panopticon he might forget to schedule them.

Due to the hour Team #2 was in place, and Jake had not met with these eight analysts before. Since he would be running several of his own searches outside the original parameters of the Geneva Project he felt comfortable not clearing the room while he manipulated the display panels. The research he was doing was related to the project, but was not proprietary in nature. He would compile some initial queries from his office and then load them into the panopticon so he could overlay the data to search for patterns.

Jake began the process of identifying every DNA-testing facility, including all law enforcement and independent laboratories worldwide. He searched for all ownership, operational control, and location of all DNA databases. He then searched for any reported breaches or hacks into these databases. In an entirely new set of commands, he established a listing of keywords and ran a global search across all data sources, mining for information on cultural anthropology and genetic studies. He knew this output would be so large it would require further refinement. He also ran searches related to all reports of stolen antiquities, biblical relics, and ancient scrolls of any kind. In addition, he searched for every active archeological dig and their funding sources. His queries were extensive, and the yield would be voluminous.

In the back of Jake's mind were several hypotheses as to what was behind the Geneva Project, but unless he found the supporting evidence, it would only be pure conjecture. His goal was to add some additional background to their 10:00AM briefing that would solidify his theories.

It was nearly 4:00AM when Jake entered the panopticon and notified the lead analyst he needed access to the data he had been mining. All standard protocols were enacted to log the activity and Jake was confident enough to deflect the accounting code request to Harper. It was not unusual for him to be the one to fill in the blanks when he arrived later that morning. Jake's higher level of security clearance and the early hour were enough to convince the Lead Analyst to yield.

Jake entered the capsule and the data began to populate the monitors. He rearranged the monitor's output until he had reassembled it into a useable configuration more suited for his purpose.

The first two hours of Jake's analysis was educational and informational. The sheer volume of data related to his areas of interest was monumental. He would need to run many refinements to hone in on specific links to the Geneva Project.

There was a new trend that Jake was seeing in his analysis of the data. Law enforcement agencies around the world were gathering DNA samples from individuals at the same time they were fingerprinting them upon arrest. In 2010 there were over 13 million arrests made in the US alone, and all were entered into the CODIS, the nationwide Combined DNA Index System. In England's system, United Kingdom National DNA Database (NDNAD), they have on record the DNA of over 6 million residents. The wealth of DNA samples worldwide was staggering, and when he added the numbers of independent testing laboratories for both medical and genealogical testing worldwide Jake estimated there were well over 250 million DNA records in secured and unsecured databases. There was pending legislation throughout many nations in Africa, The Middle East, Asia, Australia, and Europe to establish new DNA databases. Twenty-five of the 27 European Union countries currently maintain DNA databases. Interpol, itself, maintained a database of DNA profiles from 69 countries.

At present there was no official centralized repository for DNA data. There were a number of groups with less noble purposes than curing diseases and solving crimes looking for ways to breach these databases and use the information for their own agendas. Jake noted that there were recorded breaches of every agency listed, but no specific references to DNA hacks. Jake sensed that no agency would be willing to admit what data had been hacked since public trust and national security were always in jeopardy if too much information was shared publicly.

The listing of archeological digs was also enlightening. In his own native Israel there were over 14,000 sites listed in 1998 with more than 11,000 of them having been robbed. Since that time, thousands more sites had been uncovered along with unreported sites in territories not under Israel's direct control. Antiquity-related crimes ranked right behind trafficking of narcotics, weapons and people. The Middle East was a hotbed of illegal trade in archeological treasures of all kinds. Because of the tension between governments, there was little cooperation among law enforcement agencies. This would be harder to uncover than Jake had originally thought. He would also have to refine his searches in order to uncover what he was trying to find.

By 8:30AM Jake had come to the conclusion he would need to request a full-time data analyst who could run more queries on his behalf. This would allow Jake more time to piece the puzzle together. Tired, yet not weary, Jake exited the panopticon to prepare for the 10:00AM briefing with Max. He would share his hypotheses then after comparing notes with Harper and Carlson.

He was certain Max would have some new light to shed as well.

Harper and Carlson were waiting outside Jake's office upon his return from the panopticon. Instead of the standard "good morning," Jake was greeted with puzzled silence. Once inside his office with the door closed, Jake filled the other two in on his late-night activities.

Carlson was the first to speak after Jake finished. "Maybe I'm missing something, but what does all this have to do with the Geneva Project?"

Before Jake could reply, Harper said, "I'm not sure we need to know right now what he's thinking. It might be best if we waited until the briefing at 10:00AM."

Carlson shrugged his shoulders and nodded his head.

CHAPTER 52

Max was right on time as he entered the Situation Room promptly at 10:00AM. "Good Morning, gentlemen," he began. "Before Jake brings me up to speed on what he has learned about the Geneva Project, I want to hear from the others. Carlson, you're up."

Carlson began, "Everything is on track. Aaronson has been brought up to speed on the command capsule and has already logged solo hours just as we had forecast. There is more data than we can possibly process with this small a team and, to be quite honest, I still don't see the threat to national security."

Max responded, "I appreciate your position on this. I'm confident it will become clear to you once the magnitude of this threat is revealed. For now, I need your total commitment and trust. You were hand picked for this assignment and your role is vital to our success. I understand there was a lot thrown at you in a very short period of time. Right now you just have to trust me and roll with it. Harper, your turn."

Harper did not have much to add as he, too, wanted to hear Jake's report. He simply stated, "All is as it should be. No one is asking any questions at this point and the feedback from Team #2 was that Aaronson handled himself well overnight. I gave them the accounting codes they needed and they were satisfied."

Jake should have known Harper would have his ear to the ground and had been around long enough to gather internal intelligence. It was his turn to offer his update and hypotheses.

Jake began, "I have been running multiple searches on the areas we had originally targeted and added a number of new parameters overnight. I found the link to the four financial backers, and I am sure it will be no surprise to Max that the common connection is my old roommate Hakeem Baba. It appears he has masterminded a plan to assemble a duplicate genetics lab in Geneva. I can only assume it is for work not currently sanctioned in his official capacity in Tehran. There are connections to archeological digs and the acquisition of biblical artifacts, antiquities, and bones all being transferred to the Geneva Project. I have more data than I can possibly process and need an additional analyst to join the team. I think they need to be well versed in forensic anthropology and have field investigation experience. I am estimating that in the next few weeks we will have to mobilize our resources across the Middle East and Europe to uncover the real plot behind all this activity. Max, can you rustle up an analyst with the skill set I need?"

Max nodded and then said, "She is already on her way. Once you expanded your search parameters, I was notified and began to reach out to Dr. Melanie Paris. She is one of the foremost experts in forensic archeology and received extensive field training in archeological digs throughout Egypt, Israel, and Jordan. She has been a part of a number of worldwide inter-agency cases and was instrumental in solving a number of them. She is fluent in Arabic, Farsi, Hebrew and French and can handle a gun as well as she handles a shovel. I think you will be impressed on multiple levels."

Jake asked, "When will she be here and when can I review her file? I need help right away and she sounds like the right skillset to help me sift through a ton of data."

Max replied, "I have her file for you now and she is due to arrive at Dulles in a few hours. I think it best if you pick her up at the airport so you two can have some one-on-one time to familiarize yourselves with each other."

Jake thought for a moment and then said, "Sounds like a good idea. While I'm gone, I want Harper and Carlson to review the data from last night's run. There is more to this than genetic research for cures to the world's diseases. I don't know about Hakeem yet, but the other four are known members of old-school radical Muslim factions looking to employ Jihad and advance their ideology. All indications are the Geneva facility is being set up for that purpose. The big question is how it all fits together. Once we know what they are up to, we can deploy and take that facility offline. I want Harper and Carlson by my side in the field. You ok with that, Max?"

Max quickly responded, "That's been the plan all along. I think you will want to add Dr. Paris to that field ops team, but I will let you make that decision after you meet her. Here is her flight information. Her photo is in her file and you can review that while you wait for her arrival. I think it's time for you to head over to Dulles to meet her. Bring her straight back here and she can at least meet the others before Breakstone gets her over to her hotel."

As they all rose to leave Jake looked over at Max and noticed he had that look about him that made Jake wonder what he wasn't telling him. He took the file and left knowing he would find out soon enough.

CHAPTER 53

Jake opened the door to the government-standard black sedan and tossed the file on Dr. Paris onto the passenger's seat. He knew the way to Dulles and had no trouble maneuvering around the Beltway. He also knew he would have no trouble pulling right in front of the baggage claim exit as his government plates and NSA ID gave him all the rank and privilege he needed to satisfy the airport police. He double checked the flight schedule, pulled in front of the baggage claim, and parked his vehicle right under the No Parking sign. Within seconds a uniformed patrolman began waving his hands at Jake motioning him to move. As soon as Jake opened his door to try and speak, the officer's hand moved quickly into position on top of his holstered 9MM Glock. Jake knew not to reach for his credentials, as any sudden movement other than reentering the vehicle was out of the question. He eased himself back into the driver's seat and started the car and began to pull out. He stopped short of the officer and held up his NSA credentials. The officer looked at him, shook his head in frustration, and motioned for Jake to pull over. He approached the vehicle and asked how long he would be and if this was official business. Jake told him he would be no more than thirty minutes and yes, it was official business. The officer walked away without saying anything else.

Jake put the car in park, turned off the ignition, and reached for the file on Dr. Melanie Paris. He opened it and immediately saw many pages of material for him to review. As he opened the folder the rest of the way and saw the photo on the inside front cover, he was glad there was no one else in the car with him to hear the audible gasp. He had expected a middle-aged, horn-rimmed, glasses-wearing, cropped-haired, scientific geek. Unless the picture was someone's idea of a joke, he was looking at one of the most stunning women he had ever seen. Her blue eyes were riveting and her smile was a radiant source of light. She had long, dark hair, and the full-length photo showed her in high heels and a designer pants suit. He was sure this was a mistake and could not stop looking at the picture long enough to fully digest the briefing package. Time passed more quickly than he was aware, and he was startled when there was a sharp knock on the passenger window. He looked over, and there in front of him was the exact same woman whose picture he had been staring at for most of the thirty minutes.

Jake fumbled for the door handle, dropping the file folder as he rushed out the door to help Dr. Paris with her luggage. He was feeling awkward in her presence and tried desperately to regain his composure as he attempted to introduce himself. She took the lead and extended her hand and said, "Dr. Aaronson, what a pleasure it is to meet you. I have read so much about you and look forward to working with you."

Jake knew he was staring, but could not seem to do anything about it. He did not take his eyes off hers as he took her hand and shook it slowly to make sure the contact lasted as long as it could. She smiled brightly and said, "Maybe we should load my bags and be on our way."

He let out a nervous laugh and reached for her suitcase, but she had already picked it up and was on her way to the back of the car. He opened the trunk, loaded it, and then walked her to the passenger door and opened it for her. As she slid into the seat she responded with, "Ah, a gentleman. I thought that was a lost art. Thank you."

Jake used the short walk around the car to try and regain his composure. With renewed confidence he sat behind the wheel and pulled out of the parking space. Without taking his eyes off the road he said, "I am very glad to meet you too, Dr. Paris. I thought it best to let you tell me about yourself on our ride to the office rather than read some impersonal briefing package. I find it more refreshing to hear directly from the source."

"Very well," Dr. Paris began. "I was raised in a small town where family and faith were the center of my life. My parents stressed education and held me to very high moral and ethical standards. I discovered a perfect balance between faith and science and found that one supports the other. I have two doctorates, one in Forensic Archeology and the other in Biblical Studies. I obtained both at the same time, but from two different universities. I have spent the past fifteen years working with various agencies ranging from the CIA and NSA to Interpol, Europol and Mossad. During those assignments, we have been able to use my forensic archeology expertise to uncover and solve a number of cases. Most involved conspiracies to market stolen biblical antiquities or assassination attempts. I have found my biblical training to be quite useful in not only solving or stopping crimes, but also keeping a balance in my own life. Certainly you can relate to how stressful our work can be. I am sure you have many more questions, but let me list the obvious to save you the trouble. I am thirty-seven and have never been married. I speak Hebrew, Farsi, Arabic and French fluently and can field strip and reassemble any number of weapons as fast as any soldier with whom I have served. If you want any more details, I suggest you read the file folder given to you."

All Jake could muster was a one-word response, "Impressive." They rode in silence the rest of the way to the office. As they pulled into the parking spot at NSA Headquarters, Jake walked around the car, opened the door, and extended a hand to help Dr. Paris. Their eyes met and locked on to each other's without a word being spoken. Jake was aware of his increased heart rate and was slow to let go of her hand. He opened the trunk and removed her bag. This time he would carry it for her. He walked her into the security area where she would pick up her credentials. He left her there with instructions for the Security Officer to escort her to his Situation Room as soon she was processed. He stole one more glance as he walked out of the security office and headed to his own office to immediately read her file. For some strange reason he found himself with a deep-seeded desire to learn everything he could about his new associate.

He barely had time to begin reviewing her background when Breakstone's voice broke the silence summoning him to the Situation Room. He closed the file and arrived in time to see Max, Carlson, and Harper already there. It was all smiles as they welcomed their newest team member, Dr. Melanie Paris. Jake took his seat and waited in silence for the welcome reception to die down. He used this time to steal a few more glances before they began the day's briefing.

CHAPTER 54

Max and the others took their seats, and Jake began the day's briefing. "I am glad you all have had a chance to meet our newest associate. Dr. Paris is a welcome addition to our team. We have a full day ahead, and our overnight data runs have yielded a number of seemingly random purchases and thefts, but, as we all know, nothing is random in our line of work. In the past six months there has been a rash of thefts from museums and an increase in black-market-traded antiquities with a common theme. These activities surround bone fragments ranging in age from 2500 years old to less than 250 years old and of all things, teeth. Several major universities have reported break-ins and thefts of artifacts from their anthropology and archeology departments. We are trying to cross match these incidents to see any patterns. We have localized the geography to the Middle East."

Before Jake had finished Dr. Paris spoke up, "I have a number of sources of information that may not be on your radar that may give us some insight into any black-market activity. I will need to see a list of items that have been reported missing."

Jake continued, "That would be very helpful, Dr. Paris. Intelligence out of that region, other than Israel, is sketchy at best. We need some reliable assets willing to work with us on this investigation. Max, what financial resources are available to us and when will this become a sanctioned project?"

"I'm working my end, you work yours," Max firmly answered.

Carlson was quick to offer his services to Dr. Paris saying, "As the senior analyst on the team and the one most familiar with the panopticon, I would be happy to show you around and let you review what we have collected so far."

Dr. Paris smiled and thanked Carlson saying, "How kind of you, but I will be collaborating with Dr. Aaronson on this as much of the documentation is in Hebrew and Arabic. As I understand it, we are the only two on the team fluent in both languages."

Max took the discussion over by saying, "I guess you two better get to work then and see what and who is behind all this bone and teeth stealing. I will start talking a few of my Congressional oversight friends into shifting some funds around so we can bankroll this project and get some more resources assigned to it. I expect to see a report in the next few days with some actionable intelligence. Dr. Paris, I know it's just day one for you, but I need you fully engaged on this right away. Your intel may be the key to us figuring out just what they are up to in Geneva. Reach out to whomever you need to and use Harper and Carlson to assist. Jake, I have Dr. Paris at the Candlewood Suites nearby. Please make sure she gets there and settled in before we take full advantage of her expertise. Breakstone has the keys. Keep me posted and maintain as low a profile as you can until I get this moved up the ladder and secure the funding we need. Any questions?"

Dr. Paris spoke up and asked, "What latitude do we have in bringing other international agencies in on this investigation?"

Max answered, "At this point none. Until we have enough evidence to substantiate a threat to national security or international targets, we are operating independent of any agency. This operation is beyond top secret and your clearance was elevated for this project so we could bring you onboard. I think we are on to something, but until we have solid evidence and have uncovered their plan, we are in an unofficial role. If this is what it appears to be, there is an apocalyptic plan being formed and this team will be fully operational and funded in short order. For now, do what you have to do, but do not draw any attention to your activities. The last thing we need is some insider leaking information to the world about what we are doing here. There have been enough exposé's cramping our efforts to last me a lifetime. Consider this a black ops operation within a black ops organization. Trust no one but those in this room unless otherwise instructed. Are we all clear?"

With one voice all four answered, "Clear."

The meeting broke and Jake thought it best to get Dr. Paris over to her accommodations and let her get settled before digging in to the project briefings. He had Breakstone make her a copy of the briefing packet and would pick it up along with the key to her suite on their way out.

Jake shared his plans with Dr. Paris and she accompanied him, picked up her key and briefing packet, and headed to the car. The ride to the Candlewood Suites was less than ten minutes.

Upon arrival Jake unloaded the suitcase from the trunk and Dr. Paris took it from him and started walking toward the entrance to the extended stay facility. Jake hesitated, wondering whether he should follow her in or let her handle this on her own. He didn't have long to wait before Dr. Paris looked over her shoulder, continued walking, and said, "No need to accompany me. I won't be long and we can head right back to the office and get started. I shouldn't be more than a few minutes if you don't mind waiting,"

Jake was spared the awkwardness of the situation and answered, "I'll be right here when you return."

While waiting he began talking to himself, "Man, you have got to get yourself together. If she is an attraction, she will be a distraction. Keep your mind on the task at hand. Maintain a level, professional head. She is a top-notch professional and you've got to keep your head in the game. Strictly business. Got it!"

In no time at all Dr. Paris returned and Jake was waiting inside the car. As she got in Jake said, "Ready to dig in, Dr. Paris?"

She looked over at him and said, "If we are going to work closely together let's drop the Dr. stuff. My name is Melanie. My friends call me Mel. Is that ok with you?"

"Most at the Agency just go by their last names, but I am all for informality. Call me Jake, Mel."

Mel smiled and replied, "Now I'm ready to dig in, Jake."

CHAPTER 55

By the time Jake and Mel returned, Harper had secured the panopticon. An entire quadrant of screens displayed reports, photos, and details of all the bone fragments and teeth that had been reported stolen. As Mel entered the panopticon for the first time she was overwhelmed by its magnitude. She walked the entire circumference of the room, pausing in front of a number of screens as she walked. Jake remembered his first impressions and wondered how it compared to hers. He hoped he would have the chance to discuss that with her.

After completing her first lap around the room, Mel asked Carlson to brief her on how the room actually worked and how to reconfigure the displays. She sensed he felt slighted when she picked Jake to collaborate and wanted to mend any hurt feelings for the sake of the team dynamics. Carlson seemed flattered at the request and proceeded to explain how the command capsule worked and the ability to reconfigure the displays and manipulate the data. Once Carlson was finished, Mel thanked him and proceeded to ask Jake to enter the capsule so she could get a closer view of the displays and reconfigure the data for examination.

Harper and Carlson took their places behind the data consoles as Jake and Mel entered the capsule. Once inside, Jake explained to Mel how the capsule functioned just as Carlson had done not too long ago for him. Mel was soon rearranging panels looking for patterns and any connections she could make in identifying what these thefts had in common.

It didn't take long before she asked Jake to set them down so she could brief the rest of the team on what was discovered. She also placed a call to Max to see if he could join them in person. He instructed her to assemble the team in the Situation Room and conference him in by phone.

Once inside the secure Situation Room they called Max to conference him into the briefing. Max sounded a little rushed as he said, "Bring me up to speed as quickly as possible."

Mel took this as her cue to start with her assessment of the data she had reviewed. She began, "There is a connection to the bones and teeth that are missing. I am certain someone is harvesting DNA from them and building a database. These items are all connected with sacred sites across the Middle East where the cities of the Old Testament were settled and where altars were built for sacrifices under the Mosaic Law. The highest concentrations of stolen items are connected to the First Temple. If I were to hazard an educated guess, I would say someone is looking to connect some type of ancestral line. If that is the case, then what possible reason could anyone have?"

Jake spoke up, "If Hakeem Baba is behind all this I think I might know what he is trying to piece together. Back when we were roommates I took him home with me on more than one occasion. I recall there being conversations around new discoveries back then that could link Jewish ancestry through DNA. I also remember my father sharing with Hakeem our family name and the connection with Aaron in the Bible."

Before he could finish Mel interjected, "As in the Legend of the Scrolls?"

Jake was stunned at her statement and responded, "How do you know about that family fable that my father talks about?"

"Jake," she began, "that fable, as you refer to it, is something that myself and a number of my colleagues feel has great merit. In my biblical studies I was known in many circles as one who studied the Priesthood and the miracles that Aaron performed to convince Israel that God was indeed, God. One of the reasons I served as the forensic archeological expert on a number of digs in the Middle East was to further my access to proving that the lineage of Aaron still exists today. The Bible is clear that God gave an everlasting responsibility to Aaron and his sons. If it is everlasting, then it must be alive today. I have always hypothesized there was more to the lineage than we may realize and that certain secrets were passed on from one generation to the next. That would mean there is someone living today that is a direct descendant of Aaron's son and the rightful heir by blood to the Priesthood. During the millennial reign, the Third Temple will be in full operation with a High Priest in the direct line of Aaron performing the priestly duties. The Book of Ezekiel confirms that the sacrificial system will be in place. Since those who believe in Jesus have no need of a sacrifice for sin, there will be sacrifices for the other reasons stated in Leviticus. A High Priest would need to make the fellowship, guilt, and peace offering as well as receive the portion for the provision of the Levites who will serve along side him."

Harper and Carlson looked on in amazement as they watched this story unfold. Neither was familiar with the topic being discussed, but were fascinated by the subject matter.

Max's voice boomed over the speaker as he spoke, "Well Jake, it seems there is some truth behind that story your father has been spinning ever since I have known him. Dr. Paris, what benefit would there be to the Islamic agenda to identify the ancestral line of Aaron and the Priesthood?"

Mel answered, "In my opinion there are two possible scenarios, and either one of them are quite significant. The first is related to finding the Y-chromosome that linked the Jewish priest's lineage. If a DNA sample can be identified as belonging to one or more of the Old Testament priests such as Zadok, then a worldwide hack of every DNA database in the world would provide keys to the identity of the descendants living today. If that lineage could be destroyed, there would be no living heir to the line of Aaron and that would destroy the hope of a Third[1] Temple being built.

"The second scenario is as devastating as the first. Many do not realize the significance of the words of Jesus in Matthew 23:37:

> Jerusalem, Jerusalem, you who kill the prophets and stone those sent to you, how often I have longed to gather your children together, as a hen gathers her chicks under her wings, and you were not willing. Look, your house is left to you desolate. For I tell you, you will not see me again until you say, "Blessed is he who comes in the name of the Lord."

"What he is saying here is His return is predicated on the Jewish leadership of Jerusalem, the Sanhedrin, to call for His return by their proclamation of faith in Him. If you could build a database of the DNA of all the Jewish people in the world, then you would have the chance to do what Haman and Hitler failed to do. If you annihilate the Jewish population of the world, then Jesus does not return. Not only does Satan continue his wretched hold on humanity, but Islam is strengthened and would be well positioned to colonize the rest of the world."

The room was silenced by the magnitude of these two scenarios. Even Max found himself overwhelmed by them. This was personal to him as a Jewish man and reminded him of growing up hearing the horrific stories from family and others who survived the Holocaust. He though to himself, "Could it actually happen again? The fact that it happened in the first place means there is a remnant that still wants it to happen again. We must stop this. I need to get this project sanctioned and funded right away. I have what I need to take it up the line. "

Max broke the silence, "Excellent work, team. It appears we have just uncovered the tip of an iceberg. I need this in a formal report before the end of the day. In the meantime, I will start lobbying for the funds we need to launch a full-scale international investigation. Mel and Jake, get your suitcases ready as I plan to send you two out into the field to gather as much evidence as you can. Carlson and Harper will each head up a team here working twelve-hour shifts to search and process every lead you find. We all know what needs to be done and there is no room for failure. Clear? "

In unison all four in the Situation Room spoke up, "CLEAR!"

After Max hung up Carlson said, "Looks like I'm going to have to open my Bible and read up on this." Harper nodded in agreement.

Jake said, "While Mel and I get this report written for Max, I have several more searches I want you to run. I'll write up the search strings and get them over to you in the next half hour. It seems we are about to either change or make history and I am glad we are on the same team. Thanks for your hard work."

Jake and Mel headed to Jake's office while Carlson and Harper stayed behind to wait for Jake's queries. They sat in silence as they contemplated what they had just heard. Mel noticed how distraught Jake looked and decided she would ask him outside the office what was troubling him.

She broke the silence and said, "Do you mind if we get out of here and work on the report over lunch? All I've had is coffee and I just realized how hungry I am."

Jake agreed and texted Carlson that he would have the search strings to him after lunch and maybe he and Harper should take a break while they could. As they headed out they stopped to tell Breakstone where they would be if Max called.

CHAPTER 56

Jake held the door open for Mel and walked around the car pausing for a moment before he took his seat behind the wheel. He started the car and said, "I hope you like sushi."

Mel replied, "Love it." They decided to wait until they were seated inside the restaurant before starting any deep conversation.

They arrived at Asian Rim and took a table away from the commotion of the hibachi. After they had ordered and received their food, Mel said, "Jake, I don't mean to pry, but you seem especially troubled by what we discussed. If we are going to be working closely together you have to be able to share what is troubling you."

"You are not prying," Jake began. "I am just racking my brain to understand what I could have done to drive Hakeem to hate me and my family and Jewish people so much. I thought we were best friends, and even though we have not kept in touch since he left school early, I really felt like he was a brother to me."

"Jake, you have seen it yourself many times before. Operatives assume identities, build relationships, gather information, and use it to their advantage. I, too, have been betrayed and understand how hard it is when it feels personal. We are facing an enemy who knows no ethics and lives by a moral code steeped in lies and violence.

You are not responsible for an ideology that labels us both as infidels. "

Jake thought about Mel's response and vocalized another part of his concern. "If Hakeem is behind all of this and we come face to face, I'm concerned how I will react if I have to use force."

"I can imagine how that must feel right now, but you are going to have to come to terms with that sooner than later. I need to know where you stand before I get on a plane and travel the globe to break up this plot."

"You are right. This is all just happening so fast."

"I am interested to hear more about your father's version of the legend. Do you mind sharing it with me?"

"Not at all. It seems you know about the ancestral line and the rumor of secrets passed from one generation of the line of Aaron to the next. Have you heard the part about a set of scrolls that each generation in the line was responsible for updating with prophecies and miracles?"

"I had only heard rumors, but nothing even with as much detail as you have just shared. Please tell me more."

"The story goes that during the defilement of the First Temple the line of Aaron and rightful heir to the Priesthood was replaced by a high priest appointed by whoever ruled over Jerusalem. During the inter-testament period it was Greece and then Rome who made these appointments. According to the legend, the heir remained in Jerusalem to record the prophecies and the miracles that foretold who the Messiah would be. When Rome destroyed the Second Temple in 70AD it is rumored the heir was hidden and smuggled out of the city and has been in hiding ever since. A group that is trying to rebuild the Third Temple allegedly are the only ones who know his identity. According to the legend, the scrolls were passed to the heir sewn into the lining of the priestly robe. That, according to the tale, is how Aaron passed it to Eleazar before he died. This group in Jerusalem reports they have made a new set of garments for the High Priest to wear in the new Temple. Nothing has been verified, but it is believed the scrolls are in their possession and will verify whom the Messiah is and if he has already come. If these scrolls were to fall into the wrong hands, 2500 years of history would be lost. Not only are they priceless, they hold the key to a mystery that has been debated for over 2000 years."

Mel was wide eyed and hung on every word Jake spoke. She knew what he was saying was possible, but highly improbable. That was the very reason she became a forensic archeologist. Her life-long mission was to scientifically verify biblical history. She could hardly believe she was working on a project of such biblical importance. She looked at Jake and said, "I believe every word you just spoke and am so thankful to be on this mission with you. I trust you implicitly as the leader of this team. Where you go, I will follow.

You can trust me to do whatever it takes to end this threat."

"Thanks for the vote of confidence. Let's finish our lunch and head back to the office. I've got to get those search strings to Harper and Carlson and then you and I need to list every contact we have that we can source for actionable intelligence."

As they entered the building, Breakstone passed along a message that Harper and Carlson would be back in shortly. They wanted Jake and Mel to know they were at a bookstore buying a Bible.

Jake and Mel looked at each other and laughed out loud as they made their way to Jake's office. Once inside, it was back to the very serious business at hand. They collaborated on the search strings first and sent those to Carlson and Harper's email. After they finished the report of the morning's findings and sent it over to Max, they then began the task of identifying colleagues and assets who could provide solid leads. Jake focused on Mossad and Shin Bet in Israel and a few Interpol and Europol contacts Max had provided. Mel focused on archeologists and academic contacts across the Middle East and in Europe. All tolled they had amassed sixty-five names of people to reach out to either by phone or in person.

They laid out a potential itinerary that would maximize their ability to contact as many resources as possible in the shortest amount of time. In Israel they would work independently of each other, with Jake following military leads and Mel contacting antiquity dealers, archeologists, and academics. They would fly to Tel Aviv and then make their way to Jerusalem. Depending upon the leads they uncovered, they would travel to Bethlehem, Cairo, or Amman, Jordan. Jake always preferred the Dan Hotels and would indicate his preference to Max. When he shared this with Mel she laughed and said, "I have spent an inordinate amount of time in tents on digs. I think I am going to like the travel accommodations on this project much better. Sounds like my commitment to follow your lead is going to pay off for this forensic archeologist."

Jake smiled and said, "What can I say? I've slept in the desert more times than I can count, and now that I have an expense account I am going to take full advantage. Let's write this plan up and get it over to Max. I estimate we will be in the field for at least a month. In that time we should be able to amass enough evidence to verify if Hakeem is behind this and what they are actually planning. If my hunch is correct, we will finish up in Geneva or Tehran. Our chances of making it back home in one piece are much higher in Geneva than in Tehran. That's a chance we will just have to take. You still on board?"

Mel stared at Jake and said, "I knew the risk when Max brought me onto the team. I meant what I said and will follow you until this reaches whatever conclusion it reaches. By the way, don't ask me that ever again. Clear?"

Jake nodded and said, "Clear."

By the time they were finished Carlson and Harper had returned and run the search strings. Carlson's voice came over the intercom and said, "The results are up and ready for your review. Harper and I will clear a section of the panopticon and be ready for you in five minutes."

Jake looked at Mel and said, "You heard the man. Let's go check out the results."

CHAPTER 57

The queries Jake had them run searched through millions of email accounts and text messages looking for a long list of keywords. The software that captured the data then discarded all emails from known entities that had been involved in legitimate business transactions. The remainder identified a long list of prospective interested parties, sellers and buyers who were involved in antiquities sales involving bone or teeth fragments. Jake was especially interested in any photographs being transmitted. Many contained a form of steganography used to hide encrypted messages or code not easily detected. This form of cryptography drew less attention to the message as the average viewer was focused on the image. Jake had Harper searched every image file for hidden messages and images embedded within images.

As Jake and Mel entered the panopticon, Jake explained what he hoped to find. It wasn't long before his eyes locked onto a series of screens and he began to reorder the monitors to display the data in a particular sequence. Mel watched and let out an audible gasp as she began to see the pattern taking shape in front of her.

Jake had uncovered messages related to the DNA search along with hidden images of what appeared to be a miter, a robe, a breastplate, and a staff; however, there were no images of a scroll of any kind. The identities of the authors of these messages were seemingly random and originated from four distinct locations: France, London, Greece and Antwerp.

Jake said, "It looks like our travels may take us to more than just the Middle East. I will have Harper run searches on any links in these cities to Hakeem in Geneva or Tehran. I am starting to see a pattern develop here and need just a few more puzzle pieces before I can formulate who is involved in this plot. I think we will find a direct connection to Tehran in all of this."

Mel responded, "I would like to talk with you offline about how this ties into End-Time Prophecy if you are interested. I think you will find it fascinating to learn of the alliances described in the Bible. Daniel first saw the future events in his interpretation of the king's dreams. Nations and alliances forming today are described in those passages in the Old Testament. As one who sees patterns, I would challenge you to read some of it for yourself. Maybe you can find some clues that are not uncovered through this technology we have grown so dependent upon. Many of the so-called legends passed down in your family happen to be true. I would think you would want to know who they were looking for and why it was so important. I would be happy to spend the time we have together showing you how all this fits in with the case we are trying to solve."

Jake considered what Mel had said and replied, "I am interested, but after growing up in a Jewish home and living in Israel I am not a big fan of religion. It seems to divide more people than unify them, and there is enough trouble in the world already. Maybe you can show me something that I have not seen, but you need to know I am skeptical."

"Is that a challenge, Dr.?"

"If you want to think of it as a challenge, be my guest. We will have plenty of time to talk over these next few weeks as we go after the truth and solve this case. The case comes first, and as long as what you want me to see is not a distraction, I will remain open. Otherwise, it will have to wait."

"I understand and agree. I think it will make the case more real if you knew more about the history behind it. I promise not to distract."

"Thanks for understanding. I need to get that data from Harper to determine the links between those four cities and Hakeem. Once we have that, we can follow the money and it will lead us to whatever is being planned."

It didn't take long for Harper to upload the results. They had already identified the link between the four and Hakeem, but needed to confirm that it was actually his childhood friends Numair, Mahfuz, Jafar, and Farooq. Try as they might, they could not hide the flow of money from the prying eyes of the NSA that ultimately wound up in Geneva. Mel and Jake would have to determine if this facility in Geneva was sanctioned by Tehran or was a clandestine operation. One would be as bad as the other, but it would be much easier to take down a clandestine operation than launch an attack on Tehran that could, and would, have serious worldwide implications.

Jake and Mel would have to assemble a team in Europe along with a team in Israel. They didn't have long as enough money had been funneled to Geneva to have a fully operational facility in place. Max would need to come through with the funding, and it needed to be soon.

Jake set the capsule down and he and Mel left the panopticon to call Max to inquire about the funding. As they were walking towards Jake's office, Breakstone's voice could be heard over the paging system, "Jake, Max is on line 1 for you."

Jake put Max on the speaker and said, "I was just about to call you."

Max replied, "If I am not three steps ahead of you I am behind. The funding has been approved and the project is fully sanctioned. Project Geneva is now being shared with intelligence agencies around the world. I will have a list of liaison personnel to you before you and Dr. Paris catch the 11:00PM flight tonight to Tel Aviv. An old friend of yours who has been assigned to work with you in Israel will meet you upon your arrival. He has all the connections you need to cross into wherever you need to go to follow these leads. Pick up your travel documents from Breakstone and head home to pack your bags. She also has new phones, identity packets, and cash for you. You will both be issued a weapon and the appropriate credentials to carry onboard and in every country where the United States has diplomatic relationships. In other countries you are trained to use good judgment, but are also trained to know the risks. Good luck and Godspeed."

Jake was surprised as Breakstone handed the packets to them and came around her desk and gave Jake a hug. It was uncharacteristic of her, but she spoke in a personal tone, "Please be careful. You are one of the nicest agents we have ever had here and have made a difference in just a short period of time. We need you here."

They left the building and knew what they had to do. They would meet at Dulles at 8:30PM and start their journey. The ride to drop Mel off was quiet as they both had much to think about. Jake would say his goodbyes to his mother and father and realized he didn't know if Mel had anyone to say goodbye to or not. He would have to admit he never read her file or he would have known more about her. He would have to work on getting to know more about her on the 11 ½ hour flight to Tel Aviv.

CHAPTER 58

Max had called ahead to his TSA and EL AL security contacts to be sure Jake and Mel would be cleared without issue. As a dual citizen and former IDF officer, Jake would have no difficulty. Dr. Paris had been issued a new US Passport that did not show entry stamps into Arab countries. She would keep her passports separate so her reentry into countries prohibiting Israeli travel would not be hindered. Jake also carried his US Diplomatic passport for the same reason.

Jake had already passed through security and was waiting for Mel at the gate. It wasn't long before she arrived and took a seat next to him. They had both cleared security faster than anticipated.

Jake said, "If we are going to be traveling together I would like to know a little more about you. Do you have family in the States?"

Mel looked at him with a furrowed brow. "You read my file, right?"

Jake bit his lip and continued walking.

"Right?"

"Okay, you caught me! All I really know about you is the two-minute introduction you gave to the team. I'm not great at this and it tends to come out as more of an interrogation than a conversation. Maybe you can just tell me what you think I should know?"

Mel stifled a laugh and thought Jake's awkwardness was attractive in an odd way. She began, "Yes, I did rattle off what I thought were vital statistics so you already know I'm 37 and single and was raised in a small town and have two Doctorate degrees, speak many of the same languages you do, and have spent almost as much time in Israel as you. My parents still live in that small town and my travels have kept us physically apart, but I speak to them regularly and text more often than talk. I have one brother and one sister and we are all quite close. They know I have a new assignment, but have no idea that I am on the front lines of this project. There's not much else to tell. I have been more defined by my work than anything else, and you know the digs I have been on and by now have heard about some of the cases we have solved."

Jake responded, "Yes, I am familiar with those cases and understand being defined by our work. You seem to be much more knowledgeable about the Bible than I, and I am often amazed at how little I know about my own people other than the stories that we were taught. It seems that there are people all over the world talking about the Messiah coming or returning and that has pretty much passed me by. The religious seem to be so strict, both Jewish and Christian, that I have been put off by the rules. I had no problem with rules in the military or, even now working as a civilian contractor under Max, but religion has always been, well, too religious for me."

Mel nodded. "I completely agree. Man has used religion to divide, and that was never God's plan. It's very hard to make informed decisions without the right information. I noticed Harper and Carlson went out and got a Bible. Do you have one?"

"I have my Tanach, my Old Testament, from my Bar Mitzvah and have actually planned to read it in Hebrew. I never saw it as a book before, but with all this talk about Aaron and the High Priest, I thought it best to be able to understand what this is really all about. It has been a family legend for so long, I'm not really sure I ever believed it could be true."

"Believe me, it is true and has more relevance and impact today than in any generation before us. The two scenarios I laid out both have tremendous biblical implications. If we are indeed in the End Times then you and I are about to uncover a plot that may hasten the return of the Messiah by bringing more worldwide attention to what is really going on."

"Forgive my ignorance, but what are these End Times you keep referring to?"

"Let's get on board, and if you are really interested I will show you in both the Old and New Testaments what I am talking about. It has nothing to do with religion, so keep an open mind to what I am going to share with you. This is the only chance we will have to really talk, and it is more like a briefing than a biblical education. You are a man who likes puzzles. When you connect the dots in the Bible there is one message that is clearer than any other. I will let you decide for yourself what that message is and if it applies to you."

"Since I don't sleep on airplanes, and this is a topic I have a growing interest in, I look forward to hearing what you have to say."

Max had seen to it that they had first class seating and had pre-ordered kosher meals for them. Max felt if they would ever need to develop a cover story, every detail would be important. He had not shared his thinking with either Jake or Mel, but would wait to see if it were necessary. Since each was already known and established in the circles they would be tapping for information, there did not seem to be an apparent need. Once they left the known and ventured into the unknown, he would be ready.

They took their seats next to each other and settled in for the long flight to Tel Aviv. Mel leaned over and said, "I'm ready when you are. Just let me know."

Jake just nodded and pulled out a notebook and a pen to write down anything he would need to refer to later. He also, for the first time in his life, took out his Hebrew Tanach and placed it on his lap. For some strange reason he was already starting to feel like he was becoming a better person.

Mel took this as her cue to begin. "Some of what I am about to tell you may or may not line up with what you have been taught. I didn't always believe what my parents or Sunday school taught me. I had to find out for myself. Every one of us has to come to a place in our lives when we search for a higher power. I can imagine that most of what you were taught was what your parents and community wanted you to believe. That's how it works. At some point we begin asking questions like, isn't there more to life than all this? Or, why is the Bible still the best selling book of all time if it is just filled with fables? In reality, no religion is that much different than another. Most take the position theirs is the right way and all the others are wrong. Mankind has attached all kinds of rules and regulations not found in the Bible to form religious groups that conform to the leader's teachings. The Bible is not a handbook for how to form a church or a synagogue. It is about how to have a relationship with God. That requires a belief that there is a God. Jake, do you believe in God?"

Jake looked at Mel and thought carefully before he answered, "I don't think anyone has asked me that before. Yes, I believe in God. I have seen too many patterns to think all of life is random. I am not one to accept much at face value and have probably become more skeptical the more I see of how people treat each other, but the simple answer is yes, I believe in God."

Mel continued, "Good, then we have a common ground on which to build. You shared with me that you felt like you did something to cause Hakeem to turn against you. He is a descendant of Ishmael. Ishmael was the son of Abraham who was not chosen by God to be the son of the promise. That son was Isaac and through Isaac to Jacob. God changed Jacob's name to Israel because he had wrestled with both God and man and prevailed. Ishmael was described as a wild donkey among men who would make war against the world and his own brothers. He was to inherit twelve kingdoms. Those are the Arab nations today that now number twenty-two. The Koran tells the story that it was Ishmael, not Isaac, who was laid on the altar to be sacrificed."

Jake interjected, "Yes, I recall Hakeem telling me that. I thought it was strange since the Bible predated the Koran by so many thousands of years."

Mel remarked, "If I am telling you something you already know please stop me. I don't want to bore you."

Jake quickly responded, "No, you are not boring me in the least and this is the first time anyone has ever explained this to me in a way that makes sense. I think everyone assumes that because I am Jewish I somehow know the Bible, or because I spent ten years in Israel that I am an expert on Judaism. The truth is my father was not interested in religion and we attended the synagogue infrequently. If these lessons were taught they didn't capture my interest. Now, I am interested. Please continue and leave nothing out."

Mel continued, "If you insist I will continue. The Koran is really not the source of anti-Semitism. It is how the radical factions of Islam choose to identify their enemies. Regardless of what their holy book states, they have taken the position that Israel has no right to exist since the descendants of Ishmael are entitled to what belonged to the first-born son. Israel and Judaism are synonymous to those factions and they would delight in the annihilation of all Jews. They believe in a Messiah, the Mahdi, who is the 12th Imam, who will come to rule the earth under Islam.

"I am sure you have heard about the many who have been martyred hoping to be raised to paradise where seventy-two virgins await them. Imagine how much awaits the one who wipes out the entire Jewish enemy both on earth and in paradise. You can see why this plot must be defeated.

"Without the Jews, Jesus doesn't come, period. There are those who say they don't believe he was the Messiah. There are those who say he was and will return. And, there are those who say if he is the one who comes, they are fine with it. Everyone has to make that decision for themselves.

"I know you said you can't sleep on planes, but I can and I need to. Why not read this Bible while I sleep and look for some of the answers? I have marked certain chapters that I think will make what I am saying more clear to you. I hope you don't mind, but I am going to close my eyes for a while."

Jake replied, "I don't mind at all and appreciate all you have told me. I will read what you have marked. Thank you. Get some rest." He took the Bible she had given him and opened it to the first place she had marked. He began to read the Book of Matthew for the first time.

Mel fell asleep smiling, knowing she had opened a very important door.

CHAPTER 59

Mel opened her eyes and was surprised to see light peering out from under the closed window shades. She must have slept straight through the night. She looked over to see Jake had fallen asleep with his Bible opened. He was back in Exodus, which was the fourth tab Mel had highlighted. He had been reading most of the night and could not have been asleep for very long. She knew he had a photographic memory and could have used it to recall reading from the Hebrew Bible when he was younger, but chose to read it again. She took that as encouragement.

As quietly as she could, she rose to use the facilities and Jake barely stirred. He was still asleep when she returned. She used the time to review parts of the file and read more about Hakeem. She was impressed with his accomplishments, and if she hadn't known the backstory, the number of breakthroughs attributed to his work may have swayed her in his favor.

The flight attendant's voice broke the silence in Hebrew and English announcing their descent into Ben Gurion Airport. Jake stirred and sat upright as the broken silence awoke him. He looked almost boyish as he searched to familiarize himself with his surroundings. His hair was tussled and Mel realized he was quite cute when he wasn't so serious.

Jake spoke and said, "That's a first. I don't think I have ever slept so soundly before. I read quite a bit and I must say there was a lot to absorb. I have a clearer picture now that Moses predicted one would come after him who would be like him and we are to follow the one who comes. I don't think I ever realized he made that statement. I also noticed Aaron's role was in support of Moses, yet the promise to Aaron about the Priesthood being a part of his family line was for every generation. I'm not sure how all this fits together yet, but I'm working on it. I could sure use a cup of coffee right now."

Jake asked the flight attendant if he and Mel could get a cup of coffee. She brought them even though they were landing soon, and encouraged them to drink quickly. Within a few minutes she was back to collect their cups as they began their final approach.

Once on the ground they would proceed to Passport Control. As they made their was down the long sloping walkway, Jake heard a familiar voice calling his name, "YAACOV! YAACOV!"

He dropped his bag and embraced the uniformed officer. He turned to Mel and said, "Dr. Paris, I am pleased to introduce you to one of the finest scoundrels you will ever meet here in Israel, my closest friend Shlomi."

Mel shook his hand and in perfect Hebrew told him what a pleasure it was to meet him and thanked him for his help.

Shlomi was impressed with her linguistic skills and the three of them continued their dialogue in Hebrew all the way down to Passport Control. Jake would enter through the citizens counter unescorted. Mel would enter through the foreign passport booth escorted by Shlomi. After a very brief and official exchange, Mel and Shlomi were on their way to baggage claim where Jake was waiting for them.

Shlomi had arranged for another one of Jake's friends, Reuven, to join them and act as Mel's driver. Reuven was better known in the Jewish Quarter and could run interference for a woman asking questions in a tightly knit, male-dominated society. They would ride separately to the Dan Panorama Hotel where they would get checked in and unpacked before they ventured out. They would be in Tel Aviv no more than two nights. Their rooms were across the hall from each other and both had a full breakfast awaiting them in the privacy of their rooms. They could eat, shower, and change before meeting Shlomi and Reuven for the day's meetings. Jake and Mel were very much at home in Israel and enjoyed the breakfast selection and the robust coffee.

Max had already called ahead to both Shlomi and Reuven and given them the list of people that Jake and Mel wanted to see. They had a full calendar and were anxious to get started.

Mel would start meeting with several archeologists from Tel Aviv University and Jake would be connecting with old intelligence contacts.

They would stay in touch by phone throughout the day and planned to meet back at the hotel by 8:00PM.

CHAPTER 60

Hakeem had not been able to break away from his work in Tehran as much as he had planned, and the team he had assembled in Geneva had taken the research as far as he was willing to let them. He scheduled a meeting with his superiors to request an extended leave of absence. His plan was to devote the time to finishing the last tests that would identify the location of the family directly in the line of Aaron. Once that was complete, he would dispatch a team of jihadists to eliminate the entire family. While they were engaged in their assignment, he could finish typing the genetic link connecting all Jewish descendants and take that information back to Tehran. There he would turn that data over to those who had the ability to eliminate their enemy for all eternity.

So far no one at the Geneva laboratory had asked any questions and Hakeem had been able to segregate the work, so each team was focused on just one aspect of the project. He had designed it so he would be the only one capable of linking all the findings together. As far as any of the staff were concerned, they were being tasked with locating a particular genetic link to a variety of diseases. Oversight of the facilities security was the responsibility of Jamal Ben Hassam who was a trusted member of Hakeem's staff. He sent regular encoded reports to Hakeem via special courier. These reports were part of a regular flow of data sent to Hakeem from all over the world to the National Research Center for Genetic Engineering and Biotechnology.

The work of the Geneva lab was so successful that, even while working on the hidden agenda of identifying genetic linkages within the Jewish people, they had received a number of awards for their breakthrough research in Autism, Epstein-Barr, and Lupus. With Geneva being the home to a number of genetics laboratories, little attention was drawn to the non-public activities taking place inside Hakeem's laboratory.

Fortunately for Hakeem, his four investors were actually realizing significant returns from the licensing of patents for medicines derived from the research at the Geneva laboratory. Any connections they had as investors would only bring praise, not suspicion. Everything was in place now for Hakeem to come in and tie together the pieces for the greater good that he served.

Several months prior, Hakeem had started to plant seeds that he was overworked and on the verge of burnout. He began to make small mistakes and allowed his appearance to become more disheveled. He knew there were murmurings about him, and he was delighted that his plan was working. It didn't take long before word made its way to the very group who had originally approved his work and he was summoned to appear before the Director.

"Dr. Baba," the director began, "as you can see I have assembled our oversight group to discuss a matter that has us concerned."

Hakeem responded, "And what matter is that, Mr. Director?"

"It seems there are rumblings that you are under severe stress and that your work is suffering. Do we have something to be concerned about?"

"To be quite candid, I have been working eighteen-hour days without so much as a weekend off for the entire time I have been here. The only time I have been out of the Center has been to attend several conferences in Geneva. I concur, I am not operating as efficiently as I would like, but certainly it has not affected the quality of the Center."

"Now, Doctor Baba, no one is questioning your competence or the quality of your work. We are concerned for your well being and feel a leave of absence may be in order to afford you the opportunity to rest. We have provided a generous allowance for such a leave and hope you will take this opportunity to get some well-deserved rest and relaxation. You are much too valuable to us here at the Center for us to lose such an incredible talent such as yours. Please consider this as a reward and recognition for a job well done."

"I am humbled by your kindness and concern for my welfare. I will make plans now to travel first to Geneva to meet with some friends and then on to some other places I have longed to visit. How long a period were you contemplating?"

"We feel two months should be sufficient. Any longer and the work here would be hindered. Is that acceptable to you, Dr. Baba?"

"It is most generous of you. I will make certain there is no interruption to the continuity of the work. Many thanks for your kindness. May I begin now to put my plans into motion?"

"Yes, Dr. Baba, that will be fine. Thank you again for your faithful service and commitment."

Hakeem headed back to his office and sent encoded messages to Numair, Mahfuz, Jafar, and Farooq about his upcoming trip to Geneva. He requested they make plans to meet him there as they had done in the past.

Since he had been planning for this day to arrive for sometime, he had already drawn up plans and schedules for the work to continue there in Tehran. He would require weekly status reports from each of his department heads even though he was on official leave. This would keep him in the loop and ensure he maintained access to the data he needed and his login passwords and security would not be suspended during his leave. There would be no official announcement made, and his whereabouts would simply be conveyed as extended business travel. No dates would be announced and there would be no apparent changes in project leadership or assignments during his absence. He made sure that every contingency was covered to ensure that his superiors would feel that all projects were left in good working order.

The reports he had recently received from the Geneva team seemed very promising. In addition, there was the news of artifacts being obtained from Jerusalem that contained key pieces of information. It would not be long before the forgeries that replaced the stolen originals would be discovered and time was of the essence. As far as Hakeem was concerned, his plans had not been discovered and no red flags had been raised even remotely linking him to anything other than Nobel Prize winning work to cure disease.

It had been a while, but Dr. Hakeem Baba was starting to feel exhilarated again. He was closer than ever to fulfilling his destiny. In no time at all he would be in Geneva and would tie together all the data that had been compiled over the past years.

CHAPTER 61

The flight from Tehran to Geneva required a layover of more than eight hours in Frankfurt, Germany, affording Hakeem the opportunity to meet with Farooq. His travel from Antwerp was less than 250 miles and would take under four hours for him to make the drive. He would have time to have a meal with his old friend and make a delivery of diamonds to be used as payment for several deliveries Hakeem would be receiving after he arrived in Geneva.

Farooq had become very successful as a diamond merchant, and his company and courier packs were internationally recognized. Over the years he had amassed quite a large personal collection and was a generous benefactor to multiple officials in many European countries. This assured Hakeem would not be questioned about the courier pack bearing Farooq's company seal when he passed through customs either in Frankfurt or in Geneva.

Their meeting was tinged with excitement as Hakeem filled Farooq in on some of the findings they had made in further determining genetic markers in Jewish bloodlines. He also filled him in on the acquisition of certain artifacts that would lead them closer to verifying whether the legend of the scrolls was authentic. Although they had not seen each other very often over the years, their bond was as strong as it had been in their youth.

Hakeem shared that he had two months to tie all the research together in Geneva before he had to return to Tehran. Fortunately, Hakeem's team in Tehran had already made great break-throughs in their research that complemented the work being done independently in Geneva. What would have normally taken years to compile would now be reduced to a matter of weeks.

The rest of their time together was spent talking about their plans to reunite with the others in Tehran once all the pieces to the plan were in place. The old leadership would have no choice but to yield to The Five who were hand picked at birth to take control. Many had forgotten they even existed as a number of power shifts had taken place over the past thirty-five years. Regardless of who was in the Prime Minister's role at the time, they had the full support of the Ayatollah where the real power center existed. He would let nothing stand in the way of the destruction of the vilest of Islam's enemies.

Hakeem charged Farooq with updating Numair, Mahfuz, and Jafar about their meeting and the progress being made. They were to all make plans to be in Tehran in two months coinciding with Hakeem's return.

Farooq expressed some concern about Jafar since he was married with children. He had maintained regular contact with Numair and Mahfuz, but had not heard from Jafar as often.

Hakeem shared, "I have no doubt that Jafar has enjoyed a more westernized life, but he is as aware as the rest of us of what we have been called to do. When the time comes, I am confident he will respond without hesitation. If not, then his family will grieve over their loss. Nothing can stand in the way of our calling. I trust you will do what must be done if and when the time comes."

Farooq replied, "Your trust is well founded, my brother. Come, let us leave now and get you back to the airport for your flight to Geneva."

The discussion on the ride back was filled with reminiscing about their youth. Hakeem began to laugh, and Farooq asked, "What is it that amuses you, my brother?"

Hakeem spoke through his laughter, "I was thinking about the time we were all playing in the street and you kicked the ball into backend of a donkey. Oh what a scene that was as she took off down the street, pulling the cart and spilling all the fruit all over the road. I remember how full our bellies were. What fun we had as young boys...Seems so long ago."

Farooq laughed along with his friend as they pulled up to the departing zone at the airport.

Their embrace at the airport was that of two brothers who loved each other. Hakeem walked into the airport as Farooq drove away. Neither one looked back.

Hakeem made his way through customs without any difficulty, took his seat aboard the small jet, and settled in for the short flight to Geneva.

Upon arrival his assistant would transport him to the company apartment so he could unpack and settle in for his two-month stay. He had emailed instructions for him to schedule a number of one-on-one meetings with several of the department heads. He had also requested an evening gathering in the lobby of the Geneva facility to acknowledge the work accomplished during his absence. His ulterior motive was to be recognizable to the entire staff to ensure his unhindered access to all the laboratories and offices throughout the facility. Many, but not all, had seen his photograph in various technical journals. This would be the most expedient way for him to address the entire staff. He had learned to play the part of the gracious, yet enigmatic scientist who was accessible to his staff, but not on a personal level. His work was not shrouded in secrecy, but remained appropriately proprietary so as not to arouse any suspicion.

After clearing passport control in Geneva, Hakeem made his way to the baggage claim area where his name was prominently displayed on a placard held by a uniformed driver. He identified himself and handed his baggage tickets to the driver who immediately located Hakeem's luggage and escorted him to the awaiting car. There he saw his assistant, Jamal, waiting by the opened car door. They shook hands and both entered the back seat as the driver loaded the luggage.

During the ride to the company apartment, Jamal made sure not to discuss anything more than a review of accommodations and the week's schedule. He was more than just an assistant to Hakeem. He was also his bodyguard and a trusted insider strategically placed to be Hakeem's eyes and ears while he was in Tehran. They would speak of more mission critical matters once inside the secured confines of the apartment.

Upon entering the company apartment, Jamal conducted a standard sweep for any audio or video recording devices. Once secured, he gave Hakeem the signal they were free to speak openly. Jamal assisted Hakeem in unpacking and afterward sat down to share a cup of coffee and talk about more serious matters.

Hakeem asked, "When can I see the items from Jerusalem? Are you sure no one has touched them from the time they were taken until now?"

Jamal replied, "You have my every assurance they have been undisturbed. You will be pleased to know there have been no reports from any of our sources that the forgeries have been discovered. Only you will be able to determine the authenticity of the items we have waiting for you. All other research has gone according to plan and all the data sent to you in Tehran has been verified. Everything is waiting for you as you instructed."

Hakeem commented, "I appreciate your attention to detail, and that is why you are in this most trusted position. I have purposely kept you insulated so that you would not be put in a position to divulge anything that could hinder our plans. You have served me well and I want to give you this gift as a token of my appreciation." Hakeem reached into his pocket and pulled out a small velvet bag. He placed it in Jamal's hand and closed his fingers around it saying, "Thank you, my faithful brother."

Jamal was humbled at the kindness shown to him and slowly opened the pouch. He looked inside and then poured the contents into his other hand. He was now holding four high-quality diamonds with a value in excess of $25,000. He was so moved by this act of generosity he could barely get the words "thank you" out of his mouth.

Hakeem stood signaling the end of their time together and said, "You are most welcome. I will see you downstairs at 7:00AM. We will stop for breakfast on the way to the center. Good night."

Hakeem closed the door and sat back down, taking a moment to bask in the moment. There was still work to be done, but he was well on his way. In the coming days The Five would be reunited for the first time in a long time. He was tired, but it felt good to be back in Geneva.

CHAPTER 62

The ride to the Geneva facility was quiet and uneventful, but Hakeem was nevertheless quite excited to be back in the genetics lab that held the keys to unlocking mysteries that his superiors in Tehran knew nothing about. His entrance into the facility was the same as any other employee. He had to pass through a number of security stations in order to take the elevator to the secured floors.

Once through the final security station, he entered into the laboratory and made his way to the last examination room. His handprint and retina scan unlocked the door and he took a deep breath upon entering. There in front of him was the object he had longed to examine. He placed his hands in the protective sleeves that gave access to the contents of the sealed Plexiglas containment box. With surgical precision he took a pair of tweezers in one covered hand and a scalpel in the other. All he needed was a thread with a bloodstain on it. He made the tiny cut and placed the strand of fiber into a rotatable tray. He withdrew his hands and made his way to the tray, activated its movement, and retrieved the strand with another pair of tweezers. Just as he was about to examine his sample under the microscope, an urgent voice came over the intercom summoning him immediately to his office. Exasperated by the intrusion on his work, Hakeem stormed out of the laboratory and made his way down to his office. He greeted Jamal with a stern look and barked, "What is it that is so urgent?"

Jamal was taken aback by the sharpness of Hakeem's tone of voice and took a moment to compose himself before answering. "Dr. Baba, my most humble apologies for the interruption. Please forgive me, but I have a matter of the utmost importance to bring to your attention. As you are aware, we could not communicate with you in any detail while you were in Tehran about our work here. New information has just been brought to my attention. It appears our efforts to collect the artifacts on your list did not go unnoticed by the authorities as we had been led to believe by our inside sources."

Hakeem cut Jamal's words off at that point and shouted even louder, "Do you think this comes as a surprise to me? Surely by this time someone would have noticed the number of items that have gone missing. Either tell me something I do not know, or leave me now before I show you a side of me that you have never seen before."

Jamal lowered his head and spoke, "The head of the investigation is in Israel now, and our sources say they are getting close to connecting us to the missing items. A Dr. Jacob Aaronson leads the team along with a Dr. Melanie Paris." Before Jamal could finish, Hakeem had motioned him to stop speaking. Jamal knew by the ashen look on his face that Dr. Baba was stunned at the sound one of those two names.

Hakeem was noticeably shaken as his voice quivered saying, "How long do we have before you think they can find us? I have the final analysis to complete before I can verify the last piece of the puzzle."

Jamal replied, "Maybe two weeks at the most."

Hakeem took a deep breath and spoke with a tone not of this world and said, "I am to be undisturbed up until the last possible moment. Only you are to bring me meals and enter my laboratory. I want a second set of locks installed that only you and I can access. Station armed guards at every entrance. Send every other worker here on a two week paid leave. I need no assistance other than meals. I will stay in the living quarters connected to my lab and am only to be notified of urgent matters. Send a message to the other four. Dr.'s Aaronson and Paris must be stopped before they leave the Middle East. They will know what to do.

"In the meantime, I want everything you can find out about Dr. Jacob Aaronson. I want to know who he works for, where he has been, and where his family lives. Find out how to reach him. I want his cell number, email address, and any other way of contacting him. You are not to leave this facility as long as I am present. I am placing my life in your hands. Are we clear?"

Jamal looked directly into Hakeem's eyes and said, "I will not fail you." He turned around, left, and began the process of clearing and securing the facility. He summoned his trusted couriers to carry a message to the other four with Hakeem's instructions regarding Dr.'s Aaronson and Paris.

Hakeem looked out the window, but his eyes were looking more inwardly than at the wondrous view that lay before him. His thoughts now were on his old roommate Jake Aaronson. Hakeem thought, "I never presumed that the thefts would go unnoticed, but it was beyond my imagination that the sands of fate would rush together in such a way that I might come face to face with the part of my past where all this began. How fitting that the very one whose family opened my eyes to the possibilities of cleansing the world of their kind would be the first to fall at my hand. Too bad he will never have the chance to say his final good-bye to me. Nevertheless, the taste of victory will still be just as sweet."

With a smile on his face, Hakeem turned his attentions back to the laboratory to finish what he had just started. He stopped at his desk to mark a calendar to start the two-week countdown. Even if he had Jake eliminated, another would be right behind him. The final confrontation was inevitable. It was just a matter of time.

CHAPTER 63

Mel made her way from one interview to the next, and each story she heard was the same as the one before. Each Archeologist or Museum Curator reported that only select artifacts had been taken. Items of much higher value were left untouched, while seemingly valueless teeth and personal items were taken. After hearing this report for the fourth time, she decided to head back to the hotel and wait for Jake. They had agreed to meet at 8:00PM and it was only 6:00PM now. Maybe she would treat herself to an Aroma coffee loaded with chocolate and pass the time enjoying this slice of Israeli life. While enjoying her coffee, she reviewed the list of people she would be meeting with the next day in Jerusalem. It wasn't long before a young man sat across the table from her and told her in Hebrew not to make a sound. He went on to tell her she was to act normal, finish drinking her coffee, and then slowly leave the café without drawing any attention.

Dr. Paris lifted the cup of coffee to her lips and suddenly threw it in the face of the man across the table. He cried out in pain, and while his hands frantically tried to wipe the hot liquid from his face she stood to make her escape. As she approached the door, a young security officer was waiting there for her. He sat her down, and as he went to detain the man she doused with coffee, he was knocked to his feet. After striking the security officer, the man who threatened Mel ran past her and out the door before anyone else could stop him.

Mel reached for her cell phone and immediately called Jake to warn him that someone was trying to stop their investigation. He was not surprised to hear that they had already garnered some unwanted attention. He told her to go right to the hotel and he would meet her there.

Mel hailed a taxi and rode to the Dan Panorama Hotel expecting to meet Jake there. What she was greeted with was not just Jake, but Jake with several of his friends from Israeli intelligence. Jake had already filled in his old friends and they were now able to assist in the investigation. They quickly escorted Mel up to a suite and began the debriefing.

She described the man and repeated everything he had said to her. From the description they were able to pull up some photos on their iPhones to see if she could identify the assailant. On the fifth photo she stopped them and identified the man. He was a suspected arms dealer with links to Iran and Syria. They would research his known associates and try and locate him. In the meantime, they recommended Mel and Jake leave Tel Aviv early and make their way to Jerusalem. Two cars would accompany them to watch their front and back along the route. They would make the change in arrangements in

Jerusalem for them, through secure channels, so that no one else would know their whereabouts for at least the next eighteen hours.

Mel and Jake, flanked by two agents, headed to their rooms to pack and leave. They would exit through the service entrance. By the time they finished packing and exited, their car had been brought around to the back of the hotel where no one would see them. The security cameras had been turned off and no video record of them leaving existed.

It was now after 9:00PM and the drive to Jerusalem would take a little over an hour. By the time they arrived they could still meet one of Mel's contacts and start piecing together what they had learned in Tel Aviv with whatever new information could be obtained in Jerusalem.

Jake's associates had already checked them into the hotel in Jerusalem under assumed names. The meeting would take place at the Center for the Friends of the Third Temple. Mel had worked on a research project with the curator there some years back and they had maintained contact over the years.

They pulled up to a loading door in an unlit alleyway. The large steel reinforced door had no handle or lock on the outside. Even the intercom was recessed into the wall to draw as little atten-tion as possible. They approached the doorway and looked around, but could see no sign of sur-veillance cameras, yet they knew they were being watched. Before they could shine their flashlights on the intercom to announce their arrival, the door opened with an audible whoosh. The light in the hallway was too blinding for them to see anything more than an outline of someone standing several feet away. Jake's associates were preparing for any encounter as Mel broke the silence. "Rabbi Mizrahi? Is that you?"

The soft voice of an older man answered, "Yes, Dr. Paris, it is I. Please come in and leave your armed guards behind. I don't think that an old man such as myself can do you much harm."

As Mel and Jake stepped deeper into the hallway their eyes adjusted to the light and they could see their host. Rabbi Mizrahi was a slight man with fuzzy gray hair flying in every direction. At first glance it was hard to imagine this man being at the forefront of a movement to restore or recreate all of the garments and utensils to be used in the building of the Third Temple. They followed him through a maze of hallways into his office. His office had three walls of shelves overflowing with books, and there were stacks of journals and papers covering almost every square inch. He reached over and lifted piles of books to uncover the only chair in the room, other than the one behind his desk. Without hesitation he pointed to the chair looking at Dr. Paris and said, "Sit." As his eyes turned to Jake, he simply stated, "You stand."

They sat in silence for what seemed like an uncomfortable amount of time. Looking only in Mel's direction, Rabbi Mizrahi broke the silence.

"I would offer you something to drink, but there is no one else here to make it for you. It has been a long time since we last saw each other. I am sure you have had many adventures since then. I have followed your work over the years with great delight. Have you made any new discoveries that I have not read about?"

Mel replied, "No, Rabbi, I have not. My forensic work here has put me on the trail of missing artifacts. I am working alongside Dr. Jacob Aaronson who I mentioned to you on the phone."

The Rabbi looked in Jake's direction and said, "Aaronson? Who is your father?"

Jake replied in Hebrew, "I am the son of Norman, the son of Samuel, the son of Levi, the son of Jacob, the son of Benjamin, the son of Yehuda, and all the way back to the son of Aaron."

Rabbi Mizrahi first looked sternly at Jake, and then softened as he stood and walked over to him. He took his face into his frail hands and kissed him on each cheek and whispered into his ear, "You are welcome in this place."

Jake was overwhelmed with emotion as he had never been received in such a manner before. All he could muster was a very emotional, "Thank you."

The Rabbi sat back down and asked what he could do to assist them. Mel began by explaining, "Rabbi, there have been thefts all over the Middle East of teeth, bones, and other artifacts that hold DNA from ancient times. We believe they are all linked to the Priesthood. During our investigation, we uncovered hidden pictures of garments we suspect have either been stolen or are on the list of items the thieves are targeting. We are here seeking your insight into these thefts and to see if you can guide us in our search."

The Rabbi hung his head low as he fought back tears. His broken voice was barely audible and Mel and Jake leaned in to hear him say, "I had hoped we could retrieve them before it was made public. Please tell me you are the only ones who know about this."

Jake probed, "We are here searching for answers. Rabbi, what is it that grieves you so?"

Rabbi Mizrahi regained his composure and began, "As you are aware, our mission here is to restore or create the items necessary for the building of the Third Temple. Our work here is funded by people around the world who long to see the day when Israel is restored to its biblical role. During our more than thirty years of existence we have acquired some amazing items that have not been made public. Some of those items, we believe, date back to the Second Temple and some 300 years prior. The items you see on display in our gallery are replicas of some of the items we had locked in a secret location. Only a select few of our team have ever seen the actual antiquities themselves. The facility was under twenty-four-hour surveillance and was environmentally controlled to preserve the original items. As impossible as it may seem, there was a theft of the original robe of the last known High

Priest in the line of Aaron. It has to be someone on the inside, as we have never revealed its existence to the public. We do not know who it is or how to identify them without revealing the theft itself and the existence of such an item."

Jake moved closer to the Rabbi and said, "Rabbi, I know this must be devastating to you. I have heard many legends about the robe. Why would someone want to steal this particular item?"

Rabbi Mizrahi paused for a moment and sighed as he started, "Jacob, my son, you ask a question when you already know the answer. Whoever has the garment has more in their possession than they can possibly imagine. As a scientist, I am sure you are aware of the blood that is splattered on the robe. It would serve to date the robe and authenticate it. We had not performed all the analysis on the robe, but used it so we could replicate a new garment so that the original would always be preserved. We knew if we wanted to unlock all the secrets of the robe, we would have to perform some tests that could and would be of a destructive nature. Although the lining was old and decaying, it was still intact. We chose not to remove it, but subjected it to x-ray and other imaging techniques. We know that something was written inside, but would not risk the loss of the robe to extract the writing. None of our tests revealed what was inscribed and that is a part of my frustration. I was the one who was violently opposed to destroying any part of it to unlock its hidden message."

Jake responded, "We think we know who has the robe, but we need a list of everyone who knew of its existence in order to be sure. I promise you that this will not be made public and we will do everything in our power to return the robe to you. Are you willing to help us?"

Rabbi Mizrahi looked at Jake and said, "I believe you are the one chosen to return this piece of your heritage to its rightful home. Meet me here tomorrow morning at 10:00AM and I will have the list for you."

Mel spoke up, "Rabbi, I don't mean to alarm you, but our presence here has not gone unnoticed. If it is not too much trouble, can you please give us that list now?"

Without saying another word, the Rabbi opened his desk drawer, took out a pen, and began to write. He handed the list to Mel and walked them out of the office and back through the hallways leading to the rear exit. As they approached the doorway, he stopped, laid his hands on both their heads, and blessed them. Afterwards, he pressed a button and the door opened with the same whooshing sound as before. Once they stepped through into the night air, it closed without any other words being spoken.

Jake's associates escorted them to the hotel where they would get some much needed rest. It was too late to do anything with Rabbi Mizrahi's list. By the time they put their heads on their pillows it was after 2:00AM.

CHAPTER 64

Jamal delivered the meal to Hakeem and used the opportunity to offer an update on the whereabouts of Dr. Jake Aaronson. Hakeem listened without interruption to the account given of how Dr. Paris eluded the attack in the Tel Aviv coffee shop. He also heard the update that neither Dr. Paris nor Dr. Aaronson had been seen since they entered their hotel in Tel Aviv.

After studying the report on Jake's military and intelligence career, Hakeem knew that Jake would use his skills to cover his tracks more carefully now that he knew they were targets. He ordered Jamal to activate cells in Jerusalem and to post a lookout in and around the Center for the Friends of the Third Temple. If Jake were on his trail, he would most certainly pay Rabbi Mizrahi a visit. He also ordered surveillance on the King David Hotel, the Dan Panorama, and the Waldorf Astoria. He knew that if Jake were still working with Max, his accommodations would most certainly be first class.

Hakeem hurriedly finished his meal and returned to his lab. He knew he had to complete his work before Jake had enough evidence to convince the Swiss authorities to cooperate in allowing the Geneva facility to be breached. He was thankful they did not subscribe to the European Union and were not under their rules of law, thus making it more difficult to maneuver through their legal system. That assumed that Jake was working through established channels and not operating outside the constraints of traditional governmental agencies. If that were the case and Jake was privately funded, he would be able to assemble a tactical team without any government knowledge or interference. Either way, he needed to complete his work and return to Tehran where he was less vulnerable to attack.

Hakeem completed his first examination and knew he had acquired an authentic piece of biblical history. The blood on the thread he had extracted was bovine and the material dated back to approximately 200BC. This would put it in the timeline appropriate to the history of the Second Temple. Further nondestructive examination would be required to determine if this was, in fact, the priestly garment from the House of Zadok. If this was the garment, did it contain any writings? Regardless of whether it contained writings or not, it was a priceless object that had tremendous negotiating value. How he would use it would be determined by what he found after examining it in its entirety. The best method was to employ 3D printing technology to make an exact duplicate of the item sealed in the case. The lab was equipped with a state of the art imaging systems that integrated multiple scanning technologies to create full duplication of every detail inside and out of the object being scanned. The transparency of the enclosure made this possible and no further manipulation of the garment would be required. Fortunately for Hakeem, the deep pockets of his benefactors provided him with all the equipment he needed.

Hakeem double checked his settings and started the scanning process. Multiple red lights danced across the garment enclosed in the Plexiglas case, capturing every detail. He estimated it would take between 8 to 10 hours for the scan to complete. In the meantime, he would spend those hours mapping out a more detailed strategy to thwart the efforts of his old friend Jake.

The file Jamal brought to him on Jake was rich with information about his military training and his education. His distinguished service in the IDF, combined with his academic accomplishments, reinforced Hakeem's assessment that Jake was a worthy adversary. It was foolish not to consider him anything less and Hakeem had to be prepared for a confrontation. He made note that Jake's parents still lived in Bethesda, but were now enjoying a life of travel out of the public's eye. If he had to, he would use them as leverage. He would notify Jamal to find out where they were and have them under surveillance by a team that could take them hostage if necessary.

He had scheduled a call with Numair, Mahfuz, Jafar, and Farooq to find out their plans for meeting in Geneva. The call was deliberately brief as Hakeem was focused on the ticking clock. He would give them a full briefing when they arrived the first day of the following week. In as short a time as possible, he shared the latest update on Dr.'s Aaronson and Paris and advised each of them not to underestimate the abilities of these two. Their credentials were impeccable and they were following up on the thefts that had taken place over the past two years. It would not take Jake long to piece together this puzzle and figure out that Hakeem was the common denominator.

For the first time Hakeem felt anxious about the future and his confidence was shaken. His mind raced as he examined every angle to be sure he had not overlooked anything else.

CHAPTER 65

To avoid as much detection as possible, breakfast was delivered to the suite on a different floor than Mel and Jake were staying. They were each notified and spaced their arrivals several minutes apart to make sure their whereabouts went unnoticed. Guards were strategically placed both inside and outside the suite to insure their safety. Jake entered clutching the list of names Rabbi Mizrahi had provided. He was anxious to review it, but wanted to wait until Mel's arrival. He poured steaming black coffee from the silver pot and had just taken his first sip when Mel arrived. He poured her a cup and they sat down at the table to look at the list together.

Mel had prepared a list of significant donors to the Center for the Friends of the Third Temple. She recognized most of the names and highlighted the ones she did not recognize. She and Jake would cross reference the list of donors to the list Rabbi Mizrahi provided to see if any names appeared on both.

Jake took Mel's highlighted list along with the handwritten list from the Rabbi and took pictures of them and sent them to Interpol, Europol, CIA, and Mossad contacts. He also sent them back to Max, Trevor and Harper. They would run the list of names through a series of permutations to see if they could be linked to any person or organization with known ties to the Muslim Brotherhood, Al-Qaeda, Hamas, Hezbollah, and any group associated with radical Islam and anti-Israel activity. They would have to search through many layers, but the algorithms already existed and the searches would be automated. What would have taken weeks or months in the past, could now be done in as little as a few hours. In the meantime, Mel and Jake would perform their own analysis and connect whatever dots they could.

All tolled, there were twenty-six names on the Rabbi's list. After crossing off known philanthropic Jewish based organizations and their leadership, eleven names remained. Jake could identify two of them, leaving a shortlist of nine names. He emailed the narrowed down list of names to the same agencies he sent the originals to and advised them to focus on those nine first. Since they were already in Jerusalem, he requested an immediate screen for any of the nine that happened to be based in or around Israel for direct contact.

In less than thirty minutes Jake received word that one of the names on the list resided and worked in Jerusalem. It was unlikely that this individual was a viable suspect as he was on staff at the Hebrew University as a tenured professor and a distinguished member of their Board of Trustees. In addition, he managed a private endowment fund that awarded millions of shekels each year to fund local and international research into Jewish life. Nevertheless, he needed to be vetted and no stone unturned in the search for the missing artifacts.

Jake used his contacts within Shin Bet to leverage their high level relationships to set up an impromptu meeting with Dr. Mordecai Oppenheimer. They would meet him at his office located at the Mount Scopus campus of Hebrew University.

Jake had the sensation that he was being watched and advised that Mel go in one vehicle while Jake rode separately. If they were being tailed, it was less likely they could both be followed at the same time. Jake advised their escorts of his suspicion they were being followed. A plan was laid out for different routes to the rendezvous point and they decided to stagger their departure and arrival times. Under this scenario, one of them would be able to interview Dr. Oppenheimer and report their findings. If they did get separated, they would meet back at the hotel in the same suite where they had met for breakfast. An additional team of intelligence agents was deployed to backup both Jake and Mel to insure their safety. If they were being tailed, this team would be prepared to intervene as required.

Mel and her security detail drove up to the building that housed Dr. Oppenheimer's office on the Hebrew University campus. The plan was for Mel to go ahead and find his office and wait for Jake there. Instead of the expected sight of students walking around carrying book bags, they were greeted with flashing lights from police cars and a Magen David Adom ambulance. They did not see any signs of a bomb squad, but access to the building was sealed off. It wasn't long before they saw a gurney being wheeled out of the main entrance with an older man strapped to it. One paramedic was administering oxygen through a resuscitation mask, while the other pushed the cart towards the ambulance.

Mel made her way to the front of the crowd that had gathered to see what was going on and looked for someone in a position of authority. She approached a uniformed officer from behind the barricade and asked what was happening. He asked her to identify herself and state what her reason was for asking. She explained her appointment with Dr. Oppenheimer. It was then that he informed her that it was actually Dr. Oppenheimer being transported. He had suffered a major heart attack and died in his office. They were administering oxygen to make it appear that he was still alive, so that the students would not be alarmed.

Mel was stunned by this news and knew she had to find a way to get to his office. She asked the officer if she could go up to his office to speak with his assistant and he let her pass. She told her escort to wait for her and to call her if anything seemed amiss. She went straight up to the office and saw a group of people crying and comforting each other. Dr. Oppenheimer's office door was open and the people assembled were far enough away that they would not notice her. She walked in and saw on his desk a set of keys. On the key ring was a jump drive. She carefully looked around and quietly lifted the keys and removed the drive. She slipped it into her pocket and left unnoticed. If he were involved in any way, the drive would contain some clues. At seventy-eight years old and a prestigious member of the academic community, she doubted he had any involvement whatsoever.

She peeked around the corner of the office door to see if anyone would see her leave, but no one was looking in that direction. The stairwell was closer than the elevator, and Mel decided to take the shorter route. Upon exiting the building she saw Jake standing by his car watching the activity. She signaled him, and he got back into the car and waited for Mel and her escort to return to their own car.

Jake called Mel and she explained the entire situation. From all appearances there was no suspicion of foul play as there was no police presence anywhere inside the building. She told him about the jump drive and suggested they should meet back at the suite to regroup, examine the drive, and map out their next steps. They would know soon if the list of nine had just been reduced by one.

CHAPTER 66

Hakeem called Jamal into his office and gave him the following instructions, "I want you to assemble a team to install explosive charges strategically located throughout the entire building. If there is, as you have warned, a team headed by Jake Aaronson, we have to be prepared to level this facility at the push of a button. I want it to be a fully redundant system that cannot be disarmed. If they cut one circuit, it should not disable the others. You have three days to accomplish this. The master switch should be able to be activated by me alone. I want it linked to my computer and my phone. It will be to the glory of Allah if we sacrifice ourselves for him. It is imperative that none of our work here is discovered. You know what must be done. Leave me now and do what I have instructed."

Jamal nodded and left Hakeem and immediately summoned his chief security officer. They gathered together blueprints of the building and set up a meeting with a team of demolition experts they had worked with in the past. They would be able to supply all the materials necessary for this job and Hakeem's authorization meant they would be well paid for their work. Even more valuable than their expertise, was their ability to be trusted.

In less than two hours a utility van pulled up in front of the building. The crew remained inside the van as their leader and his design engineer entered the building to meet with Jamal and his team. After reviewing the building plans, the design engineer took out a scanning wand and uploaded the blueprints to his laptop. He did the same with the electrical schematics. In less than thirty minutes, he had sized the job, designed the wiring, and determined the most strategic locations to set the charges. The work would begin immediately and the building would be ready for implosion in seventy-two hours as required.

CHAPTER 67

Jake inserted the jump drive into his laptop and began to search for any clues that would link Dr. Oppenheimer to the missing garment. It didn't take long for him to locate a file named The Chronicles of Aaron. Jake opened it and found over 100 pictures of the garment from every vantage point. He made note that all of them carried the logo of the Center for the Friends of the Third Temple. These were internal photos all provided by Rabbi Mizrahi. There was a series of document files that Jake opened one at a time. Mel sat next to him as he scrolled through the text contained in each one.

There was nothing contained in any file linking Dr. Oppenheimer to anything nefarious. On the contrary, he was an avid supporter of the Center and devoted a large portion of his personal study time to analyzing the vast research available concerning the Priesthood of Aaron and his descendants. It was Dr. Oppenheimer's conclusion that the robe housed at the Center was authentic and contained text woven into the lining that held an accounting of the fulfillment of prophecy and evidence the Messiah had come and would return to rule and reign from the Third Temple. He also concluded the text inside the garment was written in a code that would only be known to the rightful heir. No existing software could decode even the small segments of text that were visible. It was a mystery that consumed the last twenty years of Dr. Oppenheimer's, life and his research was extensive.

Jake and Mel sat in silence for quite a while pondering what they had just read. They both felt the weight of the responsibility entrusted to them to not only thwart the diabolic plans for the extermination of the Jewish people, but to retrieve this artifact that held such biblical importance.

The ringing of Jake's phone roused them out of their contemplation and Jake took the call. It was his friend Avi with Mossad with an update on the other names. Three more could be crossed off the list as they could be cleared through the system. That left five remaining for them to investigate. Of those five they had secured addresses on three of them. Two were in Greece and one was in Saudi Arabia. Access into Saudi Arabia, even with diplomatic passports, would require more paperwork than time permitted. They made their plans to go to Athens and booked the one-hour flight out of Ben Gurion Airport for later that afternoon.

Mel had a number of contacts in the archeological community in Athens; however, since nothing about their investigation centered on anything stolen from that area, they would be of no help. Jake on the other hand had a number of intelligence contacts there and set up a meeting at their hotel for that evening.

Once again Max booked them into the finest accommodations at the King George Hotel. It was atypical for members of the intelligence community to stay at such high-end hotels, but Max was an expert at avoiding attention and using every resource to ensure the safety of his team.

Mel and Jake arrived at the airport, checked in, and boarded the plane separately. No one would connect the two of them in any visible way. Upon their arrival at Athens International, two different drivers, holding up two different name placards greeted them. Neither bore their real names, but displayed code names provided via separate text messages to Mel and Jake upon landing. Once again, no one would be able to connect them to each other.

After checking in to the King George, Jake would text Mel the suite number where they would be meeting. The same arrangements had been made for them to be escorted and guarded wherever they went. Max would notify Jake's contacts the details of the meeting room.

The suite had an amazing view of the Acropolis, and Jake and Mel took a moment to enjoy its beauty and history. There brief sightseeing was interrupted by the knock on the door and everyone took their positions. Regardless of the security measures taken, they had to prepare for any eventuality. Once it was verified these were the expected visitors, they could stand down.

Jake greeted his old friends and they exchanged pleasantries as introductions were made. These operatives, like everyone else Jake was connected with, had vast experience and networks. They poured some coffee and sat down to review what the team had been able to discover about the two names on the list of suspects who lived in Athens.

The first name was Dr. Dmitri Pappas. He could be crossed off the list as he was a well know pediatrician and had no ties whatsoever to anything criminal. He was a religious man with a heart for the Bible and supported many Jewish organizations.

The second name was more promising. Jake's friend Peter explained, "The name Nicholas Giannopoulos was on your list. He is in the Petroleum business and at first glance would not raise any concerns. He is a prominent member of the community and his known associates are well known business leaders. He has a number of charitable trusts that support a variety of archeo-logical, anthropological, and biblical work. He chairs the board of the trust and approves all the major donations. He was a special guest of Rabbi Mizrahi at the Center and was shown the private display. Although he has personal ties to the oil cartel, he is not the one we suspect.

"Upon further investigation of his banking records, we noticed a number of sizeable trans-fers from one of his subsidiaries to an Investment Banking firm that has been on our watch list for some time. His son-in-law runs that subsidiary and we have been keeping him in our sights. His name is Jafar Akbari from Tehran and his mother was European and his father Iranian. His mother died at birth and our sources tell us his father died several years ago. While in Tehran attending the funeral, he and three others met with Dr. Hakeem Baba. It seems they share this macabre connection that all five of their mothers were European and died at childbirth. They grew up together and were all the sons of diplomats. All have dispersed and live outside of Tehran with the exception of Dr. Baba. We believe that Jafar Akbari has been making large payments to this investment firm and we have a plan in place to acquire their records this evening. If our suspicions are correct, we will be able to link Akbari to the funding of the laboratory in Geneva and bring him in for interrogation.

We will meet you back here at 10:00PM tonight and should have what we need in hand. If, by chance, we should be able to locate Akbari and bring him in, we will notify you where to meet us. Enjoy Athens while you have time. We will see you here or elsewhere later tonight."

Jake wished them good luck and walked them to the door. After they left he turned to Mel and said, "I have a good feeling about this, but we can't ease up until we are sure this is the name from the list. There are still two names that we cannot identify. In this amount of time we should have been able to locate them in some database somewhere. They must be aliases and that usually means they are hiding something."

Mel responded, "I am inclined to agree with you, but we have cross-referenced all the aliases in our databases and there have been no hits. We need to find out when these two visited the center and if Rabbi Mizrahi can shed any light on their identity."

Jake replied, "That's a good idea. Let's get him on the line and hear what he has to say."

They placed the call and after a brief hold they heard the familiar voice on the other end, "Shalom, my friends. I trust you are well. Are you calling me with good news?"

Jake spoke up, "Shalom, Rabbi, we are in Athens hot on the trail, but needed some more information form you about two names on the list. Can you tell me when Francis Donnelly and Timothy Bartholomew visited you last?"

Rabbi Mizrahi began laughing and through his laughter spoke, "Of all the names on your list you call me about two Catholic Priests sent from the Vatican? Are they suspects?"

Jake and Mel both began laughing along with the Rabbi and Jake spoke up, "Rabbi, please forgive the intrusion. Had we known they were priests and had their names changed by the church we would not have made this call. No wonder they did not appear in any of our searches. May I ask, did the Vatican really make a contribution to the Center?"

"My boy," the Rabbi began, "you know I cannot verify that the Vatican was our biggest donor.

That would not be appropriate to share with you. Understood?"

Jake replied, "Loud and clear. I believe we have narrowed down our list to one and should have news for you soon. Thank you, Rabbi."

As the call ended, Jake and Mel looked at each other and laughed again about what they had learned. They would be sure to update the teams with the newfound information on the two missing names. They used the remaining time to call Max to discuss plans for assembling a team in Geneva. Jake wanted to be sure that certain personnel would be there when they had the final confrontation with Hakeem. Max assured him he would have everything he needed.

CHAPTER 68

Hakeem went in to check on the progress of the scan, and this time when he looked upon the garment he saw it in a different way. Up until this moment, it represented a hidden secret that he could exploit in the battle against his sworn enemy. Now, as he looked upon it, he began to wonder if this truly was a sacred garment. Something began to stir inside, and it was a very unfamiliar and unsettling feeling. Never before had he ever considered that he might be wrong. What could possibly have affected him this way?

He sat down across from the Plexiglas box and hypnotically watched the scanner lights as they moved across the garment. His thoughts were not his own, and it was almost as if he was hearing a voice he had never heard before. He called out, "Who is talking to me? What do you want from me?"

Except for the movement of the scanning equipment, there was a silence in the room unlike anything he had experienced before.

Hakeem looked back at the garment, and now it was radiating light. It was not reflecting the lights of the scanner, but was aglow with its own radiance. There, inside the sealed case, stood what appeared to be a man draped in the robe. The image lingered for only a moment, but

Hakeem knew he was in the presence of God, and it wasn't the god in whom he was raised to believe. Before the image disappeared, Hakeem was certain he heard a voice say, "I am."

He fell to his knees, wept, and humbled himself before the presence of the one true God.

CHAPTER 69

Evening fell in Athens and Jake and Mel were anxious for the hours to pass. Both of them were used to being in control, and neither was blessed with an abundance of patience. Mel decided to use this time to probe deeper into Jake's understanding of what Dr. Oppenheimer wrote in his notes regarding the encoded writing and how only the heir would be able to decipher it.

Mel began, "Jake, when we first met Rabbi Mizrahi, you introduced yourself in a rather unusual way. What was that about?"

Jake replied, "The Rabbi would not recognize me by a passport or some official document. He asked me who I was. He was asking me for my family lineage to be sure I was not someone who knew nothing about his heritage."

Mel questioned further, "Do you think there is any connection between your ancestry and this robe that seems to belong to someone in your family line?"

"Are you asking me if I think there is some personal connection between me and this mission other than protecting what's left of the Jewish bloodline and the protection of the State of Israel?"

"Yes, I think that is exactly what I am asking. Dr. Oppenheimer's research said the text inside the robe was encoded in such a way that no technology existed that could decode it. You have that gift. You have been able to see patterns that no one else could see. You told me you had this gift from the time you were a small child. Your profile says you have savant gifting in this area. If you saw the code, don't you think you might be able to decipher it?"

"Is this some type of challenge or are your really implying that I could be the rightful heir to the Priesthood?"

"I have only been working with you for a short time, but I can see things in you that you do not see in yourself. When you were speaking to the Rabbi, you spoke as one who had authority. I believe that is why he entrusted us with his deepest secret. What makes you think your name is not a clue? The Jewish prophets spoke of God's promise to return His people to their land. He promised that the Temple would be restored and that His kingdom would come and His will would be done on earth as it is in heaven. God has used men and women just like us from ignoble beginnings to do great things for His kingdom. If He chose you, would you resist?"

"When you put it that way I would be a fool to turn away from God."

"Maybe He wants to use this as a way to turn towards Him now. Maybe He wants you to know the real truth."

"If you would have said this to me when we first met, I would have scoffed at the very idea of me being used by God. Now that I have gotten to know you, I have seen something in you that makes me want to be a better person. You have a certain peace about you that puts people at ease. They feel comfortable around you. No one would ever know that you are capable of defending yourself or taking a life if you are forced. There is something you have that I have not seen in others and it makes me wonder what it is that makes you different. Let me give this some more thought. I'm starting to believe I might be open to the possibilities."

"That's all I could ask or hope."

They both laughed as they looked at their phones at the same time to check the time. It was 9:30PM and they knew the team would be on time. The next thirty minutes would probably feel like hours as they anxiously awaited some word. Fortunately for them, word came sooner than expected. A text message came through with an address. That meant they had Jafar Akbari in custody.

They quickly packed up their paperwork and notified their drivers of their destination. They arrived at the warehouse where the team was already interrogating Jafar. The ride was only twenty minutes long, but they had already started and finished the questioning.

Jafar Akbari was a quivering ball of fear as he sat at the table talking as fast as he was able. He had already admitted to syphoning money out of his father-in-law's company to fund Hakeem's laboratory in Geneva. He disclosed the travel plans for the rendezvous of The Five in Geneva that coming Monday. He confessed that he knew Hakeem had the robe in his possession. He shared Hakeem's plans to release the results of his DNA typing that would identify every Jewish person whose name was in any database to Tehran so they could systematically eliminate anyone with Jewish blood. He reported that Hakeem was planning to take over the leadership position in Iran after he deciphered the writings in the robe and announce to the world his discovery that would tear about the foundations of the Jewish faith.

Jake and Mel joined the others across from Jafar and listened to him disclose more and more information. All he wanted was to keep his family safe. He admitted to playing along and funding the operation, but not really committed to Jihad like Hakeem and the others. They were not married and had no family. They did not know what it was like to be accepted into a family and feel the love of their own children. He would go along with anything they wanted him to do as long as they did not harm him or his family. He would help them stop Hakeem, but they could not expose him to his family, especially his father-in-law.

Jake agreed to the terms and told Jafar that he would have to move up his travel plans and tell his wife he had to fly out of town the next day. That would put him in Geneva on Saturday, two days before the rendezvous. He assured him that every move he made would be watched and every word he spoke would be heard. There was no turning back now, and any sign that he was planning on running or tipping off the others would be dealt with in a final manner. He would not have to worry about his reputation, only his life.

Jafar agreed to the terms and gave them every assurance he was too fearful to do anything other than what he was told.

The team left one man to sit with Jafar as they moved out of range to talk. They agreed Jafar would be a valuable asset and that this part of the plan would give them the element of surprise they needed. They would put a small tracking and listening device on Jafar's phone that would keep him on a short leash.

Jake and Mel would leave for Geneva before the others, and a two-man team would escort Jafar on the next flight after theirs. The flight was a little over 2 ½ hours long and they would stagger their departures. Jake and Mel would depart on the 8:40AM flight on one airline and Jafar and his escorts would fly out on the 10:20AM on a different airline.

Max would make the arrangements for their accommodations and transportation and have the team assembled to meet on Saturday night in Geneva. They would have the full set of building plans for the Geneva Project and would plan their attack to coincide with the other members of The Five. They wanted to catch them or take them out all at the same time.

They left the warehouse, and Jafar was escorted home after the tracking and listening device was in place and checked out. Mel and Jake and their drivers returned to the hotel to prepare for an early morning departure. It had been a very good day and there was much to think about and plan.

CHAPTER 70

The scan was now complete, and Hakeem transferred the digitized image to the 3D printer. This part of the process would take all night and into the next day. Hakeem decided to use the time to go online and read the Hebrew Bible. He knew that the clues to understanding the significance and the content of the robe would be disclosed there.

He was driven by something not of this world and in his seclusion would use this time to follow the path on which he was being led. The same passion he had for destroying his enemy was now being applied to searching for a new truth. He had no idea what he was to do with this revelation of God, but was intent on finding the answers. The same diligence he had applied to every other endeavor he would now apply to this.

Monday was just a few days away and he had to prepare himself mentally, emotionally, and spiritually for that meeting. It seemed his focus had changed in the blink of an eye, and he would trust that he was being led in the right direction. He would not worry about Monday until Monday.

Today he had enough to occupy his mind.

CHAPTER 71

The arrival in Geneva was well orchestrated, and everyone executed perfectly according to plan. The team gathered Saturday night in the suite Max had provided. Present were the team members Jake had requested, along with a local team that had been keeping the Geneva facility under surveillance. After all the introductions had been made, Jake asked their team leader to report first on the level of activity they had observed.

Captain Culpepper reported, "A little over a week ago all regular staff was furloughed. A security team was put in place, and only Dr. Baba and that team is in the building. Four days ago a known group of demolition experts were observed working around the clock for approximately seventy-two hours. It appears that have wired the building with C4 as an added failsafe in case the facility is breeched. We have on our own team of an expert in disarming such installations, but we suspect every floor is wired and the systems may be independent of each other. If that is the case we would need several hours to disarm all of the floors. We do not anticipate that being an acceptable scenario and therefore must prepare ourselves to eliminate all personnel since we do not know who holds the trigger switch."

Jake interjected, "I know Dr. Baba, and he would not let anyone other than himself make the decision to detonate. We have to disarm all security personnel and make our way to his location without setting off any alarms. We will need sharpshooters on the roofs of the buildings on all sides and infrared vision to see into the building. My reports show the building is equipped with one-way glass so that no one can see what is going on inside without the aid of thermal imaging cameras."

Captain Culpepper continued, "Sir, our reports are the same as yours. Here are the blueprints and wiring diagrams of the building. We have already run these through our design systems and can identify where the explosive charges would be placed. Dr. Baba's laboratory is designed as a self-contained bunker. There appears to be only one way in and one way out. It has its own access controls and is surrounded by reinforced concrete walls. Someone knew what they were doing when they designed this. He does, however, have one window in his office that allows us to monitor his motion. "

Again Jake interjected, "I appreciate the assessment, but once again, knowing Hakeem as I do, he would have designed an escape route hidden within the bunker. It may not appear on your plans, but have your analysts run some scenarios and see if they can determine the most likely location and how it would be laid out. If we can come at him through a secret passageway, we may be able to circumvent the added security focused on the main entrance to the lab."

Captain Culpepper concurred and dispatched one of his men to get the design team working on that.

Jake asked if that was the entire report before moving to the next part of the briefing. Captain Culpepper confirmed that it was and thanked Jake for his guidance.

Jake then moved on to the briefing and asked Mel to describe how she envisioned this lab being laid out. She described to the best of her ability how a forensic DNA laboratory would be set up. Based on the amount of money Jafar had sent, they could only imagine how much sophisticated equipment he had on hand. Since he had the sealed box with the robe in it, Mel was confident he would use digital technology to recreate it, rather then destroy it by opening the hermitically sealed container. Everything would feed into a single computer system controlled by Dr. Baba. It was her assessment that he would also have the detonator programmed into his computer as well as his smartphone. She advised they would need to do whatever was necessary to keep him from accessing his phone or keyboard once the lab was breeched.

Jake filled in the rest of the blanks and the teams huddled around the blueprints pointing and commenting as they looked for any and all potential entrance points. Two carts of food had already been delivered to the room and night had fallen in Geneva. Two whiteboards were delivered along with flipcharts and easels and different scenarios were proposed, discussed, and supported or shot down.

While this team was analyzing the attack scenarios, Max was tracking down the travel arrangements for Farooq, Numair, and Mahfuz. Their arrival at the laboratory would be critical if they hoped to capture or eliminate them at the same time. The team had already been advised that Jafar Akbari was to be spared if at all possible, but not at the expense of anyone on their own team.

They discussed how Jafar would be delivered to the airport and his arrival timed to match his original flight plan. All the required security passes would be in place to have him appear to deplane with the other arriving passengers. If anyone was watching, they would see nothing out of order.

By midnight everyone was bleary eyed and needed sleep. They had narrowed it down to three possible scenarios and agreed to regroup on Sunday morning at 9:00AM to finalize their plans. By then Max would have determined the arrival times and that piece could be plugged in as well. A two-man team would stay in the suite to make sure that no unauthorized visitors or hotel staff entered. They took turns sleeping so that one was on guard at all times.

CHAPTER 72

The team gathered at 9:00AM and exchanged morning pleasantries, drank coffee, and enjoyed the large breakfast spread in front of them. The surveillance team gave their overnight report and commented on the unusual lack of activity inside the building. They could see into the office portion of the laboratory through its only window and saw Dr. Baba sitting at his desk, but did not log any movement from that same sitting position for over twelve hours. He did not appear to be asleep as they could see some minor hand movements throughout the night, but he never left his desk. They would get a noon update from their relief team who was also keeping an eye on his activity.

There was much speculation as to what he may or may not have been doing, but no one really knew for certain. Jake had them refocus and give their thoughts on the three scenarios laid out before them from the night before. The had to use this time to agree on the plan of attack and then review each person's assignments until every contingency could be addressed.

They went around the table and the consensus of opinion was to time their entrance to the arrival of Numair, Mahfuz, Jafar, and Farooq. Max had determined they were all arriving within thirty minutes of each other and were scheduled to be picked up and delivered by one limousine. It did not appear they had any concern about being seen together. They would use this to their advantage and use them as hostages to gain access to the upper floors. If they happened to be taken out by one of Hakeem's security forces, then that would be his problem, not theirs. If they timed it just right they would catch the internal security force off guard and overtake them without any alarms being tripped. The glass used in the building was only one-way, not bulletproof, and the guards were stationed so they could see out the windows. If they could see out, the snipers could see them with infrared. It would be a synchronized operation requiring expert marksmanship and timing.

Jake cleared the other two scenarios off the whiteboards and focused on every aspect of the agreed-upon approach. By 7:00PM they had worked the plan over and over until every team member had his assignment memorized. They would be in place by 3:00PM on Monday, as the Four were due to arrive at 5:00PM.

The surveillance team was notified to give hourly reports and to keep two sets of eyes on Dr. Baba. They had reported he had only left his desk twice in the last twenty-four hours and that was for only a few minutes at a time. It did not appear that he had slept at all, and most notably was he was no longer praying five times daily as he had been doing except in the past forty-eight-hour period.

Jake pondered this and wondered what was really going on inside that lab. He would ask Mel for her thoughts the next chance they had to talk in private.

The team took a dinner break and then headed to their own rooms for the night. They would meet again to go over the plan on last time at 10:00AM the next morning. That would give them time to meet at the secure warehouse near the lab by noon to change and arm themselves for the operation.

Jake wanted to talk with Mel in private and asked the two assigned to guard the suite if they would give them a few minutes to talk. The two left and Mel asked Jake what was on his mind.

Jake began, "I am puzzled by these reports from the surveillance team about the change in Hakeem's routine. I wanted to see if you had any theories as to what he might be doing."

Mel thought for a few minutes and then spoke, "If he is scanning and creating a 3D replica of the garment, then he has a lot of down time waiting for those processes to complete. It is not unusual for a dedicated scientist to get lost in research. I have been engrossed in several projects where I studied until I could not keep my eyes open. What is it that makes you question this?"

Jake replied, "It is not the studying part or him being consumed by some research. It is the break in his prayer routine. Even in prep school, he prayed five times a day and carried that mat with him so that he would not miss that routine.

If he has continued that tradition for all these years, why would he suddenly stop?"

Mel responded, "I had not considered that and agree that is a striking change in behavior. Hopefully you will have the chance to speak with him face to face and ask him that very question."

Jake answered, "For all of our sakes, I hope that is true. I remember what you said when we first discussed the possibility of the two of you coming face to face. I just may need you to do what you said you would. The more I think about seeing him, the more I remember how close we became. He really was like a brother to me. Thank you for standing by my side in this. I have come to appreciate you as a friend and a colleague."

Mel replied, "I take that as a very high compliment. I have come to appreciate you as well. I will see you in the morning. Try to get some rest."

Jake said goodnight and waited until Mel had entered the elevator before he headed that way. He signaled the two waiting at the end of the hall the all clear and they made their way back to stand guard over the suite until morning. Jake bid them goodnight and went to his room.

His thoughts were still consumed by Hakeem's strange behavior. He hoped he would have the chance to get his answer the next day.

CHAPTER 73

The next morning everyone was on time. Unlike the day before there was more edginess to the team. They still drank coffee and ate before they sat down for the day's briefing. The surveillance team brought the same report as the day before, noting the lack of movement in the lab and the eerie quietness of the entire facility. The security team was still in place, but they, too, seemed to be less alert and made more frequent breaks from their post than in previous days. No one seemed to be on any special alert for arriving visitors, and from what they could tell, no preparations for their arrival seemed to be taking place.

Jake again asked for any new assessments and none were offered. They reviewed their plan one more time and each member of the team recited their assignment, timing, and follow-up position without error. Everyone was on the same page.

The plan was to take out the limo driver and take the four visitors into custody. At the same time the sharpshooters would take out every guard posted at a window. That would reduce the inside forces to just four and the advance team would go in before Jake and Mel and disarm or eliminate them. They would capture Jamal, the security chief, as he had the access codes to the lab. While they were coercing him into granting them access to the lab, the team charged with breeching the escape route would make their way to the outer entrance to the lab and wait there for their signal. If entrance to the front of the lab could not be gained, the team waiting at the escape door would enter and secure Dr. Baba before he could detonate the explosives. They would then open the front door and let Jake and Mel and the rest of the team into the lab.

Everyone was clear on the plan and their assignment. They would leave immediately and meet at the secure warehouse to arm and armor up.

Before they left, Jake gathered everyone together and spoke with compassion, "Thank you all for being a part of this team. I want you to protect yourself at all cost. Do what you must. I trust your training and your instincts. We are ready to face whatever lies ahead. I could not be more proud to serve with such a talented group. I will see all of you on the other side."

After a lot of hugs and handshakes, everyone departed and headed to the warehouse. Max called to get any last-minute updates from Jake and to wish him good luck. Nothing had changed, and the plan that he shared with him the night before was the plan they were implementing. Max had checked flight status and all were on time. The go time was 5:00PM.

All arrived and were accounted for at the warehouse. Every type of weapon and armament needed was there. Members of the team had chosen their weapon of choice and it was provided for them. The sharpshooters had the latest technology available and a supply of armor-piercing bullets. The assault team had a variety of grenades ranging from smoke grenades to flash-bang stun grenades. Each assault team member had an automatic assault rifle, side arm, and was fitted with the best ballistic-grade body armor available. The explosives disarmament team was equipped with the latest jamming devices and circuit interruption equipment to do their best to disable as many floors as possible during the operation.

Jake and Mel wore body armor and carried 9mm Glock side arms with extra magazines. They were not expecting a large resistance, but needed to be prepared in case any reinforcements appeared.

You could tell by the silent preparation that all the members of the team were focused on their assignment. The warehouse was within walking distance and they had worked out the staggered deployment of each team. The last to take their position would be the forward assault, team with Mel and Jake right behind them. The forward assault team was divided into two groups. The first was to disarm the guards at the front entrance, while the second secured the four arriving visitors. One would approach from either side of the entrance and the other would surround the limo upon arrival and secure the driver and his passengers. Mel and Jake would then join that team as they walked into the building with four visitors in custody.

The hardest part of this entire operation was in the waiting. Once they took their places, they would have to hold their positions for two hours. They were all trained professionals, but even the most dedicated soldier doesn't like waiting.

At the appointed time, each team made their way to take up their positions. Like clockwork by 3:00PM every station had reported in and was in place.

Now the wait began.

CHAPTER 74

At 4:45PM, Jake had each station check in and then called for radio silence until the limo arrived. Once the advance team engaged the security forces at the front entrance, the snipers were to take out their assigned guards.

The limousine pulled up right at 4:59PM. As soon as the driver opened his door, the front doors to the building opened and the advance team engaged, the snipers' shots cracked, and the sound of shattering glass could be heard all around the building. The second assault team surrounded the limousine and extracted the four passengers without any resistance. Mel and Jake joined them at this point and followed the assault team into the entrance to the building. The explosives disarmament team was already inside and had begun their work.

Jake and Mel, the assault teams, and the four hostages met little resistance as they made their way to the stairwell leading to the upper floors. Word was received that Jamal was in custody and was being strongly encouraged to grant access to the lab.

No alarms had been sounded and it appeared that every guard had been eliminated. The team in the rear of the building identified the escape passageway and made their way to the outer back door to the lab. They signaled Jake they were in place.

The next rendezvous point was the secured outer door to the lab. There, Mel and Jake, along with their hostages, would meet up with the team who had Jamal in custody. By the time they arrived, they had hoped he would be willing to grant them access without any further encouragement.

The team executed silently until everything was secure. The sound of anxious breathing was the only thing that broke the silence.

They used the four hostages as a barrier in case they had missed one of the guards. One shot rang out and Numair took a bullet to the shoulder. He fell to the ground in pain and Jake was able to see the shooter. He took quick aim and fired three shots. All hit their mark and the last guard was eliminated. After checking Numair it was determined his wound was not fatal and they proceeded with the rest of the plan.

In spite of this incident, it appeared to Jake that Jamal was still unwilling to cooperate. Jake took him off to the side and had a lengthy conversation with him in Arabic. By the time they were finished, Jamal had agreed to grant them entrance into the lab on one condition. That condition was that only two could enter to make it less likely that Dr. Baba would be injured. Jamal was a loyal and faithful friend to Hakeem and his only concern was for his welfare. Jake agreed, but had one condition of his own. That condition was that Jamal would have to disclose how the explosives in the building could be detonated.

Mel asked Jake, "What's he saying?"

Jake quickly replied, "He is willing to cooperate, but I had to promise him we would not harm Hakeem unless it was absolutely necessary. Only you and I can enter the lab. That's the deal. We'll have to take our chances and hope for the best, but prepare for the worst."

Jamal was reluctant to share this, and Jake knew the only leverage he had was to threaten to take Hakeem's life. He knew this was Jamal's only weakness and finally he relented. He confirmed what Mel had speculated—that he could trigger it from his keyboard or his smartphone. He also confirmed that no one else in the facility could detonate the explosives.

Jake advised the teams to stand down, as only he and Mel would be entering the lab. Captain Culpepper voiced his protest and Jake gave him a look that conveyed everything he needed to convince him to yield.

Jamal entered the first set of codes, and Mel and Jake followed closely behind him. The outer door closed behind them and a second set of keypads was revealed. Jamal entered the codes and another set of doors opened. There was one last set of biometric controls that had to be accessed. Jamal paused at this point and looked at Jake. He asked him one last time for his assurance that no unnecessary harm would come to Dr. Baba. Jake gave him his word, and Jamal placed his hand into the scanner to gain entrance into the lab.

The door opened and Hakeem was startled at the intrusion. He looked completely disheveled and was typing something on his keyboard. Jake pulled out his sidearm and called out to Hakeem to stand up and step away from the keyboard. Hakeem continued to type and then stood to his feet. Now Mel drew her sidearm and took aim. Jake pleaded with Hakeem to please step away from the keyboard.

Hakeem looked at Jake and in a very calm voice he said, "My dear friend Jake. It has been so many years since we have seen each other. So much has happened that I wish I could tell you about, but it seems we will not have the luxury of having that conversation."

Jake looked at his friend and pleaded once again, "Hakeem, it does not have to end this way. Please step away from the computer and let us have that talk. Our differences can be resolved and no more lives need to be lost."

Hakeem looked peacefully at Jake and said, "I have come to find a truth and a peace I have never known before. You must do what you have come to do and I must do what I am called to do."

Hakeem's hand moved toward the keyboard, and as promised, Mel was there to take the shot. Unfortunately it was a split second too late, and Hakeem's finger pressed the enter button before the bullet tore through his heart.

Mel and Jake instinctively covered their heads anticipating an explosion, but none came. There was total silence in the room with the exception of Jamal's quiet sobbing.

The silence was broken by Jake's smartphone signaling he had received an email. Without thinking about what just happened he looked at the phone and let out an audible gasp. Mel asked what was going on and Jake replied, "It's an email from Hakeem."

Mel said, "What does it say?"

Jake read out loud, "My dear friend, I am certain these are the last words I will share with you. I am sorry for all I have done all these years hating what I should have been loving. I pray you will forgive me. This robe is a sacred garment and I could not bring myself to destroy it. I believe the God of Israel has shown me it is to be in your possession and that you are the one to decipher the code. The scrolls are real, as is the legend. You hold the key now. Answer the call as I have and I trust that we will see each other again. I have left my computer unlocked and connected to the center in Tehran. Destroy my work and shut down the computers connected to it so that God's chosen ones will be protected. Until I see you again, I am your brother, Hakeem."

Jake and Mel stood there with tears streaming down their faces. What was supposed to be the end, seemed to be just the beginning.

To contact the author visit
www.TheCodistBook.com